ADVANCE PRAISE FOR *THIS GARDEN OF WEEDS*

'The pomp and glitter of art, emerging in India somewhat belatedly, seem to conceal its underworld, the anxieties and contradictions, the poverty of taste and vision, the inadequacies of appreciation and evaluation. As an insider for long, V. Sanjay Kumar has narrated the world of contemporary Indian art through an engaging tale and, importantly, explored its underbelly. There is mischievous playfulness, empathy for art, and a clever coalescence of fact and fiction. The ridiculous and the fake, the banal and the laughable, sadness and delight all go to make the book a riveting, readable tale. In the end, there is deep wisdom laughing with tears in its eyes!'

Ashok Vajpeyi, poet, critic, and art lover

PRAISE FOR *ARTIST, UNDONE*

'Art, in Kumar's novel, is life distilled. Most importantly, despite its philosophical depth and the erudition of critics like Hoskote and his fictional colleague Ekbote, it's fun. The world of contemporary Indian art has been begging to be brought into the world of fiction. Kumar does this ably, with clever storytelling, a fluent style and oodles of wit. He pokes fun at everything and everyone, but his fondness and respect for this little niche and its conceits are evident'

Tehelka

'The story wanders from the known, the familiar, the oft-seen, to a world where reality merges into artistic dreamscape. The author uses his own life and work as a springboard, vaulting into a seemingly messy situation and navigating it with humour, warmth and a certain special madness that only a creative soul can produce'

The Hindu

'Kumar breaks several conventional patterns of novel writing with *Artist, Undone*. One gets to see a lot of images in between and there is a mix of poetry, twisted prose and long dialogues. The narrative is not linear. Probably this is the first time someone has attempted this pattern in English fiction'

BW Businessworld

'A wickedly humorous book – finely written, marvellously layered, intricately crafted and psychologically curious. The book is about hell, of self-discovery, and the price of self-discovery'

Deccan Herald

'Sanjay Kumar's *Artist, Undone* is a superb tale told with zest and cunning, a literary romp that both excites the reader and brings her or him to a sobering wisdom. Kumar wields the dagger of irreverence to telling effect, modulating a Salingeresque tonality... An elegant literary achievement!'

Ranjit Hoskote, art critic and poet

'Remarkably insightful and witty... A trippy, irreverent, yet passionate outsider's journey into the art world, and whether you're an art enthusiast or not, you are certain to enjoy this refreshing first novel which boldly goes where few Indian novels have gone before: to the artist's studio, the gallerists' office, and the collectors' psyche'

Artinfo

PRAISE FOR *VIRGIN GINGELLY*

'The book certainly isn't a romanticist or nostalgic novel that builds narratives to describe the city of Chennai, but it captures many truths about the city nonetheless. The xenophobia, the family ties, the class hatreds and the lost potential for old world charm all come out without expressly labelling themselves or choosing to stand out – and that is actually an achievement'

The Indian Express

'V. Sanjay Kumar is no hairy bearded guy from the land of the Gurus, and there is no endearing tone, but there is fun in the chaste Tamil he uses in his *Virgin Gingelly*. And it is largely expletives! Kumar's book is set in that city (Chennai) but packs in much more of Tambrahm language and culture than most books have. The abuses are not for good measure but the main menu… There is a rare sparkle in the way the Queen's language has been used'

The Week

'The cover illustration prepares the reader for the cultural hybridism of V. Sanjay Kumar's imagination and creative goals. The writer attempts to amalgamate the triple influences of English language training, North Indian "Baniya" parentage and Tamil Brahmin milieu of domicile in his writing. The innovative nature of the two opening sections of the novel bears testimony to this. The opening section is narrated in the first person, rather startlingly, by a mongrel street dog'

Earthen Lamp Journal

PRAISE FOR *THE THIRD SQUAD*

'Kumar's style, blunt but often by turns poetic and droll, is arresting even as his idiosyncratic plot roams far and wide, switching perspectives and pursuing twisty subplots with vigor. As unusual as it is compelling, this entry lays the groundwork for an entertaining series'

Kirkus Reviews

'Kumar has created some thoroughly intriguing characters… But the most fascinating of Kumar's characters is Mumbai itself – enormous, crowded, hyperactive, roiling, stunningly rich and grindingly poor, and teeming with almost unfathomable energy'

Booklist

'Kumar's understated, deadpan style cloaks his wit, poetic intelligence and impressive perceptiveness. Beneath the novel's anomie and shadowy atmospherics is a humanist inquiry into the worth and dignity of life… *The Third Squad* ends with an emotional wallop, making it stand out among crime novels. It has the chiaroscuro effects of classic noir, but also the philosophical depth of highbrow literary fiction'

Shelf Awareness

PRAISE FOR *A TAMIL MONTH*

'An irreverent look at Tamil Nadu in which crime, caste politics, and art come together to make an eclectic cocktail'

Mani Ratnam, filmmaker

'Funny, melancholy, full of off-kilter sentences that capture life's shifting, unexpected registers'

Amit Chaudhuri, novelist and singer

PRAISE FOR *RUFFLED FEATHERS: STORIES*

'They are all distinct, interesting stories, indicating a well-perfected but hardly uniformly applied formula for compelling world-making within the meagre space of twenty pages or so; at the same time, they manage to build up to and frame human sensibilities and instincts that are often so particular to their respective contexts that their capturing in words seems a feat by itself...the stories traverse known anxieties and alien terrors with a dexterity that betrays both astute observation and profound imagination. In this pursuit, of interest is not their distance from reality or common logic, but their proximity to the many meanings of living in a world that moves faster than those living in it sometimes grasp'

Scroll

'Kumar's amazingly powerful prose transforms reading every story into a joyful experience. While his narrative technique is captivating, his style lends special appeal to the stories, all of which are tightly structured and pacy. The storytelling is straightforward, simple, and accessible and their narration, honing on powerful images, has rewarding effects. He reveals, yet withholds, making the readers his fellow travellers in the journey of the narrative'

Deccan Herald

BY THE SAME AUTHOR

FICTION

Artist, Undone
Virgin Gingelly
The Third Squad
A Tamil Month
Ruffled Feathers: Stories

NON-FICTION

View from the Edge
Amitava: The Complete Works (co-authored)

THIS GARDEN OF WEEDS

V. Sanjay Kumar

BLOOMSBURY

NEW DELHI • LONDON • OXFORD • NEW YORK • SYDNEY

BLOOMSBURY INDIA
Bloomsbury Publishing India Pvt. Ltd
Second Floor, LSC Building No. 4, DDA Complex, Pocket C – 6 & 7,
Vasant Kunj, New Delhi, 110070

BLOOMSBURY, BLOOMSBURY INDIA and the Diana logo
are trademarks of Bloomsbury Publishing Plc

First published in India 2025

ISBN: PB: 978-93-61312-62-5; eBook: 978-93-61318-75-7
2 4 6 8 10 9 7 5 3 1

For sale in the Indian subcontinent only

Typeset in Minion by Manipal Technologies Limited

Printed and bound in India by Thomson Press India Ltd

FSC www.fsc.org MIX Paper | Supporting responsible forestry FSC® C010615

To find out more about our authors and books visit www.bloomsbury.com and sign up for our newsletters

For Rekha Rodwittiya, Surendran Nair,
and Mani-da

Contents

Contents

I

The glue holding this together had dried. There was this small matter that one of us was dead. No hard feelings, but this story has too many beginnings. Each of us had been in this for many years. Each of us had a story. But only one had an ending.

Hindu Lodge, Baroda

Baroda is a short overnight journey from Mumbai, and the train reached before I awoke. The lodge was near the station. Stumbling past cows flipping tails, I lurched through the lodge's doorway. It smelled old and musty. The place was a blunder. Goosebumps were sprouting on my forearms.

Karsan bhai was quick on the draw. 'Sign this register,' he said.

He turned a large, lined tome towards me and pressed a pen into my hand. 'Government ID, please.' I placed my driving licence on the counter. 'You are from Mumbai?' I nodded. He handed me a small soap, a shampoo sachet, and a towel. He herded me by the arm to a room with a plywood door and shut himself out behind me.

I was woozy, a little confused. It felt confining, that small hostelry called Jagdale Hindu Lodge. A room where nuance was missing, a bed where gandus had slept. The queen-sized bed gave, with a rhythmic creak. The sheets had stains, the ashtray had two crooked butts, and the notepad had telephone numbers scribbled on it against names like Manju and Rita. I sneezed as I dusted a well-used chair. I stood around; I couldn't sit.

I roamed the place, clicking with my phone, making square constructions of decay that looked sexy on Instagram. The room smelled sweaty; the air felt breathed. I opened a window. There was a door that led to a balcony overlooking a busy road.

I walked to the wardrobe, dragged it open, and panned the inside with my phone. A handwritten sign said 'Do Not Disturb'. There was a cockroach next to it, belly up. It waved its many legs at me like an infant. There was a faint smell of naphthalene and there were two bills from a shopping mall in Alkapuri.

That room was a treasure house of clues. I could tell who was there before me. Varun Mehta, a travelling salesman, a salty badwa who brought in dirt with his shoes. He smoked Benson and Hedges till the filter edge. And he misused the bed. There was a thin cigarette butt that had a gold insignia and some cherry lipstick. That must be Rita. Later, Mehta stepped out, went to Alkapuri, and shopped for his family. A silk sari for Mrs Mehta and some toys for the children. He left the bills behind.

I needed a strong coffee. 'Room service?' I whispered into the intercom.

'Sorry, ben,' said Karsan bhai. 'I have no staff today.'

'How about housekeeping?' I photographed the dented ashtray and kicked the metal dustbin. 'Do you have a room freshener?'

'Tomorrow, ben.' There was a dull click and then silence.

I struck some poses before the mirror near the bathroom; nothing to cheer me up there. I walked to the window and peered at the city.

I was in Baroda to hear a man called Varadarajan recount his days when he played host to four young artists, one of whom was my mother. He was a literature graduate and said to be a sentient being. I had met him in my growing years, but I didn't remember him too well.

He had called me when my mother offed herself. 'I am so sorry for your loss.' Pain, Varadarajan, how about my pain, the one I lived with? He didn't show up at the funeral.

He called a few days later. 'Please come,' he said. I was at a loose end; I didn't know what to do with my time. I was also curious. Questions were bothering me. How was my mother as a student? Was she any different then? The person I knew lived by the hour and died by the minute.

I was disoriented the next day. When Varadarajan arrived at the lodge, I tried to hug him and he wasn't ready for that. There was an awkward shuffle and we stepped on each other's toes.

'Sorry, so sorry,' he said.

I stepped back. 'No, no, I am sorry.' Hugging was such a habit with me.

He was staring at me, searching for a resemblance. I waited for him to say something.

'Tara ji, you look quite fashionable,' he said.

'Like my mother?'

'No,' he said. 'I mean…' I knew what he meant.

We stood for a while, fencing with air, before I asked him to please be seated. We arranged chairs near the table.

He adjusted his round spectacles and patted down the wisp of grey hair that remained on his head. I observed him closely. I liked vanity. This Brahmin wore his caste mark on his forehead just above his spectacles, which rested on a perfect nose. His teeth were in order and his eyes were droopy, with one eye that seemed to follow the other.

'You are younger than I thought,' I told him with a straight face, and I shot him with my phone.

His face creased as he smiled. 'You can call me Varada,' he said.

I was not good with small talk; neither was he.

'So, you came by train?'

I nodded. 'Always,' I said. 'You want some tea or coffee?'

He hesitated; dissuaded perhaps by the lodge's looks, he shook his head. 'Shall I begin? How do you want to proceed?'

'Whatever comes to mind,' I said, opening my notebook and testing my pen.

He wiped his forehead carefully, cleared his throat like a musician, and in a sing-song voice that I got to like, he began. 'It was a strange year in Baroda.'

'Why strange?'

'The river breached its banks and entered our homes.'

'Oh no.'

'Yes. I got typhoid. It wouldn't go away, it just camped in my veins. And my poor parents, they passed away quietly within a few weeks of each other.'

'So sorry,' I said. Passed away quietly? That sounded abject. I mean, what was the point of dying like that?

'I had a low-grade fever and I was weak and exhausted from doing nothing. On New Year's Day I was all alone in the house.

There were two rooms too many, you see. The sun took an age to rise and I woke up with a pain in my legs.'

'You remember all that?'

'Yes. I remember I dragged myself to a mirror and looked at my face, thinking, what is wrong? Everything felt different. Then somebody knocked on my door.

'It was a total stranger. Hello, I am Krishna Kumar, he said.

'Behind him was another boy and two girls stood on the side. They looked apologetic.

'Do you have rooms to let? We are students.

'This Krishna Kumar had a beard and the eyes of a revolutionary. Something welled up inside me. I said, yes.

'He looked surprised. He turned towards his friends. What the fuck, he said. He looked back at me. You said yes?

'I nodded. In the coming months, that is what I did, I said yes to life.

'The four of them moved in, two to a room. They told me I had nothing to fear. They spent four years in my house and took over my life. They were my best years. I began to fear their departure.

'There was Maya, your mother, who wore bangles and a nose ring. She was always on edge, wanting to take on everybody. Within minutes I realized I would never understand her fully. I never knew what to expect from someone so intelligent, who smoked so much, drank at 10 a.m. on a Sunday, rolled grass into a cigarette with expertise, and spent the rest of the day trying to destroy her good looks. Her close friend was Anjana, the voracious one. She had her hands on everything: books, music, film, food, liquor.'

'Men?'

'Anything and everything, which she would slice, dice, and critically examine like she was some social scientist. But she was also the maternal one. When she was unoccupied, she sat around, frowning, looking like Mother India.'

I burst out laughing. 'Sorry,' I said. 'Please continue.'

'There was Girish – a wordsmith, he called himself. He cooked a lot and gave each dish a name. He was an insecure fellow: uncertain, self-deprecating. The only discourse he was capable of was a long one on failure. And Krishna Kumar was their spokesperson. A part-time Che Guevara. He took offence very easily. He was always borrowing money and wasting it on visionary projects. They were doomed to fail.'

'Tell me more about Anjana. Any early pearls of wisdom?'

'Early on she asked me not to meander. She said I was like driftwood in the Sabarmati. She told Girish to get a grip. She asked Krishna to phut le. And your mother was her bestie – isn't that what you call it? She would shout in the morning, arrey behen! Once, I asked her, what is it you like, if anything? She said, people who didn't ask such questions.'

'That sounds like her,' I said.

'She even had some unkind words for Baroda – Tamil words she learned for my benefit. The city has become too commercial, Uncle, she said. If you ask for pichai here, you will get kuppai. I was upset with her. I told her one day she would be badly hurt because of all that she said and then she would cry, she would weep. I told her she would sit and sob like Shabana Azmi in *Nishant*.'

'*Ankur*,' I said. 'Shabana wept beautifully in *Ankur*. Tell me more about my mother.'

'One day Maya spotted me in the morning, standing, facing the sunrise with folded hands. She told me I looked like the artist K.G. Subramanyan. I looked like KGS? That made me happy because I knew who he was. In the Shantiniketan gurukul set up by the great Rabindranath Tagore, KGS was a doyen. He signed his works as "Mani" in Tamil and he was called Manida. I had met him when I was a student and he had delivered a lecture on aesthetics. He had a piercing gaze, Manida, and he could see the person you were, the one behind your eyes.

'The face is a mask, KGS once said. He painted faces that looked like masks. And the body is a garment, he said. He painted bodies without garments.'

'So you were a proper landlord?' I asked.

'I tried to be. I tried to keep my distance. I knew full well that arts students were a tribe that drank, smoked, consumed substances, ate at odd hours, and usually went to sleep when I awoke. I wasn't like them – ever. Except that I liked my drink. I also liked KK, maybe because he was older than the other three and closer somehow to me. Our age difference was a decade and more, yet we got along.'

'And his favourite phrase?'

Varada smiled. 'You know, don't you? "What the fuck." I don't like saying it but he did very often and its meaning varied. We were evening buddies; we shared a bottle of rum on most days and once he had had enough, he would say silly things.'

'Like what?'

'Like: "Why are you alive, Varadarajan?" You know, I thought about that for a whole day.'

Varada paused and took a deep breath. 'How am I doing?'

I gave him a thumbs-up and a bright smile. He looked reassured. In truth I was quite confused. I got up from my chair and started pacing because the beginning was off-key.

Three steps were all that was necessary to take me from the wall to the window. Outside in the distance I saw the Baroda railway station. A swarm of two-wheelers surrounded it. Away to my right, behind some trees, was the large campus of a university called Sayaji that was built by a maharaja called Rao. Its large domes flirted with Mughal architecture. Between us was a road, traffic, and some pigeon shit.

Varadarajan continued, his voice seeming to fade into the background. 'Girish roamed the campus like a fakir. He came down with a fever. And he fell in love with Anjana when she tried to nurse him. Ask me, I know. Their idea of love was to take the afternoon class off and sing elegies in the bathroom – together. There was something poetic about their lust.'

I said something rude in an undertone.

'Can I get something to drink?' asked Varadarajan. 'And can you please stop pacing up and down?'

I ran down into the bright street and found him a cold sherbet. He wiped the rim of the tumbler, sipped the drink, wiped his forehead, and sipped some more.

'Should I have allowed these youngsters to smoke all that stuff in my house?' he asked.

I did not answer. I could not imagine him influencing my mother in any way.

'The first time I saw Maya roll a cigarette I should have stopped her. Instead, I was watching her long fingers smoothen the white sheet, her painted nails slitting open the plastic packet that had the grass, her pink tongue as it wetted the length, and finally how she tapped the rolled cylinder, held the slightly irregular cheroot, placed it between her lips, lit a match, and then showed me her profile while she inhaled, then threw her head up and exhaled. I was hooked as much as she was, addicted to observing them. This was a life that unfolded like a television serial. Imagine a group of creative youngsters mixing alcohol with art, drugs with critical theory, and sex with philosophy, and you have a ringside seat. Would you want to intervene and risk their going away?'

'No,' I said.

'I was standing on the sidelines, looking. I was a bystander. I was truly a K.G. Subramanyan character, one who pretended to be involved but was in truth a mere observer.'

'Nice,' I said. I liked the image; I had seen works of KGS that depicted an old man whiling away time at the margins, looking at a pastoral.

'Do they hire these rooms by the hour?' asked Varada, out of the blue.

'Do I look like I would know?' I replied.

'Touché,' he said.

'I can't afford anything else, Mr Varadarajan. We can make too much of it or we can proceed further.'

After an eon, he resumed.

'I thought I knew about artists till this foursome came my way,' he said. 'I had read about artists, the well-known ones like Leonardo, Rembrandt, Goya, and Picasso. So, I told my four young tenants: I know where art comes from and what it can do. You should join this pantheon and make us proud.'

A memory rankled and he frowned before he continued. 'Girish punctured my sentiment. Don't take us so seriously, sir. We artists are just a handful of freaks, he said.

'True, I replied, and he looked surprised. You agree?

'Wholeheartedly, I said. What are artists really in today's world?

'You tell me, he said.

'I said, they are fodder for museum-goers and plunder for thieves.'

Varadarajan sat with his mouth open. We heard a rumbling sound and it wasn't a train. He looked sheepish as another rumble emanated.

'Can we have something to eat?' he asked. 'Somewhere decent?'

We descended the staircase carefully. My shoes were well-heeled. I wasn't. Decent in my book meant a modest eatery. Karsan bhai directed us to a nearby place that served a Gujarati thali.

I trailed behind Varadarajan and caught a glimpse of myself in a shop window. I looked like a ramp model for Fashion Street, the roadside paradise in Mumbai that sold cheap rip-offs. I thought I had the advantage over those who could afford bespoke, people who bought labels like Gucci and Versace so they could look like a million bucks.

Varadarajan would have done his village proud. He wore sandals, pants that needed ironing, and a bush shirt that hung past his hips. He held his hands above his eyes, shielding them from the sun, and looked around as if surveying his paddy fields, like his ancestors must have in Thanjavur or wherever else rice grew. He sneezed a few times. Each sneeze was followed by an invocation to a god. 'Muruga,' he said, one last time.

The small eatery served affordable meals. The place was run by a gruff, unshaven man and a young lad who plied us with local dishes. They hovered, urging us to eat. Varadarajan eyed his food with distaste; he poked at it, drained oil onto the thali, and looked at me accusingly.

An hour and a snooze later, he was enjoying a cup of coffee in the room; I waited for him to finish.

'And they did not suspect you?' I asked, as he wiped his lips with his hand towel.

'Suspect me of what?'

'Did they realize you had become a voyeur?'

Varada seemed upset with the term. 'I never peeped, I never asked questions, never took sides or got involved.'

'Then how do you know so much?'

'I had become a confidant. They would come up to me and chat. Because they trusted me.'

'All of them?'

He shook his head. 'Maya less so.'

'Was there a puja room in your house?' I asked. It was a good question. The idea of a Tamil Brahmin of Varada's vintage allowing youngsters to drink and smoke in his house was hard to swallow.

'There was one when my mother was around.' He became thoughtful. 'She was quite religious and the house always had the fragrance of incense and jasmine flowers.'

'And the flooring was mosaic?' I asked.

Varada smiled and looked at me as if to say, 'Look how bright she is, she knows so much.'

'Did they dirty your place, Uncle?'

'Initially, yes,' replied Varada, frowning, perhaps at being called uncle. 'Only Maya was fastidious. She was such a good housekeeper. She kept them in order. The boys had strung a rope in their room and hung the washing inside. Imagine! And they would never clear out the rubbish. If they needed a plate, they washed one and left the rest of the dishes in the sink.'

This was freaky. My mother – who would rather bungee jump than have a bath, whose house had a layer of dust on books and shelves, and whose personal preference for mouthwash, cologne, and other masking devices was legendary among her boyfriends – seemed to have had a change of heart at some point.

'What were my mother's paintings like? Do you have any of her work?'

'No, not even one. She used to destroy her own work those days. Just like that Girish who would tear up his own writing. Maya used to paint like Marlene Dumas, or at least that is what Anjana said.

I did not know who Marlene was but it was always about her body and men and…'

'Men with their…?'

'Yes. And it was awkward and provocative, almost crude in execution. Initially the work looked wishy-washy because her paint application was diffuse and her colour palette had only shades of grey. But very soon I woke up to its depth.'

'Depth?'

'Anjana said something remarkable which has stayed with me to this day. She said that women had to battle to reclaim their bodies from their men and their children. Which is why in their art the body became a site where wars were fought, and often, they were the ones getting hurt.'

'Heavy,' I said. 'But so relatable.' I rearranged the table, made a show of pulling up my chair, then sat and inclined my head.

Varada watched me; he was done for the moment. 'Your turn now!' he said. 'Please, I really want to know more about you. Is this your first trip to Baroda?'

I spoke at length. I was comfortable with this old comrade, landlord, and outright decent soul. In so many words I travelled back to my time in this city that was a crucible for memories, my mother's and mine. These weren't my best memories. I am not sure which ones are but Baroda certainly isn't one of them. I get lost when I think of Baroda, and even as I am speaking to Varada, my mind wanders.

Baroda isn't new for me: that was what I wanted to tell him. I went to the same college as my mother, and the same damn departments. I wore my hair in plaits at the time and my lips were pursed. Art was what I wanted to study and it was a strong enough urge. I remember exiting the railway station; it felt like I was retracing my mother's footsteps.

It had rained in the night and the air was cool and fresh. Leaves and flowers had fallen on roads and pavements. Morning walkers followed me and walked abreast. A few smiled welcomingly. They were used to the sight of students dragging a large suitcase, looking anxiously at signboards. I found my hostel room, dumped my bag, and headed for Vishnu ki Laari, the tea shop outside the campus. I looked into my cup and found pieces of cardamom.

The Maharaja Sayajirao University of Baroda (MSU) had shaped art history and I arrived at the campus expecting to see some stirring works. There were none. I had been to the sprawling Visva-Bharati campus at Shantiniketan in Bengal and every doyen there had left a mark. There were murals on buildings, murals in corridors, and iconic sculpture in prominent locations. It was a robust and masculine display – not surprising, as all the doyens were male. At the film institute in Pune there was anonymous graffiti on studio walls that paid homage to greats like Ray, Ghatak, and Tarkovsky – again, all male.

While the MSU campus was bare, there was a record of sorts in the library. There were dozens of catalogues, a busload of books on artists from the Baroda school, and a few manifestos. There was a manifesto written by the artist Anita Dube and essays penned by the curator/critic and Indian modernism's custodian, Geeta Kapur. She had written movingly, among others, of Nasreen Mohammedi, Amrita Sher-Gil, and Nalini Malani.

'Have you heard of them, Mr Varadarajan?'

He nodded, up and down – good for him, I thought – and then shook his head sideways. Was that a yes or a no?

'Mr Varadarajan, I was a legacy student and the arts department in MS University was aware of this.'

'You met her professors?'

'A few. I liked the professors who were practising artists. Their practice had not flourished. They had struggled, each of them, and that struggle made them the teachers they were.

'The first show makes a man out of you, said one of them. Forget all the hard work you put in making art. On opening day, you stand in a commercial space, naked, and money walks through the door. You can see the cruel gaze of the buyers sizing up what you have slaved over and suddenly you want to go up to these people and explain. You want to talk up your art, and make it valuable.

You want to reduce the price you have set. You want your work to bloody sell. What a lovely show, they told me. Really great work, they told me. These were epitaphs. I was dead by then, having stood on one leg for luck, then the other, a smile plastered on my face.

'If our work found a home, we lived, and we returned to our cute little barsati, to the corner we called our studio and worked some more, said another professor, a quiet one who seemed to carry with him a tinge of regret.

'It was a minuscule market, said the first professor. It had a handful of collectors and there was one government museum. Curators doubled up as critics, and artists doubled up as curators. Nobody criticized art seriously in this merry-go-round, and nobody swiped at established positions. We were bold in our art but very afraid otherwise.

'Successful artists dropped anchor, said the other, but the water was shallow.'

'Ouch,' said Varada, and he laughed.

'I was told then that my mother's first show did well. The professors were there at the opening. She was exultant when the first sale happened, they said. She said it was better than sex.

'There was an indigenous creed that I took to, one fanned by the likes of J. Swaminathan and K.G. Subramanyan. I was told that in art the nation is not a boundary. But for me it was a rich lode for mark-making.

'I cut my teeth at a time of transition, when the moderns, those who were alive, were in their late eighties and they still held sway. The next rung was just a decade behind and yet it was lost in a pond that was called post-modern by some and pre-contemporary by others. The contemporary movement was already middle-aged. There were young contemporaries in their thirties and they were on life support. Their concoctions were thoughtful and clever. Some of them refused to go to market with an object. It was a dumb practice, I thought, to flaunt your socialism when art had no pension. We are artists, I shouted, not poets! Why bugger around with philosophy when someone had made this big bad market, gilded our creations, and telescoped art valuations?'

I looked to see if Varada was listening; he was.

'The sun rose in the west in our little world, Mr Varadarajan. We went west early, shaking our booties, or we ended up looking naïve. I was asked to try for residencies because they help you stay current. Go, they said, or you will be stuck. I struggled, Mr Varadarajan, how I struggled! I needed to evolve, find a voice, make something that spoke to me and others in equal measure.'

'Is art so difficult?' asked Varada.

'Not just difficult but also wilful,' I said. 'At times an adversary and in the beginning an unending quest. My first few works paid homage to my gurus, then they looked like building blocks made from my confusion, and then they wrapped their arms around me to stave off the cold, cold feeling of emptiness. The hunt for the elusive was palpable. Western artists had covered so much ground, it wasn't fair. What could I add to this discourse? My mother had found a way. I have to give her credit for that. She had evolved in her deep blue haze. She had truly felt what was missing. She had travelled far into a realm that few understood.'

'Beautiful,' said Varada.

I think he was moved. I can be honest, you know, and it always affects people.

'Damn,' I said, lost in a haze. 'I miss her.' I truly missed my terrible mother at times. So badly behaved she was, and so vulnerable.

I realized Varada had wise eyes. They spoke even as his voice stayed silent. He pulled out a piece of paper; it was an envelope, a registered letter. I guessed what it was.

'Police summons?' I asked, dreading his reply. He nodded, looking pained.

'I am so sorry,' I said.

'Not your fault,' he said. 'What is happening? Please tell me. Please tell me who is this Pandey who has signed this summons?'

I told Varada of my meeting with Inspector Pandey of the Special Branch a few days after the incident. He was the case officer.

He said he had waited a week before he called. 'We need to meet at the crime scene,' he said.

I arrived early at the apartment; the police had already searched it thoroughly. I tried to clean up the place, dumping the expired meds, some nasal sprays, and many attar bottles. There were encrusted paint tubes, unwashed brushes, and unfinished works in the studio. All of them spoke of a rude interruption.

He was younger than I expected, and standing in the doorway, he looked like a Bollywood actor. He was medium height, very fit, fair, with dark eyes. He spoke in Hindi at first and switched quickly to English. He surveyed the place. 'Habit,' he said, as he continued to look around. His eyes settled on the bathroom door. 'Crime scene,' he said.

He had brought a box file with him that had sections and he had flagged them with coloured stickers that bore titles. There was a section labelled Suspects, one that said Motive, and another section was called Accessory. The largest section simply said Victim.

'Can we do this quickly?' I said. The place made me uncomfortable.

'No,' he said. 'Today is just the beginning and this is not a simple case.'

I expected cops to be cold, humourless, and business-like. This one was; he wasn't looking to make friends. He lifted the file cover and opened it slowly.

'This is an astonishing case,' he said. 'There is enough in your mother's history to support the suicide theory and all the circumstantial—'

'It wasn't a suicide,' I interjected. 'Forget everything and believe me. My mother would not have done this to herself.'

'Your mother wasn't your mother when she had so much inside her. Toxicology reports—'

I interrupted again, nodding vigorously, 'Exactly. I have seen her in that state. She worked in that state. Sometimes it was rubbish and occasionally it was art.'

'I understand,' he said. 'Look, I don't mean to be rude, but—'

Again, I interrupted him. 'You don't understand, do you? She never had that kind of initiative. I don't have a better way of putting it.'

'And all that self-abuse?'

'Inspector, for her, it was life experience. In her mind that's what it was: a mind-altering, heightened state. That's what her groupies kept telling her.'

'Fine,' he said. 'If it wasn't suicide, what was it?'

'An accident,' I said. 'She went over the edge that she always flirted with.'

He turned the file towards me.

'Look inside; my predecessor has marked it as closed. You know why? Because your mother was considered scum and we really don't care about scum. No, don't get upset. Alcoholics and drug addicts get no respect from cops. And your mother was special, she was a narcoholic. She ran a circus when you were away, you know that? Her lovers disappeared, her friends were desperate, and finally they brought a Brahmin from Baroda to try to reason with her. They couldn't wean her away from drugs. The cops got complaints from neighbours. They did nothing. But I am different. I got involved because I don't judge people. I came to your place after one noisy night and it was a mess. No problem with that. Night after a party so what do you expect? Your mother, she was seated on the sofa, looking regal. She struggled to make me some tea and we sat next to some fresh flowers and we chatted. I don't want to go overboard but she was a lady. Your mother wasn't who I expected to meet. She was interesting.'

'Thanks, nice of you to say something like that. You could have busted her that day but you did not.'

'Well, I had a selfish reason,' said the inspector. 'I asked her for the names and numbers of her dealers, her heroin suppliers. She said she would give them to me.'

This was news. I had no idea my mother was planning to rat on some hoods.

'Did she?'

He shook his head. 'I got the details from someone else. An anonymous man called me and gave me the information. We busted that gang soon after. And your mother had no supply for a fortnight before she died. I was told she went wild from the withdrawal. They should have put her in a facility.'

I felt sick. This whole retelling brought up bile. 'Inspector, I want to know what happened that night as much as you do.'

'Of course,' said Inspector Pandey. 'Should I continue?'

I shrugged, quite tired and confused.

'This case is what we call an inside job, which is why it is very difficult to crack. There is no apparent motive and everybody wants to get on with their lives – except the two of us.' He looked at me and I nodded. 'The setting was too perfect for it to be a suicide. The cuts were too perfect for someone as drunk as your mother that day. She was drugged out as well. But I have no proof, no evidence that she was done in. We will have to work very hard to uncover the truth. I can't do it alone. You will have to help me ferret it out.'

Ferret, he said. 'How?' I asked.

'By meeting everyone concerned, listening to them, being patient with their stories and with what we call extraneous material. You are someone they will talk differently to. They will open up and chances are we will uncover something.'

Extraneous, he said. This was something I might actually like doing. I wanted to know more about my mother's stint in Baroda. What was she like as an artist? And was she ever in love with someone besides herself?

'What is your theory on motive?' I asked him.

'Money,' he said. 'The prize money is large, as you know. This could have been a prize-winning performance, and someone could have assisted her.'

'Who?'

He looked hard at me, making me uncomfortable. What the hell? Really?

'I have come to know that you and your mother have a large debt burden.'

I was horrified. I had been warned that the police would go hunting anything and everything; this was too close to home.

'But you don't look the type,' he said. An uncomfortable silence followed.

'My friend Nupur has received a summons to formally appear at your station. Why?'

I think he was a little embarrassed. Finally, he shrugged.

'Aiding and abetting,' he said. 'She and her father set up this prize. We have sent him a notice as well.'

This wasn't happening, I told myself. It was. An adventure in the art world had turned hostile.

'In the meanwhile, you can travel like you wanted to.'

I was planning to head to Baroda to meet people who had known my mother.

'How do I go about this? I mean, I can't just walk up to these people and ask them.'

'Yes, you can,' he said. 'They would expect you to do just that. They would be happy to speak with you because each of them will be harbouring some guilt.'

Harbouring, he said. 'Are you going to give me the file?'

'No,' he said. 'You don't need it. You don't need to act like the police. You are on a personal journey.'

'Where do I begin?'

He thought about it for a moment. 'Not for me to say,' he said.

Varada looked sad. 'So the police are fishing around and calling everyone? I know how they operate. They will play us against each other.'

'This Pandey is a clever fellow. That much I can tell you. He is convinced it wasn't an accident.'

'Let him do his job,' said Varada. 'So you studied here, like your mother did? I had no idea.'

'That is because my mother never spoke about me to anyone. I wasn't good enough, you see? I hoped to be an artist like she was but it was never going to happen. I should have known better.'

'You are not a successful artist?'

I shook my head. 'I am just a wannabe. Anyway, forget about me, tell me more about my mother.'

'One day I held her,' said Varada. 'I actually held your mother. I don't know why but she broke down. She spoke to no one about her past, her parents, her young life. Nobody asked her. I should have; I am sure she would have told me so much more. I think she needed that: to be able to talk to someone, to go to her memory rooms and walk through them again. She was like an orphan. It was almost like she never had a family.

'And then she started drinking. She went hard into everything, unmindful of consequences. She said she liked the slow blurring, the laxity, the dulling of conscious awareness. In this state, she would work. She would draw and the next morning she would say, look at this line – I could never draw it when sober.

'She called me a darpok. She said, you should see yourself, the look in your eyes. You are afraid of what?

'The last year they were here, there was full-on drama. I don't know how they managed to stay together. Krishna Kumar and Anjana hated each other. Can you imagine the dynamics?'

'When did you get to know she was an unusual person?'

'I kept looking at her drawings. She drew all the time – day and night, without pause, and sometimes without thought – till it became like breathing, she said. And she was careless about these sketches and studies. They would be everywhere, in everybody's way. I complained at first and then I began to gather them and file them by date. I would look at them when I had nothing to do. And they began affecting me. I understood her better; I could see her struggle, her journey, her exploration, the quest that came from deep inside her. It was so beautiful.'

'Then?'

'I noticed she was getting stuck in her drawing and I was afraid. I thought here is where it all goes to waste. She said that when you are young, there is a poverty of ideas and a shallowness of experience. She was impatient; she felt she could remedy this by living life on the edge, an induced edge.'

'And the other three?'

'Krishna Kumar had a rich motherlode where he came from. Kerala is the land of magic realism and dramatics, performances like Kathakali and theyyam. Girish wasn't an artist in any case. Anjana was the one who worried Maya. She was a budding critic who cared little how art got made. She looked at what Maya did from time to time and said nothing, and that by itself was damning.'

'What did my mother submit for her final year?'

'A set of paintings. No drawings. She displayed three paintings at the students' display.'

'Did you encourage her?'

He laughed as he remembered. 'She wanted one big moment on the campus. But that moment never came. That public acknowledgement that she was in some sense special – it never came.'

'The students' display?'

'Went off well. Bombay came: the gallery people, the odd critic, some curators, friends. They were there and there was palpable excitement. She was noticed, and one or two discussions happened. But that was all. No pedestal, no podium.'

'She realized she was just a student?'

'Yes, and not an overnight prodigy in art.'

There was so much more we could have shared with each other but I had to process what I had heard. I was also done. I was so tired and I wanted to leave that city, go away once again. It happens to me often – this urge to just get away.

'You are leaving,' said Varada, 'When will you—'

'I don't know,' I said.

I caught the night train. I sat by the window and stared into the darkness. I was headed home: would it feel like home, like it used to? Would I get that special feeling of coming home again? People make so much of living with art. I lived with an artist. That's a whole new world, a different dimension. Would I recommend it? Depends on who you are. I had no choice. My name, by the way, is Tara and this could have been my story. In my heart I know it will never be but I cling to that thought, that belief.

II

Behavioural scientists say it is greed, lust, jealousy, and pride that drive people to attempt the irrational.

There was this khandani baniya I got to know. His name was Gupta. He bought art.

Sarla Gupta

The first day of school was hurried. Nupur stuffed her bag with what she could find and ran down the stairs, where the house help was in a flurry and her anxious mother was shouting instructions. The yellow bus arrived with a hydraulic hiss.

'Bacha party, where are you?'

Nupur fled, her sandwich in her mouth, her bag slapping one side, her lunchbox the other. She muttered a hi, a good morning, a kaise ho, and got to a window seat. The bus was air-conditioned; she took a deep breath and looked outside. Some sky was visible, some sun. It was a spring day in Delhi. A hot summer waited in the wings.

They drove through traffic onto a six-lane highway. They passed wheat fields and livestock and hoardings that offered villas with amenities. Her new school had a sprawling campus in the neighbouring state of Uttar Pradesh.

She sat, nose pressed on a windowpane, her breath forming continents.

'Shy one, what's your name?'

'Nupur,' she said.

'Where are you from?'

'Lajpat Nagar,' she said without thinking.

Three generations of Guptas stayed in Lajpat Nagar. Grand-uncles, grandaunts, their children, their grandchildren. Some dogs without collars wagged their tails outside, some cats roamed like they owned the place, and two cows from the neighbourhood bellowed till they were fed.

'I am a Gupta,' said Nupur.

This was a declaration of belonging, not exclusion. Guptas were common in Delhi, as were Goels, Agarwals, and Mittals.

The caste grouping was baniya and they were middle class to the bone. In an earlier time, almost by common law, baniyas were shopkeepers. Some were halwais who sat in community centres in Delhi behind a board that said 'Agarwal Sweets'.

'Nupur Gupta. Business family?'

'Yes. We have a factory.' She thought for a while, then made a clean breast of it. 'We make mixies in Naraina.'

There were a few giggles. Naraina was a grimy place with sheds where small units made parts that were often sold in the grey market.

A girl came and sat next to her. She smiled warmly. 'Anaiya Goel,' she said. 'My family has shops in Sadar Bazaar.'

More giggles followed. Naraina and Sadar Bazaar were parts of Delhi that tourists did not visit.

'What is the mixie called?'

'Toofan,' said Nupur.

It was a noisy processor that went after Indian ingredients with the required tenacity.

'Does your family pay tax?'

Nupur laughed; the whole bus laughed. The question was a good one and it came from what baniya children overheard. The bus was full of new money; some were richer than others depending on which business the family had stumbled upon or which corner they had cut.

'Where do you stay, really?'

'Noida,' said Nupur. 'Just like you.'

The house was a kothi with a large garden and a roundabout. The windows were French, the mirrors Belgian, the floor Italian marble. In the garage were two Bavarian SUVs.

'I love Noida,' said Anaiya. 'I like what they call it – Jamuna paar.'

'My father wants to move to south Delhi, to Vasant Vihar,' said Nupur. 'He is busy making enough money.'

'So who stays in Lajpat Nagar?'

'The joint family, the extended family. My father broke away.'

'I like him already.'

Nupur smoothed her skirt. 'He is a tech entrepreneur.' It was a badge he wore with pride.

They passed a traffic island that had a life-size public sculpture. It looked like most public sculptures did – trauma with a blunt instrument.

'And mummy dearest?'

'She is Christian.'

'You are full of surprises. What about you? Are you Hindu?'

'Am I Hindu?'

Nupur had asked this question of her mother. 'Beta,' Ma said, 'when you grow up, you decide.'

'Where are you from, Ma?' was Nupur's favourite question.

'Bombay,' was Sarla Gupta's favourite answer. Every time Sarla uttered the name, she paused, and she remembered.

'Where in Bombay?'

For as long as Sarla knew, her family had stayed in Bandra. Some relatives stayed in Santa Cruz. She belonged to the island dil se, a strip of land that she travelled south by train, alighting at Churchgate. She walked to Colaba, roamed the pavements, and bought trinkets. She walked to Kala Ghoda and listened to poetry. She sat on the parapet in Marine Drive, where the sun – a lazy orange ball – sank into the sea.

Most people in Sarla's city were playing a role in a film. There was one that unspooled in her head.

'Don't ask me where I am from,' said Sarla, a sad heroine in her film. 'Ask me what I left behind.'

Nupur was born in a plotted pura in north Delhi. Pitampura then was a bizarre place with barren plots on derelict roads. Dust storms swirled in the hot summer. Atop a television tower in nearby Rohini, a restaurant began to revolve. Nupur arrived in its vicinity like a flash of lightning. She grew up an only child, sucking her thumb.

Her father travelled on work, her mother coped. Salil had to amass a fortune; Sarla had to move home – bag, baggage, and frail temperament – to middle-class Mandakini Enclave near Nehru Place, then to a posh sector in Noida.

At each location Sarla was bemused. 'What is this Delhi?'

It was Dilli, it was Dehli, a sheher, a basti. It had naalas, a river called Yamuna, and it had hives called DDA colonies.

'When will it grow up?' she asked Salil.

New Delhi was where sane people learnt rash lessons. The city stoked their insecurities, fostered in them a degree of recklessness. Old Delhi was a record of invasions. It had a skyline with forts, mausoleums, ramparts, and thickset gates. New Delhi had concrete flyovers and gleaming towers. The really old Delhi was captured by a sound-and-light show in the iconic Red Fort. In New Delhi, there was a sound-and-light show on every road at rush hour. It was a civil society if you spent enough time in it. You learnt quickly. You lowered your standards.

There was a Delhi that Sarla grew to like. It had an auditorium called Kamani, the Triveni Kala Sangam, shops in Janpath, street food in Bengali Market. 'That's what I am,' she said when someone called her a tourist. There was more for people like her. Art galleries in south Delhi, a private museum in Saket, and the National Gallery of Modern Art in a red-brick building called Jaipur House.

She fortified her home. In the evening there was gin and tonic on the sideboard, and the company of artists, poets, and dancers. School-going Nupur was privy to this world. Randy visitors who lounged on sofas and then stretched out on the floor. Smoky air filled with naked arguments. Late nights were followed by quiet mornings. Nupur stepped gingerly past debris and let herself out. Her yellow school bus hissed and lowered its stairway.

Sarla saw herself in her daughter. It was a cause for worry. She had given up her job, raised the child, and was at a loose end with her time. Her husband was lax in domestic situations. 'You have a free hand,' he said. He was particular about school grades, mark sheets, metrics.

'Only child,' he said, 'needs to stand up and swim. You know what I mean.'

Sarla wasn't into grades. She dragged her daughter to her galleries and museums.

'Open your eyes. Do you feel something?'

Nupur would be in her school uniform, her school shoes biting her feet.

'Feel the excitement?'

Nupur would nod, trail behind her mother, stand in front of paintings, and draw circles with her toes.

'You told me it would be an adventure?'

Sarla snorted. How was she to explain – and why did she have to? What was art if not an adventure?

Salil Gupta, a graduate of the Delhi College of Engineering, viewed the world through the prism of science. At age forty-five, he was a technology entrepreneur and a ruthless user of business aids, toolkits, and life manuals. Competitors admired his vision and envied his focus.

He had a mixed record at home. He hadn't logged the required hours; he hadn't spent enough time with his daughter. His wife, piqued by his hours at work and frequent travel, once asked him for his visiting card.

'What will Nupur do in life?' asked Sarla. 'Do you have time to answer that question?'

Salil sat at his computer and mapped out Nupur's future. He drew a chart that had goalposts, cut-offs, and percentages. For good measure there was a Plan B along with a Plan A.

In Plan A, Nupur would complete high school at Modern School, Barakhamba Road, and graduate in commerce from Shri Ram College. In Plan B, she would opt for an Honours in economics from St. Stephen's College.

Sarla held the printout against the light. 'Wah,' she said. 'So simple.'

'Just plain foresight,' said Salil.

'Foresight that may be in vain,' said Sarla. 'Nupur has a mind of her own, have you noticed? If she sees this, she will do the opposite.'

Nupur had no idea where she was headed. Middle school was a confusing time; teenagers had other important questions and discoveries. Sarla alerted her to the best-laid plans of her father.

'I can't think right now,' said Nupur. 'Can't I just enjoy this moment?'

Delhi was seeing a rash of new schools advertising an international curriculum. The International Baccalaureate programme was making waves with youngsters. Stories were being told about its rigour, the course called Theory of Knowledge – how we know what we know – and the torturous exercise called the Extended Essay. Youngsters, some still wearing braces, had to prepare a mini-thesis that required an original research question.

Sarla was enamoured with this approach. Nupur found it interesting as well.

'This will cost me,' said Salil, looking at the glossy prospectus.

'Merely a nibble,' said Sarla.

Nupur decided on a new school on the outskirts of Delhi; she chose the IB programme. She would be schooled in a stream called the humanities.

A Ring Road circled the city. When the city expanded, an Outer Ring Road described a larger circle. Nupur's junior college was at the North Campus. It was a haven of fast friendships, canteen link-ups, and the odd break-up. She was in love with her history professor. He had grey hair, a beard, and wore a scarf in summer.

'Imagine Delhi as a conqueror's muse,' he said. 'A revolving door through which many rulers swept, leaving a fresher ruin.'

She spent a Sunday with him. The day was punctuated with ragas; he listened by the clock to ustads and pandits, to Kesarbai Kerkar. And while Nupur appreciated the atmosphere, and what he called the prosody, she came away with a headache.

A longer stint at a bristly Delhi college would have toughened Nupur but she was shipped prematurely to study in a college in America. She added five kilos in six months: the freshman minimum. She decorated her room wall with family photos. Soon she was a double major, having mixed business with art, history with calculus, and PowerPoint with Adobe. She wasn't a topper, but she was voted class something.

'No need for you to come to the convocation,' she told her parents.

She made the trip home with a bunch of her peers. They were from the science stream and were focused; their life plans were ready. She came from the humanities; she arrived in bits and pieces.

Salil and Sarla showed up at the airport to receive her.

'Look, Ma,' she said, holding out her hands. 'No tattoos.'

Sarla looked around her, behind her. No boyfriend either.

The ride home was quiet. Nupur stared out of the window. She found the same chaos she had left behind.

'You don't travel enough,' she told her mother. 'You need to get away to see the well we live in.'

'What do I look like to you?' asked Sarla. 'A frog?'

Nupur, fresh from years abroad, saw history that crisscrossed centuries. People stood and stared. Why? They spat into corners, threw packets, sat on stairs. Pithy comments followed her; she could sense ugly intentions.

She could sense tiredness at home. Everything was in its place; the furniture was new, the art was new, and servants were everywhere, dealing with dust, looking for bugs, for things to do. Her father stood tall and looked proud; her mother looked like Nupur did after listening to an hour of Radiohead.

Four long years away from home and Nupur's lens had changed. In her mind she was a protagonist in an art-house film, facing existential moments. Traffic chased her as she shimmied and scaled a divider. A dog followed in her wake, a street dog seeking protection. She helped it across, then turned to pet it. The dog bared its teeth.

'I won't be here long,' she promised her parents.

They called her out when she complained.

'How do you drink this?' The water left stains on vessels.

'How does one breathe?' It was winter; the sun was hidden by smoke from burning fields. Nupur looked up at the grey sky and coughed.

'You will get used to it.'

Particulate matter settled in Nupur's ears, on her collars, in her sleeves. She coughed again. 'Ma, have you heard of dusting?'

'Dusting doesn't help,' said Nupur's grandma. 'Dust has nowhere to go.'

'Nani, you should go out and see the leaves on the roadside trees. You will weep.'

Leaves were covered by reth, by mitti. Brown was the colour of photosynthesis.

'Will I die early?' asked Nupur.

The city she had grown up in had succeeded in unsettling her. She was wary all the time, particularly of the quiet moments when the unexpected lurked. There was a new syndrome she had fallen prey to, like most returning Indians.

One weekend there was a party; Salil had drawn up the guest list. There were many interesting people Nupur met, who seemed to have been picked from a roster that his office had prepared. The guests seemed surprised to see each other. They held their drinks, their eyes roamed, their minds sketched vectors, searching for intersections.

'A party without an occasion,' mumbled Sarla Gupta. She had started drinking before the guests arrived. 'Trust Salil to assemble a Serengeti. If this isn't an example of haphazard hospitality, what is?'

The guests arrived in no particular order, and they stood here and there next to furniture and works of art and some suspicious objects that could have been either. Sarla did not receive them. She had her corner.

'Look at me,' she said, perched on a ledge, her habit-forming ash, her glass listing. 'Look. What is happening to me? A perfectly normal person. A nice person.'

'Since when are you a votary for nice?' asked Nupur.

'Listen.'

Ash dropped; some whisky spilled.

'Make some money of your own,' she said. 'You hear me?' Her voice had risen, and a few people looked their way. 'Don't depend on your father's stash.'

The next morning Sarla set off to her mother's place in west Delhi. Nupur accompanied her and received a shitload of advice.

'You will have to be strong,' said her mother.

'You will have to resist,' said her grandmother.

'Look at me,' said Sarla again.

'Don't be like her,' said Granny.

Granny had a small business that she ran out of her two-bed apartment. Her own eyesight had declined but she hired neighbours on an hourly basis, and they embroidered trousseaus for a famous designer.

'Run away,' said Sarla Gupta. 'Go to Bombay.'

She remembered her glorious years there. Her film unspooled in her head. That suburb, those Catholic bungalows, a church, a school playground, the smell of bacon. Bells tolled at the appointed hour. Time froze in the afternoon for siesta. Evenings, she sashayed south in her heels, one strap loose, make-up without foundation, a hurry more desperate than the trains.

'You must make a trip,' said Sarla. 'Spend some time between Mount Mary and Santa Cruz.' Her eyes moistened. 'Is there a better name for a place than Santa Cruz?'

'Don't forget the hospital called Cooper,' said Grandma.

'Bombay is now Mumbai,' said Nupur. 'I will have to get used to Chunabhatti, Chinchpokli, and Ghodbunder.'

'Bombay exists,' said Sarla with feeling. 'Lost love of mine. Such attitude! A long history, mind you, but not pretentious and monumental. Like this Delhi. Where is the space in Bombay to cordon off history? If you have a precious Art Deco building in Bombay, you stay in it. If you have a UNESCO heritage station you buy a ticket and catch a train. You go to the imperious General Post Office to post a letter. You don't dawdle outside like tourists do, taking pictures of pigeons flying.'

'You are such a romantic, darling mother.'

A genteel person, modest in her ambition, particular about cultural consumption, critical of philistines like her husband, Nupur was fond of her mother, her silliness, her easy-going ways, her fights over unimportant matters. She was often on the phone, talking to friends and family; she leaned over the boundary wall and chatted with neighbours. She kept herself busy. She had strong opinions on things considered minor.

'Don't worry about me,' said Sarla. 'I am not a big fan of the other life. I know several homemakers are.'

'What other life?'

'The one they are not leading. My husband, God bless him, he is fine, such a pretender. It is you I worry about.'

'Don't worry about me,' said Nupur. 'I am fine as I am, even if I have nothing to prove it, and nothing to show.'

'What self-belief!' said Sarla.

'Too much,' said Granny.

'I have a philosophy,' said Nupur.

'What philosophy?'

Nupur spoke for ten minutes. Her mother smoked through it all, half-listening, and her granny kept coughing.

'Who filled your head with these thoughts?' asked Granny.

'I know who paid for it,' said Sarla.

Nupur's head was full of what her school and college had taught her. Chiefly, she was good at essays, in a style called rhetoric. It was how she was trained. She was helpless; asked a question, she became self-conscious and very literate.

'International Baccalaureate and a humanities undergrad degree have messed with her mind,' said her father.

'On the contrary, they have set me free,' said Nupur. They allowed her to roam in the lives of men and women, strange people whose pursuit was a kind of evil. One man and his feral grandson fascinated her. They laid people bare in the pursuit of their vocations. The grandfather was a psychoanalyst and his grandson a famous painter.

Sigmund Freud said what drives most people to art is the pleasure principle. The work of his grandson, the artist Lucian Freud, belied this. He highlighted angst and pain; the style was grotesque. He had his friends lie supine on couches for many long days. He bared their flesh, skinning them like a butcher would. As a painter he had an omnivorous gaze.

Nupur feared the worst for her mother, whom she regarded as vulnerable; she imagined her ageing, wrestling with the meaning of life.

'I worry my mother wears a mask, behind which is… I don't know. Lucian knows. And Sigmund understands.'

In the matter of looks Nupur was uncertain. She caught fleeting glimpses of herself. It was better that way.

'I am not good-looking.'

She was sure of that. But was it possible that she was? And somebody might say it? The thought teased her.

'What do I care?'

That question served her well.

'Does it really matter?'

It did. She looked around her, at her room, at her things. At herself. Everything, waiting to get noticed.

'I am not a good housekeeper.'

Odds and ends cluttered her dresser. She kept a special hairbrush for split ends, some make-up that she never used. Her colognes were stale; the fragrances, it seemed, had expired.

She had a wheatish complexion. Salil called it savla rang. Sarla said it was baniya brown.

'Looking at myself again, carefully, things aren't so bad. Some angles suit me. And there is always Daddy. He says my smile lights up the room.'

The boy she was dating was good-looking. He took care not to emphasize those good looks. Why did he want to spend time with her? He liked her father. That made her suspicious.

'He admires my father, makes no secret of it. His traditional family and their dated business are in his past. Could my father with his tech company be his future?'

She met his family.

'They treat him like a prince. He is so comfortable in his skin, in the knowledge that one day he will be the karta of his joint family. Why don't I feel the same way?'

She asked him about his family business, and he didn't say much. She realized he didn't know much of these things. He had been granted a licence to do what boys do: chase girls, party, wake up at noon, press repeat. This was a window of time in which he could live without holding back. One day the family would rein him in, and he would settle down.

'I could be like him. Silver spoon, business on a platter. What makes me uncomfortable with the idea? Why does my stomach churn?'

She liked him – kind of. He was a refreshing change from young men in sneakers and obvious brands, who watched films, not cinema; who saw more than they read; whose tastes were less refined. She was a sucker for subtlety, for an evening well put together, for a gift that was thoughtful. She could deal with the crass ones who hung around in community centres, who made a hole with their left thumb and forefinger, and yo-yoed their right forefinger in between. She had trouble with the ones in between.

They went out a lot. He knew where to go and what to order. It was always money well spent. Good taste, admittedly, but a surfeit that was beginning to pall. She was looking forward to one bad meal, one disastrous evening, spoiling for one proper fight.

'I am uncomfortable,' she told him, 'spending so much money that I haven't earned. You should be too.'

He did not respond. He stayed away for a few days, hung around with his friends. He returned, it seemed, to the same places and did the same things.

The fight never happened.

It wasn't worthy, she felt, a relationship without a proper confrontation, without cringe-worthy moments, without regret.

She spoke to her mother.

'Marriage?' said Sarla. 'Why? There is so much life has to offer.'

'Ma,' said Nupur, 'answer my question.'

Sarla said, 'He is a little soft around the edges. Not like your father. Salil has rapier-like precision. Does that help? I mean, you will keep comparing them all your life.'

Facile as it sounded, what tipped the scale was her beau's driving. He accelerated hard, he braked hard, and he honked in between.

'Marriage to this man will be a train wreck,' thought Nupur.

'My parents hug, they kiss. They do a lot more behind closed doors. I was embarrassed but then I thought about it. Isn't it nice to know they can be tender? Vulnerable? Playful? Downright silly?'

'So why the frown?'

'I can sense their boredom. Home is so dull.'

She tried to provoke her mother, tried to disturb her set routine that she seemed to be using as a shield. Rummy was her anchor. She had others like her addicted to a six-hour daily dose of twenty-eight-card rummy. Salil was happy she was busy; he, in turn, was practising some form of Zen, using it to good effect in the art of marital maintenance.

'My mother is beautiful. She has effortless skin and thick, wavy hair. She isn't rounded and proportioned in the manner baniyas call classical beauty. Her mixed blood has made her quirky and interesting. When she sits in front of her dresser, she is quite funny. She imitates people. She mimics Salil and members of his family. On random occasions when truly inspired she is a riot. I come close to loving her. It is a side of my mother that only I get to see. These are moments when she is herself. A child, an actor, rueful, a not-so-simple person.'

'I am not very useful with my time, you know,' said Sarla. 'Your father cannot stomach that. He wants me to value time. Perhaps mourn its passing.'

'He said something?'

'He said, you can't just waltz through life.'

'What did you say?'

'Nothing. I went back to my reading.'

'I wish—'

'Don't.'

'But—'

'Leave me alone. Just let me be.'

'Daddy sounds excited. I wish you could be there when we chat about business. He has so many ideas. He is planning a new project. He said he would discuss it with me.'

'I know all about his new project,' said her mother.

'What?'

Sarla hugged Nupur. 'You are his new project,' she said. 'Haven't you realized by now?'

'Not really. But it makes sense. Knowing him, I mean.'

Sarla poured out two glasses of her homemade wine.

'Think about the big question that life asks,' she said. 'What will you be up to in your best years?'

The wine was sweet and convivial. Nupur took small sips. 'It will be a business,' she said.

'And?'

'I have an idea it will be in the arts. I will use the next couple of years to intern.'

'In what?'

'In what life has to offer. Then I will intern in a gallery or a museum.'

Sarla downed her glass, poured another, drank till her vision blurred. 'I am a lifelong intern,' she said. 'Poor Salil. Why does he even try?'

Salil Gupta

Sukha Niwas was a joint-family dwelling in Lajpat Nagar. It wasn't a landmark structure. Every square inch of the compound was built up. There were many rooms over its three floors, a narrow staircase, small bathrooms, small bedrooms, and a hall with a double-height ceiling where guests sat and stared nervously at a chandelier that swayed gently over them. Moderation was the moat that surrounded Sukha Niwas. Salil's father grew up there. He had three brothers. One was a bachelor; he had books. The others married; they had children, two apiece.

It was a busy place with many mouths to feed. A common hearth served vegetarian fare. Milk came from a goshala, a variety of pulses from a village. The kitchen worked on three cylinders. The puja room, where visits were frequent, was small; inside were many deities that were worshipped in rotation. Scattered chants through the day, pressure cooker whistles, and the three-speed roar of the household mixie scaled the high walls of Sukha Niwas and merged with Lajpat Nagar's middle-class thrum. Clothes fluttered on terraces in the afternoon, kites stirred the air in the evening, and vocal vendors with sing-song voices plied their wares through the day.

'Engineer?' His father looked incredulous. 'What will you become? Tell me. Will you wear overalls and work in a factory? Or will you wear a helmet and become a PWD engineer?'

Salil had decided to break away. The family fold had a vice-like grip; no one in living memory had escaped it. He was different. He was the eldest male in line so he was precious, and he was Bari Mummy's favourite, her laadla, who, as the song went, was heading towards 'bigad gaya'. Bari Mummy, the matriarch, had her aangan, an open space where she sat with her three daughters-in-law: bahus one to three. Salil would stray in and sit till he was asked to leave.

'Sui dhaaga? Why? You want to learn tailoring? For what?'

'For hostel life,' he said.

Bari Mummy smiled. 'Give him the needle and thread.'

When Salil left, she said, 'Interesting.'

She turned to her bahus, one to three. 'This khandaan has a boring history. This boy gives me hope.'

Ashok chacha, the bachelor uncle, was Salil's role model. He did not conform but his rebellion was within limits. There were arguments, fights between the brothers that nobody won. Ashok chacha would retreat to his den, ask for ice, and light a cigarette. After one such argument Salil found him seated on his armchair, smoking.

'You shouldn't come here when I smoke.'

Chacha made space by removing some books. 'I am growing old and Delhi is changing. I don't belong here any more.'

'Sit here.' He stubbed out his cigarette. 'Open the windows and switch on the fan. Let the room breathe.'

'I like your room,' said Salil. 'It has so many books.'

'They talk to each other,' said Chacha.

There were books on history. Many of them were hardbound and dog-eared. There was one on Delhi that he was planning to read. Salil sat at his feet. It was a happy Sunday. Every now and then Chacha threw nuggets of wisdom his way.

'Delhi was born over many hundred years. You took half an hour.'

'So many invasions. The latest by migrants from neighbouring states. This includes us. We are called baniyas. People say it in a peculiar way.'

'"Being Baniya" isn't a slogan to be found on T-shirts. Baniyas and Marwaris turned the wheels of commerce, and they became a social stain, at the receiving end of derision and envy.'

'Three things lie in state in Sukha Niwas,' said Chacha. 'Queen's English, poetry, and a moral compass.'

'These are strange times.'

Fifty and more years past the freedom gate and laissez-faire had gripped the nation. The English language had dripped through an Indian sieve. In Delhi, where people took things to heart, there were different communities in its middle-class localities, each with their customs, cuisine, and accent. They called out to each other, at times called each other names. Some shared leftovers.

Next door to the Guptas were the Kapoors. They were boisterous and at most times ready for a laugh and a drink. The Guptas were quieter; their ways were measured.

'Our Punjabi friend likes to complain,' said Chacha. 'Kapoor feels we are becoming prosperous at his expense.'

Uncle and nephew spent the rest of the day grappling with the family accounts. Uncle looked closely at the vouchers. He kept aside some of them, to be pursued with the accountant.

'Your father taught me suspicion. It is my constant companion. You will be surprised what people are capable of doing for money.'

'Chacha ji, who shall be my example: my father or you?'

Bari Mummy overheard that question. She pulled her laadla aside. 'All important questions you ask me,' she said.

'We never had any artistic ambition,' said Salil. 'Does that disturb you?'

'No,' said Bari Mummy. 'But what you say is true.'

'Our school had art classes,' said Salil. 'I could draw, but my teacher said I had no imagination. Who should I blame?'

His grandmother sighed.

'Look at our house,' said Salil.

'Did somebody say something?'

'Does somebody need to?'

The old lady laughed; some tears formed in her eyes. 'Listen,' she said, 'we make a living, we lead a comfortable life. I was told by the menfolk that last year we paid some taxes.'

'We could try,' said Salil. 'I could, I mean, do something creative like this chap I met.'

The youngster had chanced upon a neighbour down the lane. It wasn't much of a lane, not much of a neighbour; his lodgings were small and untidy. Untouched by a woman's hand, he had said, taking pride in that.

His name was Gabriel. Thin and scraggly, not macho in the least, Gabriel was an artist; he made lithographs and posters in numbers. A kind of labour. To be fair he designed the posters. Salil tried his hand at it under Gabriel's supervision.

'What will you bring to paper?'

'A thought? An idea?'

'Feeling,' said Gabriel. 'Try conveying a simple feeling.'

It was hard, an honest challenge.

'What does it look like? Tell me honestly.' It had taken Salil three days.

'Some work has drama,' said Gabriel. 'Some none.'

'And?'

'In your case, none.'

'My first attempt,' said Salil. 'Be kind. Tell me, how do you do it? This one for example.'

'Does it matter? Breakfast?'

Breakfast was bread toasted on a flame with white butter and a sprinkling of daal moth. 'This is the secret sauce,' said Gabriel.

Salil's uncle had his own story of pursuing art. His attempts at breaking away from the family had been lame.

'In my time the family said painting was a feminine pursuit. Like needlework. I was like you. But I was easily dissuaded. Artists were a bedraggled lot those days. And writers – they had no means. The family, particularly your father, said, why take a chance? In the end I learned accounting.' Chacha made a face. 'Accounting is a shackled discipline that believes in conservatism, for God's sake!'

Salil looked around at his home, his uncles, the Rexine thrones they sat on. A few curios made from banned items – a sandalwood elephant, an ivory Taj Mahal – rested on a glass-fronted sideboard. A side table with a sunmica top had round tea stains. There was a rug on the floor; its raised edges tripped the distracted.

The women in the household covered their heads with their saree pallus in front of the elders – and showed the world their navels. The jangle of house keys announced the arrival of Bari

Mummy. The key bunch hung near her hip, where stretch marks, the bane of childbirth, showed.

'Don't try to act smart,' Salil was often told.

'I was only—'

'Don't talk back.'

Salil read the daily newspaper cover to cover. His bookshelf had second-hand books, mostly on economics and political history. As a teenager, he came under the influence of all things American. The moon landing, a photograph of John F. Kennedy, an idea of an unsullied democracy, the inalienable right to free expression. He felt hamstrung by his surroundings. His uncles with their fissionless molecules. His aunts with their age-old remedies, sayings, and superstitions, some that were bottled as pickles, some that had wrinkled like murabbas.

He educated himself, with some help from Bari Mummy and Ashok chacha. They pushed him, they made him read, they encouraged him to break the family mould. He did well in school, college, and engineering college. As a qualified engineer in computer science, he could have chosen a tech job; he chose instead to do a master's. He was fascinated by immersive technologies that transformed audio and visual experience.

Salil was a mixed bag when he entered the corporate world, that too in a conservative Lala company trying to make its way into new technology. So many in the corporate world were well brought up, offspring of service households. They grew up as self-conscious journeymen. Correct and careful. He disliked their narrow focus, hated their bucket lists. True characters seemed to have been weeded out before they could make a difference. In a moment of honesty, he confessed, 'I may be like them, but at least I am trying to be different.'

Meeting Sarla set him right. Sarla was a secretary at the office. Trouble erupted in his joint family when he fell in love with her. The family was aghast when he broke the news. A secretary? And half Christian.

One of the first things Salil shared with Sarla was a plume of smoke. She lit up in the office pantry next to the exhaust and she blew. He coughed, wiped his tears, and stuttered. She apologized, then offered him a drag. Salil was nonplussed. He had never smoked; would refusing this offer be unmanly? He took a drag, coughed a whole lot more, shed some more tears, and started laughing. She made some coffee. Black in her case. He liked it with a dollop of milk and two heaped spoons of sugar.

'Sorry,' she said, 'but who drinks coffee like this?'

'Coffee is just to camouflage milk,' said Salil.

They stood next to the water cooler. Salil tried to straighten his shirt that bulged around his stomach.

She saw him adjusting his shirt. 'You should count your calories,' she said. 'Do you?'

'I have a weakness for sweets,' said Salil.

He watched her while he spoke. She was wearing heels and she stood with one leg bent, one hip askew, head inclined to the other side. As she held her cigarette, the ash lengthened and then curled, defying gravity. At the right moment she tapped it into her palm.

'We Catholics have an association,' Sarla was saying. 'We have a strong sense of community. And guilt. We pray together, sing together; in front of our pastor we even cry together.'

'There is no baniya community,' said Salil. 'We don't form associations.'

'No?'

'No.' He imagined his father laughing at the thought. 'Have you ever seen a protest march for baniya rights? Nobody in my family has held a candle at India Gate for any cause.'

'What happens when you are in real trouble? Who do you turn to?'

'Nobody. Give me another drag.'

She smiled at his newfound addiction.

'The baniya knows that businesses fail. Every family has seen it. If it happens you drown. If people come after you, you flee.'

A couple of colleagues came by for some water. They waited for them to leave.

'Then what is the motivation?' asked Sarla. 'Why do you take such risks?'

The question was a good one. Why do business in India, given the odds? The baniyas had reframed the question. Why run a clean business, given the poor odds? They took their chances with rules and regulations.

'My family has many retainers,' said Salil.

'Old people?'

'No.'

'Ex-employees?'

'No. People in the government. They are on our informal payroll. Bureaucrats, excise, and tax officials.'

The two met often, after hours. Sarla was refreshing. Different. Her house, where she stayed with her mother, was modest, a two-bed apartment where furniture edges intruded, finding elbows and knees. She had no airs. She was funny, a good mimic, with a full-throated laugh. They wandered the city; the two of them visited modest bars where they tried every cocktail on offer, most of them filled with innuendo and sugar syrup. She read as much as he did. But different stuff. She liked romantic literature and the classics. She read aloud passages that she had bookmarked and he listened, looking at her, enjoying her absorption. She was often moved while reading, sometimes to tears. There were musical interludes. They listened to western classical music that she had collected carefully.

'All this,' she said, pointing to her books, her music, and her posters, 'is my DNA. What is your DNA, Salil Gupta?'

'Big question,' said Salil, wiping his spectacles. 'Let me think.'

'No hurry.'

'I am never in a hurry.' He blew moisture into each lens. 'You can't force me.' He placed his specs on his nose and folded his handkerchief neatly. 'I will resist.'

Sarla held up her hands. 'Okay, okay. Cigarette?' She lit one for him. He took a couple of drags and the smoke curled out of his puffed cheeks.

'On my own I will happily run a marathon, climb a hill, or cross a river.'

'Okay, champion, got it. What else?'

'Given a convenient option, I will choose an adventurous one.'

'Really? We will see. Do you believe in God? Do you practise?'

Another drag.

'I have faith in money. And ideas. But mostly in money. The rest,' he said, waving his hands at her things, 'I am curious about, but I have yet to discover.'

'Isn't that a baniya résumé?'

He proposed to Sarla. She consented, after taking a day to decide. No tea leaves in her case, just a plain, simple feeling. She liked the fact that he could be decisive and yet in her company very unsure of himself. He would never travel far enough in the world that she inhabited; he would try and she would help him. She could imagine sad moments with him; she would treasure them. She could tease him, that was so important. And he listened; his eyes never wandered when she spoke.

Introducing her to the family was a challenge for Salil.

'Let us prepare,' said Salil. He thought he could coach her, get her to wear the right clothes.

'Shall I wear something special? A proper dress?'

'Umm, yes, sure, why not? What did you have in mind?'

'And make-up? Can I wear make-up?'

It went badly; that was inevitable. She carried a bouquet of flowers with her. It came back with them, a few petals less. She was tripping over her dress, her make-up askew.

'I am feeling small and sad,' she said. He was apologetic.

'You know what one of your uncles did? He took me aside and asked me about the two generations before.'

'He did? No harm in that.'

Sarla remembered the moment, her surprise. 'He wanted to know how long they lived and how they died. He said your family lives long and no one, repeat no one, has died of cancer. A little blood pressure and a little diabetes, which is quite natural, he said, but no cancer.'

'God!' said Salil.

'Indeed. I told him there is cancer in my bloodstream, there are platelets running riot. I told him two of my mother's brothers died from it. You should have seen the expression on his face. There goes the family tree, it said.'

'Sorry,' said Salil.

'No, please, don't apologize for family. I wouldn't.' She remembered something else. 'Listen, is the baniya waddle a thing?'

He smiled. 'You noticed?'

'Yes. They walk half sideways, the women especially. They use the sides of their feet.'

'You should check their slippers,' said Salil.

The Guptas convened a family meeting to handle the crisis and Salil, who had flown the coop by then, did not attend. He tried calling them. On the weekend he met his parents but there was no reconciliation. Once the dates were fixed Salil sent them an engagement invitation. At the appointed hour the young couple waited anxiously at the hall in Lajpat Nagar. Sarla's mother was there; nobody else showed up. They headed the next day to the registrar's office where the formalities were over in a few minutes.

His wife broadened his perspective, helped him make connections. New ones. Outside the office, she was no longer a secretary. She had a lot that she could show him, worlds that he never knew existed, a new vocabulary, people he found interesting because they came from different walks of life.

'All good things happen on a weekend,' she was fond of saying.

She gathered people in their small place and ensured there was enough food on the table. The food was freshly baked, and she served hearty portions. She loved watching people eat what she had cooked.

In her world there were no 'regular' people. Those that came seemed to have emerged from cocoons and dens, some from pedestals, some from pulpits.

'Whisky has no time of day,' said a writer to nobody in particular.

'I go for a walk,' said a painter. 'I return after a couple of days. There is so much energy when I get back.'

A poet stared at a piece of furniture. 'Nobody listens,' she said.

'What do you do, Salil?'

'I?' He was at a loss. What could he tell these cool people? 'I work in a technology company,' he said.

'No shit! Really?'

'Doesn't he look like a baniya?' Sarla asked them.

'I wish he did,' said the writer. 'I like authenticity.'

'You can stuff your authenticity,' said Salil.

'Aha,' said the painter. 'Is that all it takes to get under your skin?'

Sarla never intervened when people fought. She sat in the same place and never moved, a smile on her face, acknowledging whoever looked towards her from time to time. Her openness and her generosity moved Salil. He could not imagine such soirees in Sukha Niwas.

Salil struggled to stay awake at these gatherings. It was typically 3 a.m. when things warmed up. People ignored him. He sneaked out, crept into his bed without changing. 'Creative people suck,' he said, mimicking them. 'Big time.'

Salil slogged away, making each minute count, and the months flew by in the office. At home Sarla waited; time crawled, doing very little for her. She brooded. Salil's career progressed rapidly and he became the company's youngest vice president. At home the brooding atmosphere persisted. The Gupta marriage stumbled along.

In a few years Salil would have become CEO. But there was an unsubtle urge that lurked in his DNA, telling him that beyond a point it was stupid to make money for others. He quit his job to set up a business.

He was clear it would be in the new economy. He had learned an important lesson. Wealth was to be found in the new economy, and it came not just from value addition, but from disruption.

Outsourcing was the new mantra in India. He chose knowledge process outsourcing: a segment called scientific publishing.

He named his company Immersive Technologies. In a few months he was up and running. Tonnes of printed matter went virtual in Immersive's climate-controlled caves. His work ticked the box called value addition. Investment funds turned up at his door. In their world, value addition was nutrition, more so than quinoa and kale.

Salil became a New Age entrepreneur. He sought membership in the Young Professional Organization, an exclusive enclave for those that had arrived.

'You need to improve your CV,' said the YPO secretary. 'Expand your interests and then come back.'

Salil examined his interests. They paled under the scanner. He decided he would collect art. It sounded like the thing to do and there was Sarla to guide him.

Salil in the Art World was a title worthy of a novella. A satire perhaps. He spent one evening visiting five galleries. He breezed in, he breezed out, nothing caught his fancy, nobody gave him that all-important attention described in business circles as 'bhav'.

The private gallery space struck him as another exclusionary enclave. He was bewildered. This small, intimate subset of humanity had set out, it seemed, to exclude people like him.

First and foremost, the art was obscure and unyielding. When he tried to ask questions, he was handed a catalogue. 'Read it first,' said Sarla. She was at ease, a nodding acquaintance with art world insiders. Salil peeped into a catalogue and couldn't make it past the first page. 'They are throwing stones at me,' he said.

He wasn't one to give up easily. He continued visiting galleries in his spare time. He became a lunchtime visitor at shows. He dragged Sarla to a few openings and tried chatting up known collectors.

'They are so secretive,' said Sarla.

'You mean rude,' said Salil.

'I think they are shy,' said Sarla.

'No,' said Salil, 'they are acting superior. They don't know I am thick-skinned.'

Salil's art preferences mirrored his life philosophy: 'Keep it simple.'

He liked art that spoke directly to him, with few metaphors attached. He got no respect from the inner echelons of the art world that quickly dismissed him as lightweight. 'I heard he buys only Bengal,' was one comment. 'Put him in a room full of romantic stuff,' said another, 'and you won't see him again.'

In truth, contemporary art confused him, the medium and the message. He made some random purchases, but his heart wasn't in it. To gain more visibility he attended auctions and bought some expensive moderns. People began taking notice. Auction houses gave him more bhav than he had experienced in galleries.

Enthused, he kept buying. Every acquisition of his set a new family record. Sarla was aghast. She did what she could. She hid the family jewels and threw away the key.

In all this Salil found a backer in his daughter.

'My father is sweet,' she said. 'Right now he is buying Ara's buxom women, small-breasted Badrinarayans, and big-bindi Bikashs. He buys landscapes as well, but he prefers Manu Parekh to Ramkumar. He listens to Jagjit Singh, he drinks Chivas Regal, and he prefers Govinda films to movies by the Coen Brothers. This is his life on loop. But don't dismiss him. That would work against you. He might enter your smug little world and shake things up.'

Salil found a naysayer who gave him what he called a 'fair warning'.

'Fair warning? What does that mean?'

'An auction term,' said the naysayer, 'used when the gavel is about to fall, irreversibly consigning a lot to your possession.'

The naysayer was Ardeshir and he was from Bombay. 'The old city,' he said, 'the rowdy, good-humoured, carpetbagger version.'

'Why do I need a fair warning?'

'Believe me when I say this. Art is a privileged creature, a thug in the world of commerce. It has pissing rights on everybody, including somebody as smart as you.'

'And why have you singled me out for your warning?'

'Because it means so much to you to be a part, a player. I can see it has captured you. The art world has the power to hurt you, and it will. It will draw blood. One day it could be your nemesis.'

That challenged Salil. He had not heard this language before, nor that tone: effortless, invasive, threatening.

'Is that a promise?' he asked Ardeshir.

'No,' replied the gallerist. 'I told you what it is. It is a fair warning.'

'You don't even know my name. And you are issuing a warning for my benefit. Why?'

'Because I know you will not heed it.'

Nupur Gupta

Nupur arrived in Delhi, cleared customs. A six-month internship in an auction house in London had shaken her moorings. There was so much to discern in the art world that had nothing to do with art theory. Every fall of the auction gavel was another nail driven into theory and rhetoric. Of course, there were good days when iconic works soared, but there were also days when fuck-all got sold to fuckwits.

Her father was there to receive her. Salil kept his questions at bay, hugged her, held her, and looked closely. She looked back.

'Looks like you kept a vigil,' she said.

'How are you feeling? Tired?'

'No, refreshed.'

'What happened? Why did you ask me to book a ticket to Mumbai in the first place? That too by train?'

'I can't tell you, not now.' She kissed him on the cheek.

'It's good to have you back,' he said.

She waited till the weekend. She was restless. Sunday morning, she broached the subject.

'Dad, I need to leave home. Please. Right away.'

She was set on leaving for Mumbai, where she would open a new chapter. Salil acted like he hadn't heard what she said.

'Have you discussed things with Ma?' she asked.

'What things?'

'You know what I am talking about.'

'There is nothing wrong between us,' he said.

'Dad!'

'Fine, I will make an appointment. We will meet the counsellor. Then will you stay back?'

'No.'

He slammed his cup down, his broad shoulders slumping slightly. He tried to look helpless. She finished her coffee while they stared at each other.

'I have begun to grey,' he said.

'I noticed. It suits you.'

He smiled. 'So, you won't change your mind? I will miss you. You know all this money I have made—'

'I need to make my own, my little jama poonji. When I have it, I will come to you for what you can give me.'

She left the next day, taking with her a suitcase, a tote, and a laptop. Her mother dropped her at the station, and she caught the Rajdhani Express. Her eyes were dry. Guilt was swept away by a sense of relief.

'Will you tell Grandma?'

That was an important goodbye. Sarla hugged her, teary for a variety of reasons. 'Go,' she said.

Nupur slept well on the night train. The next morning the train left the mainland of Maharashtra and eased into the island over a creek that was grey. Still water, no splash yet in her quiet crusade. Crusade it was, a personal voyage. Her bogie had other urban delinquents.

Her father kept messaging her. Her phone pinged again when she reached Mumbai Central.

'You come to Bombay to work for money,' said his message. 'You arrive when money works for you.'

She arrived and hunted for a place to stay. Single girl. A broker met her, sized her up.

'How are you today?' He was wearing impossible rings.

'I'm good.'

'North is cheap, south is robbery. There is a one-bed place in Andheri East.'

That was quick, his assessment.

'Distance to the station?'

'Aha, you know how important that is? It is a little far.' His rings were glinting at her. Each was a chunk of gold beaten into a round with a gemstone on top.

'Why east?'

'East is cheaper by the square foot.'

Per square foot was still a joke. 'Everything is so expensive.'

'Other option is Borivali East. You are okay with sharing?'

'No, this one is fine, but no lights out, no lectures, and no peeping in.'

'No guarantees. Some landlords are good, some are crack.'

'Morning tea?'

'Maybe,' he said, looking doubtful.

There was an interview. She wasn't prepared for one and she behaved badly with her prospective landlady, who stood at the door in her nightgown and asked her about her personal habits. A few questions, and she shut the door. The broker smiled at Nupur. His phone lit up inside his shirt pocket. He wanted to shake hands and leave.

Single-girl accommodations were few and some options seemed unsafe. By then she was exhausted just thinking about travelling by bus and train from the distant suburbs to south Bombay, where she planned to work. For relief, she inspected some high-budget options.

She placed a hand on a balcony railing of a building in Ballard Estate. It was an old, well-preserved colonial structure in brown stone and there was a full-grown tree outside that had survived Indian independence. She was on the fourth floor, where the branches had thinned, where leaves had given way to a line of sight. She leaned as far as she could on that balcony and caught a glimpse of the sea. The very sight of the sea affirmed its value, the kind the owners were asking.

'Nupur ji, I told you it had a sea view.'

He was a Sindhi broker wearing a shiny white shirt with two buttons open; some grey chest hair peeped out.

It was a single room, a studio/office in the making. Money for the deposit was all it needed: ten months' rent.

She left that place swinging her bag and grinning from ear to ear. Her Sindhi agent watched her smile and to his surprise he broke into one himself. They were two grinning idiots for a while.

'No?' he asked, shaking his head.

She shook hers, her hair swung, and she lost sight of him for a while and missed his disappointment.

'Mumbai is the wrong place to rent an existence,' he said finally. 'The cost is murder.'

'I wish I was a landlord,' said Nupur.

'Don't wish that,' said the agent. 'Landlords in Mumbai die fighting an ailment called tenancy. They receive a pittance while tenants get pugree in cash as a reward for their being squatters.'

There was no money yet in her fledgling account. But she liked the idea of a studio. Nupur had gripped that balcony railing really hard. It was her only hold on reality.

After her Ballard Estate fiasco, she was looking at the middle suburbs. Accommodation in the by-lanes of Mahim was available and she was veering towards a poky two-bedroom place which had a restaurant below: the smell of Chinese cooking in the afternoon and tandoori in the evening. Next to the restaurant was Afzal Tailor and next to Afzal bhai was Santoor Bar. Santoor Bar had cold beer and a toiling lad in a vest behind the counter, cutting boiled eggs into four. It was evening and she saw people stumbling. The landlord of the apartment stood on a broken tile and asked for too much rent. And that was the end of Mahim.

A one-room set in Shivaji Park, Dadar, fell vacant on the weekend. It was on the third floor of a building called Dwarka Deep. There was no lift. The place could be hers if she did well with the owner, who stayed on the first floor. Mr Karmarkar. He conducted her interview as she stood at his doorstep.

'Single?'

'Yes.' She stood on one leg for luck. Should she call him Uncle? 'Yes, Uncle.' The other foot landed.

'Where from?'

She had made it to the foyer of his house, one small step in.

'Delhi.'

He looked alarmed. She needed to distract him. In a film that unspooled in her head, she was the heroine in *Garam Hawa*.

'My family came to Delhi after Partition,' she said. 'My grandparents settled in Punjab. My grandfather brought one memory with him along with my grandmother. He laboured till he had money to buy bighas of land. He bought land till his holding was the exact same size as what he had left behind in Pakistan. Then he planted seeds and the rains came, and when the yellow flowers of the mustard fields bloomed, he laid that memory to rest.'

Karmarkar had wise eyes. 'Take a seat,' he said. It was a cramped living room that had space for one visitor. She sat on edge. 'Now tell me about your grandmother,' he said.

'My grandmother was a farmhand. She could milk cows, she could bear the heat, and she could sit on her haunches without complaint.' Should she say it? 'And she smoked cheroots.'

Mrs Karmarkar had entered the room quietly and her mouth was open. 'Bring her some tea,' said her soon-to-be landlord. 'What about a local guardian in Bombay?'

'My father told me if you need a guardian, please come back.'

Karmarkar was genuinely stumped by her replies. He coughed while she sipped tea. His wife was giving him a look that said, enough is enough. 'Shall we see the place?' he said.

They climbed the narrow staircase. He had one last family question that he asked on the landing.

'I hope your father gave you advice before you came to Mumbai all alone.'

She imagined the scene, replayed in countless films.

'We are a Partition family, Uncle – from the other side. All he said to me at the station was, alvida.'

By now she was on her home run. There was the small issue of the rent and the deposit. And here Providence smiled. Providence sent a rat that ran over her leg as they entered the one-room set. It was a poignant moment for Mr Karmarkar for it robbed him of all he wanted to say in favour of the place. They saw it disappear into a crack in the doorway to the toilet. Nupur had let out an involuntary shriek. She realized now that it was up to her to take advantage of what was construed as bad luck in most books and bad hygiene in some.

'I can pay a six-month deposit, Uncle,' she said. 'I have only that much.'

That rat saved her. She moved in the next day. Mr Karmarkar had thoughtfully left a sofa, two buckets, and a rat trap.

On the first day of her independent existence in Mumbai, she slept. She woke up at noon, opened the windows, stretched her arms wide, and yawned. Two residents from the building opposite responded. A woman in her kitchen smiled and a middle-aged man on his balcony held his newspaper aside and scratched his armpit. She retreated, tiptoeing her way back, and looked around. No amount of new furnishings could change the place. It had been hard-coded by a middle-class Maharashtrian. It looked prissy and proud.

Nupur rolled up her sleeves, got down on her hands and knees, and started scrubbing. The washroom was a delight. The flooring was a dirt-caked mosaic that was slippery near the drain. The washbasin in the corner was so small she had to take aim, and the flush made a sound like a watery grave. She shed some tears on that first day. She was missing something; perhaps nuance.

She walked around Shivaji Park the next morning wearing a T-shirt and tracks. Eyes followed her as she crossed Cadell Road and took one of the narrow gullies that led to the sea. There was no promenade there, and worse, there was debris. A man called Suleiman heard her complain and spoke to her.

'New to Mumbai?'

She nodded. She noted his kohl-lined eyes and his flowing kurta. He was quite a sight.

'Don't worry, high tide will wash this away,' he said.

'And you are happy with that?'

She returned quickly to the park and ran around it, building up a steady rhythm. Her thighs tightened and her bobbing sports bra drew some whistles. She received many brusque offers, none of them romantic. For some reason she didn't feel threatened. She did some stretches underneath a tree as traffic hurtled past on the busy road.

She walked home slowly, testing her calves, whistling softly, and stretching her neck from side to side. She felt at ease with herself, fit, eager, and filled with anticipation.

'Ajay,' he said.

He wore a gold chain around his neck and a red thread around his left wrist. He had tousled hair, which was a plus, and he looked clean.

'Sit next to me,' she said.

He worked in a restaurant nearby.

Ajay and Nupur sat for three days on the low wall that circled Shivaji Park. Other couples dotted the neighbourhood. On the third day Ajay tried to fondle her. It took an hour for his hand to reach her elbow.

'Say something,' said Ajay.

She brushed her hair away from her face. The breeze was a lifesaver in the evening. Turning away from the cricket match underway in front of them, she looked at him. She decided she liked him. She placed a hand on his cheek and he placed his over hers.

'Ajay, do you have a sister?' she asked him.

Ajay and she became a 'jodi'; they held hands and Mumbai yielded to their discovery tour. Trains, buses, long walks, some respite in between, sitting on promenades watching debris bobbing, couples necking.

There was a Mumbai trait that Nupur found: it was panache. In turn she was becoming a Mumbai type; an aspiring youngster climbing above her station, living in the now, paying no heed to naysayers and cynics. What drove youngsters in Mumbai was an insidious feeling, one that Nupur was beginning to experience – a feeling of being on the brink.

They went to Aksa Beach to discover what killed people there every year. A signboard at INS Hamla, a naval station, kept a yearly count of fatalities. They waded into the water, stood in waist-deep waves. Nothing happened for a while. And then suddenly water rose from her navel to her neck. The sand had shifted beneath her feet.

'Scary,' said Ajay, coughing, blowing bubbles.

'Awesome,' said Nupur, wiping the salt water from her eyes.

It was a Mumbai moment; the city had led her to the brink, and she felt happy to have survived.

The following Tuesday Ajay made her walk barefoot to the Siddhivinayak Temple. It was early morning and there were many pilgrims. She had no idea why she did it or what purpose it served. The temple was not pleasing to the eye, and every addition and renovation had added to the imbalance. A modern temple like Siddhivinayak did not need stellar sculptures or fine architecture. All it needed was a rockstar following.

She started work at a five-star hotel in a euphemism called Customer Relations. She rescued herself on weekends, veering towards the sea. Standing at the water's edge, she owned the view.

Ajay looked up to her. He had never met a girl who treated him as badly as she did. They climbed some hills near Matheran. They drank in the green of the ghats, just like the brochures asked them to. They trekked to a waterfall called Chinchoti. They slipped on stones and splashed their way to a mighty cascade. They skinny-dipped in a small pond and a slight breeze gave them goosebumps. They drank rum and shared a cigarette.

'I don't understand you,' said Ajay, his teeth chattering from the cold. 'I think you are a tease. I think you are having fun at my expense.'

'Maafi,' she said. 'Listen, can we just be friends?'

Sunday loomed, an empty day. She sat idle for an hour, contemplating a bath. Lined up on the bathroom shelf were two old shampoo bottles with diluted dregs, water added to make use of the last sticky drop. She dragged her eyes to the soap dish. She picked up the bulging bar and turned it around; below the new glycerine soap were flecks of Dove and a thin slab of Lux. She had sworn she would never do this. This was stuff her mother did – and here she was, doing the same.

She stumbled to the cupboard, to the carefully arranged shelves, and pulled down all her clothes. She sat amidst them on the floor and examined each of them. She found frayed collars and split threads.

'Fuck me,' she said.

She undressed, switched on all the lights in the room, and looked at herself, head to toe, in her full-length mirror. Was that a stretch mark? Yes. Were those shadows under her eyes? Maybe, just maybe. Her love handles quivered. She held her breath for as long as she could. It was official. Her dream life was on hold; this day was not part of that dream.

Months later, there was a promotion, by which time some money had accumulated in her account. Enough for the bank to assign an account manager and offer a housing loan.

Her grandmother called, sounding distant. 'Your father has found someone,' she shouted.

What! Her father was being linked with a diva. Say what! She rushed to Delhi, as if she could do something. She returned a trifle disappointed. It was a false alarm.

Birthdays came and went, and she refused to celebrate them. Work wasn't very exciting but the affluent, privileged customers of the country kept her on her toes. She moved south into better lodgings, looked around, and felt better. The commute was shorter, the cologne was more subtle. She began to belong, not to any time or place, but to a suspended state of being called Mumbai Local.

It was time for her to move on. 'My vertical of choice,' she told her father. 'The art world.' She needed an internship. She wanted to meet the art world insiders, a secretive species that was rarely sighted. She needed to understand how the gallery world functioned. It had to be at a private gallery. It had to be with the one and only Ardeshir.

She got off the red double-decker bus in front of the hotel where she had been working: the Taj Mahal Hotel. This part of the city had career gawkers. Some stared at Shivaji astride a horse, some at the Gateway of India, and most were just taken in by this magical spot where land met sea and history met the present moment.

Nupur walked past the hotel. Down the Bunder at the water's edge was Ardeshir's art gallery. Fortuitously it had an opening for an intern.

The Bunder was a low rampart on the Arabian Sea. The wall held her knees as she leaned forward, a palm shading her eyes. In the distance an oil flame leaped out of the ocean. The tide was out, the water rippled gently, and a variety of sailboats and small yachts bobbed in the bay. It was a picture-postcard view. She stared till her eyes watered. This part of the city consumed her at will.

Her young promenade friends accosted her. Ramu was a boat tout who lived in the vicinity of the Gateway of India. He sold tickets that got visitors a boat ride to the Elephanta Caves. Raghu offered lodge rooms to all comers – by the hour if needed. There were others who had perfected the art of accosting strangers. They showed up as she walked past a row of four-storey structures on the waterfront: grand mansions that had been converted into lodges.

'Come to Elephanta, madam,' said Ramu.

'It's too hot, Ramu. And I can't swim.'

He laughed. 'I take you in a good boat. It moves like a shikara and it doesn't leak.'

'Who will pay for the diesel?' asked Raghu.

They abandoned her halfway when they spotted a French-speaking group wearing sunhats and sweating profusely.

At the bend in the Bunder was the Radio Club. Cars arrived in the middle of the day, bearing women who played rummy till sundown. One stepped out near Nupur, squeezing herself out from the rear, the driver stretching the door to the full.

'Hello, Aunty.'

Aunty frowned at her familiarity and her powder-caked face broke into lines. Her bright red lipstick, her jet-black hair, her salwar, and her jhak-mak shoes reminded Nupur of her own aunt.

Past Radio Club were some old structures. Hoardings and signboards were haphazardly strung all over them. Each building merged into the other; each had a lodge, an antique shop, a rug store, a few offices, and an art gallery. The pavement was occupied by paanwallahs, chaiwallahs, cigarette sellers, shoeshiners, and old men sitting on stools. Parked on the roadside were taxi cabs and handcarts that reserved space. A constant stream of visitors stumbled over uneven stones. Crows cawed on the grand old trees that lined the road. They sat on the same branches and shat through the day; a white coral reef took shape below.

She spotted her Multani, an old gent who used to dye his hair and then stopped. His hair was mostly orange, in parts rust, in parts brown. He wore earrings and his eyes were ringed by black kohl. She was in love with him. For him she swayed and he adopted the manner of the rake he once was. The familiar toothpick was at work between his teeth.

'What have you brought for me?' he asked.

She opened her handkerchief that had a few dry fruits. He took them.

'Bas? That's all?'

'Tomorrow we will run away. I promise.'

'Kaash!' he said.

The paanwallah outside the manor where she was headed was a Bihari. He spoke to her in English.

'One kadak saada,' she told him.

'Takeaway?' he asked without looking up.

Nupur sighed. 'Why don't you get a job? Go to a fast-food place.'

He looked pained. He applied white lime onto the green leaf.

'Supari today?' he asked. She pointed to the wet betel nut.

'Didi?' he called after her.

She turned around. 'You are looking good,' he said, and he smiled.

The juice filled her mouth as she climbed the staircase. It was a broad wooden staircase. The walls had wires that snaked up the sides and the lighting was dim. On the first floor was the Apollo Lodge, which had a glass door; the darwan, seated on an aluminium stool, gave her a salute. On the second floor were recruitment offices. Young men sat on the stairs and leaned on the windowsill, filling forms. The third floor housed the art gallery, the one where she hoped to intern. This had to happen. She would pray if need be. How else would she set up her own business before she turned thirty-five?

Every day since she turned twenty, she had imagined helming a business in the arts. What shape it would take depended on what life had in store. For now, she stood at the threshold, a large door, behind which was the Touchstone Gallery.

Every gallerist in Bombay was an anxious being, acutely aware of the mortality rate of artists and ideas. The art world was no place for faint hearts. Tentative efforts made no impact. Running a gallery was a lonely pursuit carried out in a quiet place that came alive occasionally for a show opening and then lapsed into silence. It had the same desperate question hanging over its head that a small-town airport with a flight a day had: is this a viable life form?

Those who survived were the committed ones. Over the years they became impresarios; their practice created a persona that was one with the art that graced the walls of their cube.

The Touchstone Gallery was a new kid on the Causeway, branded as brash by the entrenched establishments in Colaba and Kala Ghoda, who publicly questioned the need for another gallery.

'Where is the art that we haven't seen?' they said.

'It is waiting to happen,' was the reply.

Touchstone attracted fashionistas, hip professionals, young scions from business houses, and a bunch of wannabes who wished to graduate from what was cool to what was considered edgy.

The press gushed. 'Cutting-edge shows,' they said, 'from a new-age gallery.'

'Cut the hyphens,' said the established ones. 'Spare us the hyperbole. New art is the same as old art. The difference is packaging.'

Collectors who bought art from Touchstone were considered bold. Critics and curators were more studied in their assessment. They stood at Touchstone's paddock, brows furrowed, as a new stable of artists paraded before them.

Openings were raucous affairs. Dark rum ruled over red wine, grass had tobacco's measure, and music from a hipster DJ added to the din. Nose rings glinted, tattoos snaked across bare backs, and a variety of sneakers squeaked on the polished concrete floor. In the middle stood Ardeshir, languid and loose. He was a friend to a few and unapproachable to the rest.

The Indian gallerist was often a woman of substance; there was occasionally a male at the helm like Ardeshir – intense, willing to provoke, and willing to burn.

Every year Touchstone hosted a couple of experimental shows. Art that was art for art's sake. On other days, art and money changed hands. Ardeshir loved art but was willing to part with it. On his terms. He knew the hallmark of a good gallerist was a slow, well-considered sale. Buyers had to serve a long internship before they were allowed to buy the better stuff. Established collectors began arriving at Touchstone, willing to forsake and hoping to gain. The market was hot. They had to throw caution to the wind and dance around the fire. Ardeshir played his part in the game.

It began with, 'Beautiful, isn't it?'

A moment's pause usually followed. It was considered good taste to be less hurried, to tarry a while before a commercial discussion.

'Is it available?'

'Hmmm.'

Pause. 'How much is it for?'

'I will have to check. I think it is on hold.'

'And the others?'

'Most of them are already spoken for. Actually, there is a waiting list for this artist.'

'I see.' Pause. 'Any works on resale?'

Long pause. 'There is an old sculpture on resale. But they are asking for an absurd price. I wouldn't buy it if I were you.'

'Is it special?'

'It is an important work. It was part of a museum show and it featured in the catalogue.'

'It did?'

'A critic said it was a turning point in the artist's oeuvre. The artist wanted to buy it back herself. I had to dissuade her.'

'Wow,' the collector would say, losing it by then. 'Listen, I will take it, but don't tell me the price. Just give me a discount.'

'Ha ha. Will you display it in Malabar Hill or will you hide it in your Alibaug beach house?'

Ardeshir was articulate on odd days of the week. People he knew well called him RDX, an unfortunate acronym in Mumbai's history. He had the bright eyes of a man on speed, the languid smile of a dude on substance. He was the only son of the late Xerxes, a gallerist who, in his time, dealt with the best of the moderns.

Ardeshir had called Nupur for an interview on a Friday afternoon. He was seated on a white sofa positioned in the centre of the display space. The walls had photographs of a performance artist who had played the role of a toff in an ashram.

Ardeshir looked the part in a lemon-green linen shirt, white trousers, and red loafers. A cigarette dangled from the fingers of his left hand; the other hand ran through his long mane that ended in a ponytail.

Nupur stood before him. There was no chair nearby. He looked at a point above her left shoulder.

'Do you agree that white is a colour?'

Her first words were spontaneous. 'It's a grey area,' she said.

He smiled, took a deep drag, his eyes half-shut. He clicked his fingers to tap ash onto the floor.

'Do you pray?'

She nodded.

'Are you addicted?'

What? She shut her eyes momentarily. She could not trust herself to say anything.

'I have seen your résumé,' he said, switching tracks. 'It is like a pastiche.'

'Pastiche? I don't imitate others!' she retorted, a little hot under the collar.

'Pastiche on India,' he replied.

That sounded nice. 'Sorry,' she mumbled. She felt like doing something for him to make up for her outburst. He read her mind.

'Could you get me something sweet? I need something sticky and sweet.'

He was stretched out on the sofa and had slid down as far as he could without falling. He was flaky and far gone. It was 2 p.m. on a working day and Nupur's potential boss was smoking grass in the middle of his display space. What if a client walked in?

She rummaged in the pantry, found a variety of snacks, and got him some baklava. He put two pieces into his mouth. The sugar perked him up. He looked livelier.

'Love, what if your workday began at 5 p.m.? I can tell you when we finish. We finish at 2 in the morning. But I can't tell you where.'

She left the gallery, squeezed past Ardeshir's yellow Beetle, and took a taxi to her apartment. Her reflection in the rear-view mirror affirmed her fears: that the interview had been a disaster. She had been tongue-tied, unsure whether Ardeshir was being serious. He was a dude and he had her measure. He knew what she was thinking.

Back home, she sat in a corner, plugged into some music, and drifted off. Late at night her phone rang when she was fast asleep. It was 2 a.m. and it was Ardeshir.

'Love,' he began, 'my day is done.'

'Boss,' she mumbled.

He laughed. She could hear lounge music, glasses clinking, and soft voices.

'I like you, love,' he said. And he waited for her to say something. What?

'You there?'

'Yes. I was asleep.'

She heard him take a deep breath. 'Girl,' he said, 'you have it in you. You are a natural.'

A natural intern?

Out of habit she reported the next day at 10 a.m., wearing black. Ramu and Raghu whistled and kept their distance. Ardeshir trundled in at 2 p.m., looking fresh and alert. It was a Saturday, a day for business in the art world. She saw a different side to him that evening, a side that she liked and respected.

She handled two clients on her first day. They left smiling, promising they would pick up the works they had kept on reserve.

That night she peeped into Ardeshir's cabin before she left. He was about to get started on his first joint. He looked at her, clear-eyed.

'You played your part today,' he said. 'Know what, love, you dress well and you are stacked.'

Arsehole.

'No offence.'

Oddly she found him attractive. She had this thing for men who wore linen, grew their hair long, and pretended they didn't care.

He taught her. He taught her how the art world walked on the edge of false pretence.

'Capitalism is the iron fist, love. In the art market, you need a velvet glove.'

'Which is?'

'False pretence. What is false pretence? Professed socialist values, support for liberal causes, opposition to the wealthy and their icons.'

She was surprised that someone as direct as him could be cynical. 'Why the charade? Isn't it inefficient?'

'Not just,' said Ardeshir, examining the shiny rock on his gold ring. 'In this business it is okay if you make money as long as your heart is in the right place. While quaffing your bubbly always remember there are those who go hungry.'

She fetched him an ashtray to save the distressed floor. She fetched him a drink to help him stay in a state that he himself described as 'sotally tober'.

'Love, the art market rewards the male of the species. Female artists have toiled unseen, unheard. None have received their just desserts.'

Nice, she thought. Was he being politically correct?

'Art has been cursed by a chauvinistic market. Marlene Dumas, Yayoi Kusama, and Louise Bourgeois. You have studied them, love?'

'To death,' she said.

'Expectedly,' he said. 'Compare their prices with results achieved by Peter Doig, Richard Prince, and Jeff Koons. Get the picture?'

'The market is not the final arbiter of what is good or who is worthy,' she said. It sounded pompous the moment she said it.

He laughed. 'That sounds like a consolation prize.'

He asked for more to drink, and he smoked more weed. He spoke with utmost clarity.

'The difference is down the line. A plucked-early flower like Basquiat rules the market despite his prodigious output. Have you ever heard of Eva Hesse, Ana Mendieta, or Francesca Woodman?'

Ardeshir zeroed in on women artists in India. In his sights were ten of the best in his not-so-humble opinion. She scanned the names.

'These artists will stand the litmus test of historians, critics, and time.'

'Boss, they have not succeeded yet, honestly.' She bit her lip after she said this.

He shrugged. 'Their time will come.'

She waited.

'Do you have a handle?' he asked.

'On what?'

'Are you on Twitter and Instagram?' he asked patiently.

'I have a Facebook account.'

'Love, you need followers, you need to express your opinion and your point of view. On Twitter and Instagram, you are a Pied Piper; on Facebook, you are merely the tune.'

One afternoon he was seated on the sofa in the middle of the hall, one leg bent at the knee and one stretched over the centre table, sporting red shoes that matched his suspenders. He wore khaki dungarees, fashioned by a painfully thin young designer who ate with his fingers and then threw up with them.

'There is a system,' he said.

He dragged a bowl of grapes towards him, plucked a black round, and popped it into his mouth. 'Where was I?'

'You were telling me about the system.'

'Ah yes, the system.' He leaned back and dangled a bunch of grapes over his open mouth, looking like Caligula on a night of debauchery.

'Artists sift through their ideas, pick one, and make it. The good ones destroy their initial attempts. They make some more and keep destroying till something holds their attention. They keep producing, they keep editing. One day they get a high, a special feeling. When the high wears off they take high-res pictures, make a CD, and write a résumé. They do a round of the galleries.'

He sighed. She watched his mouth, wondering what it would ask for next.

'Most galleries do not have the eye. The eye of the gallerist is a mystical thing, like the third eye. I have it. I am blessed with the third eye.'

The profundity of this truth moved him. He was aware of his place. He was the locus of the system, the pivot around which art got made and then moved into salons and soirees.

He headed to the small pantry that had two coffee makers.

'French press?'

She nodded. Black coffee was a new addiction. She was yet to find her blend.

'Ghana?'

He heaped the powder into the press, boiled the water to 90 degrees, added some to release flavours, then poured the rest and waited for it to steep. After a while he sniffed at the decoction and served her a tiny cup. She sipped the brown coffee, the dark earth it came from. It was delicious.

'Looks like you have a taste for coffee,' he said.

'What if I don't have the eye for art?' she asked.

He shrugged his shoulders. 'You worked for an auction house, right?'

She nodded.

'Good for you, then,' he said.

What the fuck did that even mean?

'My local guardian is coming in today,' she told Ardeshir. 'He wants to see the place.'

She had been to Malabar Hill to meet her maternal uncle. This one was rich, the only wealthy one in Sarla's extended family. Uncle was curious about his niece, a little worried she was alone in Mumbai, that too in art circles that were considered bohemian. He had expressed a wish to visit the Touchstone Gallery.

'Should I buy something?' he had asked Nupur. 'I will, if it will help you.'

The uncle arrived wearing a suit, in his limousine, smelling expensive.

'Where is the showroom?' he asked.

'Showroom?' said Ardeshir. Was her uncle being deliberately naive, Nupur wondered. 'This is what we call our display space.'

'How much do you charge per day?' asked her uncle, looking around, measuring the square feet. He looked out of the window, evaluating the frontage. 'This space must be expensive?'

'We don't rent out the space,' said Ardeshir. He looked towards Nupur for help. She smiled and shrugged her shoulders. She was enjoying the interaction.

'Then what do you do?'

'We hold exhibitions, we sell the work, we make a commission.'

'I see.'

It was clear there were many more questions forming in her uncle's mind. 'So, Nupur is your salesgirl?'

Ardeshir smiled. 'We call her gallery assistant.'

Uncle walked around a ceramic sculpture, examining it closely, leaning forward. He was itching to hold it, feel the surface.

'Expensive?'

'Very,' said Ardeshir.

'You know,' said Nupur's uncle, 'from childhood Nupur has been a nervous sort, dropping things, breaking them.'

Nupur had broken just one item, an ugly pot, quite hideous in her estimation, but it happened to be a family heirloom.

'I know one thing she is careful with,' said Ardeshir.

'And that is?'

'Whisky. I have seen her drink glass after glass and she never spills a drop.'

Her guardian uncle left, shaking his head, a look of faint disapproval in her direction.

Ardeshir stretched himself on the sofa as only he could. 'Look what we have here,' he said. 'You are a social case study.'

'I am not a fish in a bowl,' said Nupur.

'In Mumbai you don't decide, my dear.'

She busied herself, moving from piece to piece, looking for something.

'What stories have you fed him?' asked Ardeshir.

'I could begin at the beginning,' said Nupur, 'and you will fall asleep. He is a jeweller, a prosperous one. He stays in Malabar Hill but his house is dated and dowdy. He grew up middle class and he stayed that way. He has no clue about anything modern or contemporary.'

Ardeshir lit a cigarette. 'You are mistaken,' he said. 'He is leading you on. You have fallen for his fiction.'

'What?'

'You may not notice but he has been to a plastic surgeon. Not for weight loss, but for a nose job. His suit is tailored, his shoes are from Milan. I know the brand. And by the way he is known for his bold investments in areas where he has no expertise.'

Nupur was surprised and tried not to show it. 'Well, he won't be buying any art,' she said.

Ardeshir took it on as a challenge. 'Give me six months,' he said. 'And by the way,' he said, 'what you are wearing, it is noticeable.'

'Is that a problem?'

'Yes. It is not expensive enough. So, till such time as you upgrade, be smart and choose plains that are elegant and match them skilfully.'

She reddened.

'And you have brought something for the evening?'

She had chosen carefully but now she was less certain. It was a red top with dark trousers; there was a scarf, and a bag that hid its credentials. They were to attend a dinner at a collector's home.

It had a commanding view of the Arabian Sea. The collector had a good wine collection and a spacious terrace where Ardeshir would smoke himself silly.

'Who else will be there?' she asked.

'Ask around,' said her boss. 'Go on, network, gossip, damn it. And by the way, eat something before you go. The gentleman is a vegetarian. There will be theplas and khandvi and paneer three ways.'

It was a warm evening and there were a hundred people. The terrace was huge, so it did not feel crowded. The wine was a full red. They met some artists, talked, and laughed a lot.

One artist came up and caught their attention. He had sent in his work and Nupur remembered: it was in the Serious file. 'Most artists,' Ardeshir had said, looking at his work, 'drink potable water and live antiseptic lives. No illness, no pain. This fellow is crooked. Up in his head, there is something delightfully off. A window is open, the curtains are blowing, and he has wiring that is shorting in the rain. One day he will kill someone, maybe.'

She kept the potential murderer company that evening. They talked about films, music, and suburban trains. 'I have a large plasma TV,' she remembered him saying. 'You should come.' As invitations went, that was new and refreshing.

'Why do you look sad?' she asked him.

'A Mumbai veteran told me to,' he said, with a straight face. 'He said it makes a person interesting. It seems people are attracted to those looking sad. They have to know why.'

'Hmmm,' said Nupur, less impressed, and less inquisitive.

Why did the city have this effect on people? The question confounded her. People came from here and there, each with potential, and they felt the need to act out a play. They were self-aware. She herself was an occasional actor; she too dreamed often, and she too performed.

'I read somewhere that art needs an illogical city, one that mocks its inhabitants.'

'That has to be Mumbai,' said the artist. 'It mocks reason, I can tell you that.'

'Everybody here says city-this, city-that, as if Mumbai is some kind of spirit that gets hold of you. I know only one thing about this city: it does not have a script. The only things that go according to plan out here are the same disasters, year on year. The founding fathers said, let's raise the level of difficulty, hoping that would keep the migrants out. They had no idea how bad it was where people came from.'

'You are a philosopher,' said the artist.

'I think I am drunk. This wine… you think we could smuggle out a bottle?'

'Are you serious?' He saw Nupur laughing.

They left the place and walked aimlessly along a well-lit street, down a slope, at a pace that mirrored life. Night revellers passed by in fancy cars, loud music thumping.

'Nupur is an unusual name,' he said. 'How come?'

'Nothing else works.'

'Everybody has a catchy short form.'

'Not me.'

He was persistent. 'So, what is Nupur to this city?'

'I am nothing, really,' she said. 'Unless listening to Fleetwood Mac counts for something.'

'Ha ha. I love that. So retro.'

They paused at a traffic light; its yellow light was flashing. 'I feel old in this city. I have to blame Mumbai. I hate more things by the day. You?'

'I am not counting,' he said, shrugging his shoulders.

'You know, most of all I hate the smell in this city.'

'Garbage? Fish? Sweat?'

'No. Potential.'

'Hoot!' he said. 'That is so deep, behen. The smell of potential. Wah!'

'Look around you, beta.'

'Okay. Where?'

'In the trains, on the streets, in the lift, if you please. Look at you, for that matter.'

'Me too?' he asked, pointing to himself.

'Yes, you too.' She smiled. 'You know why people are attracted to you? You have that slightly helpless, patented Mumbai look. Like a lucky coin waiting for a toss.'

III

Suleiman

Suleiman was a local presence in a Mumbai gully. He lived in Mahim, a central suburb that was Worli's poor nephew and Bandra's poor cousin. Worli and Bandra were exclamation marks in Mumbai's realty. Mahim was the city's colon. It had a causeway just like Colaba, but it lacked tourists. Picture framers set up shop there, selling pretty landscapes and cheap deities. They were joined by mirror dealers and woodcarvers. Water was a strong presence near these precincts. Through a small awning you could look out to the sea, past a beached boat that stood like a gazebo in the sand. You couldn't hear waves in Mahim; the bay was calm and still. On humid evenings DJ Majid surfaced, prowled The Terrace, and played the blues.

The arterial road of Mahim saw office-goers drive south every morning to the business district. They returned in the evening, ties askew, blowing horns, cutting lanes, sending chickens scurrying in their hurry to get home. The locals cursed; they couldn't do much else. The pavements had narrowed to make room for SUVs and MUVs. Lamp posts were shifted, and saplings were cut. Pedestrians squeezed past each other. Suleiman realized that like them he too was walking sideways.

The din abated past midnight. Street dogs appeared in larger numbers. A three-legged casualty called Tripod hobbled across the road. A breeze blew in from the Arabian Sea. DJ Majid lit up, leaned back, and eased the tempo. Suleiman sat at the tea stall, one leg over the other, dipping saunf biscuits into his tea.

The measure in his gully was an inch. Four-and-a-half-inch walls, thirty-six-inch corridors, and doors six inches shorter than most people. Suleiman stood on his niggardly landing smoking a cigarette. A year ago, a car park had usurped a playground. But space had been left for worship. His grandfather had planted a mosque and it had grown till it split the gully into two. The mosque had an onion-shaped dome and it was green in colour. On festive days it was lit by hundreds of small twinkles. The neighbourhood was festooned with chadors, the gully shops sold sweetmeats and trinkets, and azan rent the air periodically.

Suleiman owned three buildings in the gully. His neighbours called him Bhaijaan.

Bhaijaan loved cockfights. He called it a hobby; his family called it an addiction. He lived for the moment a fight began, that very moment, with men crouched in a circle restraining themselves, above them another circle of men standing anxiously. The crouched men held angry birds, Suleiman's heart pounding, bubbles blowing out of his spit. The cocks would squawk, blood would spatter, men would sprawl, sway against each other, chant names, scream epithets. The qawwali would continue, the swirling dust and flying feathers shielding the bloody horror.

'There is no good or bad in all this,' said Suleiman, when somebody in the family protested.

A full moon lit the night and Our Lady of Bandra sang nearby through a potent loudspeaker.

'Put him up against Timur,' said Suleiman.

His handler, a young lad, was aghast. Timur was the ruling rooster in Mahim, a killer. With his engorged neck and fulsome pout, he looked evil.

'Bhaijaan?'

'Just do it.'

The battle ended badly. Suleiman's cock lacked staying power.

'Why?' shouted a frustrated Suleiman.

'Too much meat in the belly,' said his handler, trying not to look at his boss.

Bhaijaan was in his prime, in his forties, and he was experienced in the ways of women. He was acutely aware of what went on in their minds. From time to time he spotted opportunities and then he was quick and relentless. The gully knew of his exploits.

His kajal-lined eyes were legendary. They smoked. On occasions like family functions they roamed.

He had an official business that he carried on under the name Deluxe Framers. The name board was repainted every year and the shop shutter was rolled down every night to reveal an artwork that a well-known artist had rendered on it as a measure of gratitude. It was a significant measure. The clients for his framing business were down south in Colaba so Suleiman would leave late morning in his old Fiat that had an MSG number plate. He would be wearing a white flowing kurta with ruby red buttons.

He did not need the framing business once his real estate gained value. But he continued with it and remained personally involved. He loved the ambiance of art galleries and he loved the women who ran them. Single women. Strong personalities who carried their world with them. A bubble in which there was magic.

Suleiman had lunch in Pasta Lane. There were five Pasta Lanes in the area and they were remnants of an era when they had played a useful role in the economy. There were sheds that housed karigari, a word that meant handmade. They had high ceilings, ideal for displaying art. In one such he was given some space where his men could stretch canvases, fix mounts, place paper and glass, and affix moulded frames. In the shed next door the karigari was nefarious. There were shadowy artists who worked at night, making fakes. They gave good business to Suleiman.

The framing business was on the decline. Art had turned contemporary, bought some attitude, shed its mount and frame, and leaped off the wall. The new art shows confounded Bhaijaan and he stood patiently in many of them, trying to figure out what he was missing. Installations bemused him; video works tested his patience. He was confident that none of this newfangled stuff would sell and these young boys and girls who were playing around, having fun at his expense, would soon return to painting. He asked the gallery supremo Ardeshir for a term that would capture these new paintings which had a flat surface, simple lines, and blank spaces.

'Minimal,' said Ardeshir.

Suleiman raised an eyebrow. 'You mean lazy?'

'Conceptual,' said Ardeshir.

Suleiman stroked his beard. 'Is there a word for it in Hindi or Urdu?'

'Sufi,' said the gallery owner.

Suleiman wasn't satisfied. 'What is Sufi? What makes it so superior?'

Ardeshir looked at his framer who stood there with his hands on his hips, his beard quivering. Describing Sufi was hard but he was on the mat and he had to come up with something better than 'Sufi is soulful'.

'What makes Sufi superior? I guess imperfection.'

'How do you get into trouble?' asked Zubeida, the one with all-grey hair. She was Aunty to the gully, and Mausi to Suleiman.

'You take three steps,' said her nephew. 'Draw something. Call it something. Then show it to people.'

'Who is this Charlie Hebdo?' asked Mausi, fanning herself with the newspaper.

'Big trouble,' said Suleiman.

'Your daughter is learning art?' asked Mausi, narrowing her eyes.

Suleiman threw up his hands. Praveena, his daughter, was drawing things he did not like. She was threatening to sign her name on her work. He had hoped she would stop at craft work but she wanted to become an artist. He tried to influence her work. He introduced her to the spare lines of Nasreen Mohammedi and the austere cast paper works of Zarina Hashmi.

'Sufi,' he said.

She showed him gouaches of Shahzia Sikandar. The works were on paper coated with clay, which had gained a pastel tinge. The New York-based artist travelled through history, touching on culture, violence, and religion.

'She is from Pakistan,' said his daughter.

'Trouble,' said Suleiman.

It began as a charity initiative. A painting competition for those under eighteen. They had to produce a birth certificate. They were given a number and a seat. Do not sign or write your name anywhere, said the invigilator. The hall filled up quickly and they had to put chairs on the lawn outside. Suleiman stood outside the college gate asking, 'Who is the judge?'

There were three of them. How could they be influenced, he wondered?

The day after the competition they returned, father and daughter. 'Why have you come?'

Suleiman tried to explain, 'She might have written the wrong number on her work. Please, a genuine mistake.'

'And what number would that be?'

He scratched his head. 'Just show her the works and she will tell you which one is hers.'

The judges were judging at the time and they pointedly ignored Suleiman but they watched his daughter as she picked one.

'Go home now,' said Suleiman. 'I will come later.'

She won the competition but refused the prize. 'Give it to my father,' she said. He took it. He displayed it at home, proudly. She banished him from her presence for a week. He made her chai one evening, put some freshly baked biscuits on a plate, knocked twice on her door, opened it, and tried to make peace.

'I need to go to JJ College,' said Praveena. 'Will you let me?' She saw her father hesitate. 'Abba,' she said, 'that is where Nasreen Mohammedi went.'

Suleiman stroked his chin and sifted through his scraggly grey hair.

'What is it, Abba?' said his daughter. 'Why do you keep stopping me? What is the real reason?'

Suleiman parted with his private nightmare. 'Praveena, I have done framing work for an artist called Maya for the last ten years. Yes, Maya the famous artist. I have been to her house when she was not able to get out of bed on some days. I have seen how she lives. I have seen what has become of her. Art may be precious but it is a world that can grab hold of you and tear you apart.'

'You like her?' asked Praveena.

'I do,' he said. 'She is a strong lady, stronger than men. And yet.'

'You think I will become like her?'

Praveena had taken to embroidery, acquiring the skill and then applying her imagination. She began with cushion covers; she made many of them and they were so remarkable that a customer asked her to produce thirty and they held a show in Kala Ghoda. The show sold out very quickly. People liked the unusual subject matter and the innovative use of embroidery. There were only outlines and the rendering was semi-abstract.

One of Suleiman's clients, a gallerist, happened to attend the show and she was struck by the work.

'Your daughter should go to art school,' she said. 'Her talent needs staging.'

Nothing happened for a while until the old man was given a work for framing, one that had only embroidery. He was so taken up with it that he did not notice the subject properly. He took the work home that night and showed it to Praveena. 'Made by somebody called Ghada Amer and – what is this name? I cannot read it.'

'Reza Farkondeh,' said his daughter. She was glad her father hadn't noticed what the work portrayed. She ran her fingers over the outline, over the lips of two women. A proper lip-lock.

Staying at home and doing nothing useful, Praveena paled. She lost weight and her health declined. She lay in bed during the day, sighing audibly, reading books on art: heavy, hardbound books she could barely hold.

'Don't behave like Meena Kumari,' said Mausi.

There were bouts of weeping. 'I will run away one day,' said Praveena.

'And go where?' asked Mausi.

Praveena threatened to kill herself when marriage proposals were brought to her.

Her father capitulated a few months later. Praveena joined MS University in Baroda. Suleiman travelled with her on the overnight train, sulking, toying with his food.

In Baroda they visited the campus, a first for Suleiman. He liked the quiet, the trees, and the library. He sat in the library, absorbing what he had missed all his life.

Watching his daughter in this environment he felt a pang. She looked so happy. She was, once again, the daughter he remembered and wanted to preserve. Her unbridled curiosity and non-stop chatter made his heart sing. 'Look, Abba!' she kept saying.

They ate a vegetarian meal together, made faces, and laughed a lot. And then it was time for him to leave. He returned sad, a little thoughtful.

Mausi was waiting for him, sitting in the small veranda with her newfound interest in embroidery.

'She will change,' he told Zubeida.

'How?'

'The place will set her free.'

'More trouble,' said Zubeida, missing a knot.

Years ago, Zubeida faced questions when Suleiman had an affair with a young starlet. It was a brief and intense affair that ended abruptly. The starlet walked away; she was pregnant, and a few months later Praveena was born. An amicable agreement later, Praveena came home and she was brought up by Mausi.

Mausi had no prior experience and she was tested when Praveena was in her teens. 'Your daughter is out of control,' she told Suleiman. 'She is like the raging sea.'

In the tight family circle Praveena strained to break free.

'This girl will be like her mother,' said Zubeida. 'How I wish you hadn't dropped your pyjamas.'

Suleiman adored his daughter. She was his only child and she had no mother around so he carried some guilt. He did raise his voice at her occasionally but half-heartedly.

Praveena returned from Baroda a postgraduate. In the early morning light, she stood in the gully entrance. Her family was ranged on the side, anxious, watching her closely. They watched how she walked, the dress she wore, how she greeted them, and they waited for her to speak.

'Nashta,' she said. 'I am hungry for home food.'

There was an elaborate breakfast waiting for her. She ate and they watched.

'I want to live on my own,' she said.

A chorus of voices greeted this announcement.

'I need space,' she said. A few square feet was all she wanted, at a fair distance from the family.

She slept well, awoke from a recurrent dream to find her father standing next to her bed. Behind him, wearing a frown, was Mausi. They looked like they wanted to abduct her. She flung the covers aside and tried to run for the door, but then she stopped and turned.

'I am not a child anymore,' she said.

Suleiman swallowed his retort but Mausi did not bother. She had her say. Praveena gave it back, using her newfound vocabulary. Their fight was quick and it drew blood; the bickering continued through the day.

Suleiman left the next day to look for a place in Bandra. Praveena wanted to stay in Bandra, the queen of the suburbs, and she wanted a small studio apartment that had big windows. She wanted it to look out into greenery. She wanted to be able to look at the sky. In Mumbai, and in Bandra, these were unreasonable demands.

He found her a place, luck by chance, in Pali Mala, a neighbourhood that was crummy yet considered tony. He found a chamari in a rickety two-storey structure surrounded on all sides by concrete high-rises. There were dogs and cats in the compound, a large rooster, and a few paying guests who came and went at odd hours, struggling to pay the rent on time because they spent money as it arrived, sometimes before it did. The sense of struggle left its mark on the bushes and creepers that had sprung up; they wrapped themselves around the nearest lamp post or railing and never let go. Dust clung to leaves and clothes hung heavy on lines. A clump of grass survived on drip.

Praveena flourished in this atmosphere, throwing herself into her art. Her newfound skills married to her traditional temperament produced interesting results.

The family watched with bated breath as Praveena set up an independent existence. They had heard of some activities on the college campus that were a cause for worry. Nothing happened for the first few months. Then a video surfaced on social media. It was titled 'Masti'. Over three minutes it showed girls and boys dancing inside an apartment in low light. One of them looked like Praveena. The comments section was full of 'xoxo babes', 'hawt', 'dawg alert', and 'luv u hamesha'.

A month later another video surfaced. A young bearded man, bare-bodied, and Praveena in a freestyle dance sequence. It had a frenetic track through which the young couple danced with abandon, ending with a clinch. The comments section had 'all night long', 'night without end', and 'luv you jaan'.

'Go find her mother!' screamed Mausi.

Suleiman handled Touchstone Gallery's framing requirements. The first time he did this, after he had delivered the framed art, he asked Ardeshir if he wanted a bill.

'Of course,' said Ardeshir.

'Kuccha or pukka?' asked Suleiman.

'Kuccha? What is kuccha?'

Ardeshir took offence but realized that for his framer it was a routine question. 'Do you pay taxes?' he asked Suleiman.

'I am too small,' said Suleiman. 'Actually, I do not wish to.'

'And why would you not?'

'Because Mahim has no pavements,' said Suleiman.

Most of the clients of Deluxe Framers were happy with kuccha rather than pukka. Touchstone clients on the other hand needed a pukka bill because they needed to record provenance. They also asked for an authenticity certificate. There was a cash side to Touchstone's business. Many customers discussed a 'ratio' and whether they could pay some of the amount in cash. It helped offload some of their stash and it reduced their sales tax burden. Ardeshir could not afford to refuse such business. He wished he could. He tried to keep his distance by having Suleiman handle it. The framer dealt mostly in cash and what little billing he did officially was to help him file returns. For a small fee that was never discussed or enumerated, Suleiman handled Ardeshir's cash, storing it, drawing from it, and maintaining some sort of record. All such records were kuccha.

The slush fund grew in size and when it became unwieldy Ardeshir got nervous. Get rid of it, he told Suleiman. On the latter's advice some of it was parked in art itself. Ardeshir bought selectively and the collection was squirrelled away in Suleiman's material depot in Mahim. The gallery owner was in some sense compounding a crime. Some part of the money funded Ardeshir's habit, his joints and his powder.

Suleiman kept a loose-leaf ledger. He had a head for numbers and a good memory. Over a few years this informal business became a bond between the two, a bond defined by a sense of obligation that Ardeshir felt.

'You can have some of the money,' he told Suleiman.

The framer wouldn't touch the money. 'Haram,' he said. 'I have not earned it.'

'Damn,' thought Ardeshir. 'One day this fellow will ask me for something.'

One fine day when the smog did not show up and the breeze was a cool slap on the face, Suleiman asked Ardeshir for a favour. 'My daughter paints,' he said.

It was a frightening declaration, similar to what hosts sometimes spring on their guests when post-dinner they declare, 'Do you know my wife sings?'

'I want you to see her work,' said Suleiman. It was a request only in name.

'Bring her work,' said Ardeshir. 'Show it to me.'

'She wants to do so herself,' said Suleiman. Praveena was insistent. It was how things were meant to be done.

'She is from Baroda,' said Suleiman, a little proud. 'MFA.'

'You did not tell me,' said Ardeshir. 'You should tell me these things.'

'She has been struggling for many months,' said Suleiman.

Nothing more was said and nothing happened for a while as Praveena, sifting through her embroidery art, gathered her work and some courage.

Money collected in Praveena's drawer but it wasn't enough. She wanted more and she wanted recognition. One solo show would save her. One chance. She was sure she would make an impact. She had intensity and a unique rendering.

Her father had called in a favour with the man with the Midas touch and this was her golden chance. Ardeshir was the ultimate in discovering new talent. She went.

Call it an off day. Too much vodka, stale grass, poor lighting. Ardeshir was dismissive. It was perhaps the one mistake he would ever make. It did not help that Praveena was dressed in traditional black and her work seemed like domestic craft at first glance.

'Have you been to art school?' he asked absently.

'Baroda,' she said. 'MFA.'

'Yes, of course, your father mentioned that.' He took another cursory look. But it wasn't to be.

'Come back when you have something new,' he said.

She was shattered. She gathered her work, stuffed it into her duffel bag, and staggered out of the gallery. Outside she roamed. She lost her sense of direction. She could hardly breathe or believe what had just happened. This was the end of her career. Her life.

She sat in a railway station as evening fell. When she found her way home, she was inconsolable. She did not answer the phone and when her father arrived, he found her dishevelled, alternating between rage and despair.

Her father channelled her rage. In so many words he directed it at the feckless art world, at the subjective gallery system, at the mercenary market, and the unjust mafia that controlled it.

'Not your fault,' he said, again and again. 'That fellow Ardeshir drinks in the afternoon. Everyone knows it. He smokes hashish and he has boyfriends.'

She screamed at him, and when he sat next to her, she bawled. Her father tried to hold her but she fended him away.

'How about getting back at them?' said Suleiman. 'We need to expose these people.'

She wiped her tears, then washed her face. They sat for a while and she collected her thoughts. There had to be a way of getting back at the uncaring art world. She wanted to do something, anything, to expose the skewed market, the blind critics and curators, and the whimsical gallerists. She had been spurned by the art world she loved so much and wanted to be part of. She would get back at them. With her was the power of unrequited love.

Tara

For taxpayers, the last day of March was a day of reckoning. It was the end of the financial year in India. Tara spent an hour trying to get in touch with the accountant who filed their returns. His phone was busy.

'Mother,' asked Tara, 'why have you kept these ticket stubs and hotel receipts?'

'Because I can claim them as expenses,' Maya replied, blowing smoke between coughs.

'And these medical bills?'

'Medical expenses can be set off against income. The accountant told me that,' said Maya, on her third cigarette of the day.

'This is for a strip of paracetamol. That is not even ten rupees.'

'The accountant will do his job, why do you worry?'

'You haven't paid for his services. Remember?'

'And yet he comes, poor sod.'

Tara ruffled the papers. 'Where is the income to set off all this, Mother?'

Maya stubbed out her cigarette. She lit another, absently, and coughed again.

'I will sell out my next show, just you wait.'

'Mother, after your last show's reviews you will be lucky to get another show.'

The show had been panned by critics and friends alike.

Instalments were due. Tara stared at the growing pile of registered letters, notices from the bank that had given Maya a large loan to buy an apartment in Nepean Sea Road. The apartment was 3,000 square feet of irrational exuberance in a posh locality. It was purchased when the art market was on a bull run, when artists had to merely sign a page for it to gain value. There was a waiting list at the time for

Maya's works; each of them had multiple suitors. Maya thought this was how life would be henceforth, a golden age. Nepean Sea Road was where Tara was born, where she went to school from.

The golden period was short-lived. They never really settled in; they had no time to belong, find their favourite spots, and build an inventory of things to remember. The markets crashed. Ever since they had been trying hard to get rid of the elephant and pay off the loan. There were other loans that Maya had taken from private parties where interest was deducted upfront, and where the monthly reminder was an urgent ring of the doorbell followed by a hard knock on the door. Tara fretted about the debt mountain they were buried under.

'Where are you?' Maya sounded sleepy and irritable.

Tara tried to ignore her. It was midnight or thereabouts. Tara often sensed when her mother was awake at that late hour and would herself lie half asleep.

Maya scrabbled around and her ashtray fell to the floor. The loud clang woke Tara up fully.

'Tara, where are you?!' Maya sounded petulant.

She had slept on her throne, the sofa. The pull of gravity had formed a shapely impression; two bums like vectors, in between was a birdie. Her body was wrapped in a tangle of sheets. She started rocking back and forth. 'Baby, my fever is rising.'

Tara shook her shoulders and Maya opened an eye.

'My feet are cold,' she said. They were. 'Where are the long socks? Get them.'

'Mother,' said Tara, slapping her feet, 'stop ordering me around.'

The tremors started with Maya's hands and they spread, gaining in intensity. Her bones rattled, her teeth chattered.

'Must be malaria,' she said, wringing her hands. 'Must be that blasted dengue.'

'No,' said Tara loudly. 'You can't fool me.'

Maya was in withdrawal. She was hurting, physically.

'Where is the pain?' asked Tara.

'I don't know,' said Maya. 'Please, Tara. Please find it.'

Tara gripped her shoulders and her neck from behind. 'Here?' She felt around with her fingers. Maya kept shaking her head.

'It is not the same place every day. Can't you knead harder? Press down with your knuckles.'

Tara was dying to get the hell out of the place. She couldn't stand the poky, reeking flat they had been reduced to. Her mother smoked three packets a day. As a form of revenge Tara lit joss sticks and scented candles. The place smelled like a busy ghat in a Varanasi summer. There was ash strewn around the ashtray, on the floor, and in the upholstery. A thin cloud that had formed overhead near the ceiling seeking an escape.

'Aaahhh,' screamed Maya. 'I knew you would find it.'

Tara used her knuckles to massage the area. 'Why don't you go for a complete check-up?'

Maya's shoulders hunched. She started weeping. She took deep gulps of air as though she was choking. She sneezed into a hanky, took a towel to her eyes, and looked up at her daughter. Tara watched, hating her just a little.

'Were you dreaming again?'

'Yes, I was. I was back in Baroda, in college. Bhagwan, our dhobi, had brought me my clothes.'

'Did he fetch you grass as well?'

Maya smiled and brushed the hair off her face. 'What would you know? We needed good grass to survive college. We needed a heightened state to rise above shit.'

Tara had heard this before. 'And you needed Guru?'

'Guru!' said her mother, remembering him. 'Guru crossed his legs when he sat. You should have seen his hair – it was a bird's nest. When his palm went up, something valuable fell.'

Her eyes glazed over. Her hands searched around the sofa. She lit another cigarette. 'Go back to sleep.'

'Why?'

'Go, please. I am fine now.'

Tara eyed the dark, smoke-stained spoon that her mother had managed to locate. She was reaching for the cigarette lighter. Tara hit her hand. Her mother hit her across the face. Tara fled; she slammed her head into her pillow. She was alone when she woke up. It was raining.

Mumbai knows a disaster or two. The city is a sliver of land that tapers into the sea and every monsoon it pours, sometimes without pause. A seventy-two-hour spell was threatening to bring the city to its knees. It was evening, and the office hordes had swarmed into bars for a tipple before the ride home. The tide came in with force and crested the southern ramparts. A few cops stood amidst the floating cars, smiling helplessly.

When Tara reached her apartment building the water was climbing the stairs of the circular stairwell. Tara was soaked to the skin; her clothes clung to her, and her shoes were probably ruined. Drops fell around her from the leaking skylight. A domestic helper ran past her, holding milk packets aloft.

'Namaste, Tara aunty.'

'Aunty, my arse.'

It must be the salwar kameez I am wearing, thought Tara. She had run out of clothes to wear and dredged up this behenji outfit. When college holidays approached, she got lazy and the laundry bag in her hostel room overflowed. The bottom of the pile surfaced in her almirah, showing off its creases.

She hissed as she climbed. At the third floor she sneezed as she walked down the empty corridor to door no. 37. She sneezed again as she stood at the door, dripping into a puddle. It was quiet now and she could hear him and his shallow breathing as he peered through the peephole of the door opposite. She sensed he was waiting for her, the creep next door. She bent to pick up the key below the doormat. Where *was* the doormat? 'Welcome' was a coir doormat that her mother's visitors stood on, she of the foul mouth and lit cigarette, mouthing, kya, what do you want? to visitors.

She took out the spare key she was carrying and unlocked the door. It opened inwards. The dark poured out like ink. She entered, hair raised, imagining cobwebs brushing against her face.

'Mother?'

The black drew her in and she groped for the light switch. It snapped like a twig and the room flooded with fluorescence.

'Ma?'

A surprised cockroach sped towards her and she screamed. It flew between her legs, fell over, somersaulted, and scurried behind the sofa. Tara laughed in relief. The silly sound took a while to subside.

As usual, she got the stare from the three men. One was stoic, one had a leer, and the third had a lopsided grin. They kept staring as she stepped up to them, each a pencil portrait her mother had made.

'Kya?' she said. 'What do you want?'

It was warm and stuffy; every window was shut. The air felt ripe and she felt breathless. The place was a tomb, time visibly still. An antique clock stood near the door; its two outstretched hands were inert and its pendulum had fallen. Dust had gathered in her absence, settled down, making a home on every surface. She sneezed.

'Tara?' came Maya's voice.

Tara sneezed again.

'Bless you, baby.'

'What do you want, Mother?'

'Where is the bloody loo?' Maya needed a compass at night.

'Can't you see? The bathroom is there. There! I am pointing, damn it.'

'Why can't you…?' screamed Maya, tripping over something.

'Why can't you…?' shouted Tara.

The building was fifteen years old. Walls had chipped, plaster had fallen, twisted iron rods had shown up and rusted. Fresh smoke arrived every morning from a chemical factory nearby, soft and fluffy, like daily bread. This was Chembur, darling of southern people, a suburb of Mumbai that Tara never belonged to. This apartment was where they had moved, from the heights of Nepean Sea Road. That high life, a distant dream, was now a recurring nightmare. Nepean Sea Road was where her life story began. With her mother in her queen-sized bed. A string of men showing up to serenade her. Hush, baby, sleep, play with these toys that make music, dress these dolls while I am – how shall I put it? – far away nearby.

There were two glossies that kept Tara company. *Good Parenting* and *Good Housekeeping*.

The phone would ring in the middle of the night, waking Tara up. The poor child would lie awake and hear her mother in the bedroom. Awful sounds. C-sharp (God), pitch by pitch to G-flat (yes, yes, YES), then back, slower, softer, longer, deeper. (Oh God). The sound of slapping, glasses clinking, giggling, whoops, whispered protests. Tara would make a plaintive sound, a cry that stayed in her throat.

The question that haunted the daughter was: Will I be like her? She went away to college but kept returning every three months, like a homing pigeon.

Her mother was incorrigible. Her clever lies. Her artistic license, an excuse for poor housekeeping. Her overstuffed sofa. The smell of cigarettes. The enduring image of her as she sat and read for hours into the night. The burn marks she made as she smoked and flicked ash. The occasional nosebleed, the irreverent response, the fights, the arguments.

'Just who do you think you are, Mother?'

'An artist should never be asked that question. The risk of a long answer is too great.'

'Short answer?'

'I am the pale voice of reason,' said Maya. She laughed.

'Manifestos,' she said to Tara. She gave her daughter a sheaf of papers. Tara, ten years old at the time, blinked.

'Keep it with you, but don't show it to anybody. You will want to read them one day.'

She had no manifesto for choosing lovers.

The day Tara's acceptance letter arrived from MS University, the art manifestos surfaced on the side table in the living room. Under a note that said, 'Legacy.'

'Read them in Baroda,' said Maya.

Tara read them that very night. The first two were tedious and she put them aside. There were some that were quirky. The precious few that she liked had the quality of an emptied vein. What leaped off the page was intent. The desire to provoke, to anger, and not to please.

'Who wrote this one?' she asked.

'A serial killer.'

'This one?'

'A man of God.'

'And this black folder?'

'It is the Communist Manifesto. Unite, it says, under this red flag.'

'I am strangely moved by this one,' said Tara. It was a dark treatise called *The Prince*.

'Machiavelli,' said Maya. 'A Florentine statesman – he urged merciless conquest.'

This was Tara's teenage internship. Machiavelli and Marquis de Sade.

'What do you think?' asked Maya.

'I am finding it hard to think,' said Tara.

As a child, Tara had sat on Maya's lap while her mother filled up notebooks with squiggles and stains. She was left-handed. Not that it mattered. She used both hands when she worked, drawing, smudging, occupying the page, looking for room to manoeuvre, and then, obeying some divine impulse, suddenly stopping.

In Chembur, sometimes, Tara sat by her mother's cramped workspace. Maya did not have a separate studio here. Most of her work was small format and on paper. She had a CD player which was perched atop a pile of books. Music was her companion when she sketched. When she got down to painting, she played Wagner. Tara would watch, round-eyed. The deep sound of the cello was unbearably beautiful. At moments like these, so was her mother.

'What do you think?' Maya would ask unfailingly, when she was done. She would look sad when she finished a work. She would feel lonely when the work shipped. And lazy.

'Mother, I think you should bathe more often.'

Tara veered towards making art; it was perhaps inevitable. She played Wagner on loop and she sketched. She was left-handed as well, and she drew just like her mother did. But something was missing. The work was almost a mirror image, but an ingredient, a secret sauce perhaps, was missing. Tara could sense it.

'It is a curse,' she said. 'I have to shake off your influence. I just can't get it right. This whole thing is an illusion.' She stood in front of her heartfelt copy. She blacked it out and felt better.

'One day it will happen,' said Maya. 'When it happens, it will be magical.'

'What makes you so sure?'

'Look where you have grown up.'

'In this bloody mess?'

Maya's fingers tiptoed on paper. 'Art treads water in here, my dear. Ideas eke a living.'

Tara picked a handmade cigarette from a box that said Happy-Go-Lucky. She lit it, inhaled, and lost her bearings. The mirror turned, her head spun, and her eyeballs walked out of their sockets.

'What the hell is this stuff?'

'From the hills,' said Maya. 'How many cigarettes do you smoke in a day?'

'Don't ask.'

'How is my old college?' asked Maya. 'Is it taking good care of you?'

Tara brushed her questions aside. 'Let go of this place, Mother,' she said. 'I hate coming back here.'

She was hungry and the shelves were bare. In the bathroom there were potions, medicines, and ointments. There were some used needles as well.

She frowned. She inhaled some more and blew out a plume. The smoke curled and drifted, holding its shape. She followed it to the window and let it out. A few raindrops fell on her face and she stayed still till they formed a line down her neck.

'How many do you smoke in a day?' asked her mother again.

Tara wandered into the bedroom, to the mirror, and looked at herself. There she was, looking like her mother did, staring like her mother did. Late at night, in front of her mirror, Maya would stare. First the foundation, then the stare, then rouge and some mascara around her eyes, trying to get the look. Finally, some pills, some unwelcome froth, and sleep, humming a tune heard during the day.

Tara crept up one night, held her mother's left hand, turned it over, and looked. Where did the art come from? Her eyes travelling up her mother's arm, Tara got her answer. Maya was shooting heroin and perforating her brain.

'Why do the heavy stuff?'

'Who put you up to this question?' said Maya. It did not occur to her that her daughter had grown up and could have questions of her own.

'I feel ashamed sometimes,' she said. She sounded sincere.

'Is that why you sent me to boarding school?'

'Yes,' said Maya, a tear appearing. Was it that easy? Banish the daughter and banish the guilt? Maya could not fight her habits. When she was needy, she had the eyes of a hunter. Her restlessness would be palpable, as would the hurt that she felt from a certain lack, a void that sucked her in. At times like these she was an open wound. Her fingers would twitch.

'Look at my work and be proud,' she told her daughter, her voice falling to a whisper, her tone vulnerable.

'Fuck your work,' said Tara.

Maya looked down at what she was making, smudged a line, and cried for a while. She lit a cigarette.

'You don't know the feeling,' she said.

'Feeling?'

'Unlike you, I will do anything for my art,' she said.

That was her plain and simple truth. Cause and effect. High art came from living life on the edge. In the process fuck the family, fuck your friends, and fuck the living daylight.

'Unlike you I am at my best when… You have no idea.' She picked a piece of paper that she had torn out from a book and read aloud. 'It feels as if the mind has moulted, cast off its cracked skin. And a bodyless body steps out from the wizened bones within.'

Tara knew where Maya was quoting from: the writings of the artist K.G. Subramanyan, an artist who did quite well without Maya's habits.

'So, what about me?' said Tara. 'Same prescription?'

Another drag, a flick of ash in Tara's direction. Maya had a temper, and it flared when she heard her daughter's mocking tone. She took a few deep breaths.

'You need to do more,' she said softly. 'Can you? You could carry on the way you are, or like me, you could hurtle through the wall of flesh into the heart of things.'

'My mother is forty-eight years old. She is deep in debt and her lenders will threaten her very soon. If she doesn't get another show, or if a show doesn't sell, she just might take her life. I am not imagining things. I have seen the rehearsal: a pathetic attempt with pills.'

Tara was so worried about Maya's impending death she went to the police. They could hold her on a possession charge, surely. She walked past three police stations each worse than the other till she found a half-decent one.

'She will kill herself,' she said at the station.

'Maybe,' the cops said, 'but what can we do?'

'I know she will,' said Tara. She stood there. 'Come on,' she willed them. 'One of you, please respond.'

Inspector Pandey took the bait. 'She has just the CV,' he said.

He had been summoned before to the building because people had complained about Maya. Her music, the noise, the strange hours, and the strange visitors.

'Is she a madam?' asked the neighbours. 'Is she running a brothel?'

'Such ugly people.'

The fire department had been summoned twice. They had to hammer the door down when nobody answered the doorbell. They found smoke, a whole lot of ash, and people who were draped on the walls and spread-eagled on the floor, smoking, laughing. Scattered syringes. Half-naked flesh. Music was pounding.

'Easy come, easy go, will you let me go?' pleaded Queen. 'Bismillah!'

There was mayhem when the firemen were spotted.

'No, we will not let you go, let him go,' sang Freddy and Co. 'Bismillah!'

People tried to run, jump through windows; they tripped on hash and their undone clothes.

The cops arrived and busted Maya and her friends for drug possession. They were repeat offenders. Incorrigible, helpless. They took Tara in for questioning and held her for a couple of hours. 'Kya?' she said, when they peeped into the holding cell. Inspector Pandey arrived, looking fresh. He asked everybody else to leave the room.

'I am so sorry,' he said. For what? He looked at her in a way no man had.

'Do you know me?' she asked him.

'I am not a stranger to you,' he said. This was a soft-spoken cop. 'I was there when you were born. Inadvertently.'

Inadvertently? Tara looked at him closely. Grey near his temples, lines near his eyes.

'You were born on a Sunday. Easy to remember that. Near this old-age home. Elderly ladies knitting, old men sitting and staring, kind nurses taking care.'

'Old-age home?'

'Yes, a modest place. The bulbs were naked, the walls were peeling. Clothes were hung out to dry in corridors, and there was leftover food lying on tables and chairs.'

That was some description.

'Sunday was special in that home because eggs were made to order. An old caregiver gave me the whole story. It was raining that day, a light drizzle.'

'My father?'

'Your mother never told you? Anyway, nobody knew. Your mother was gone by then. The home called the station and I showed up and asked questions. Did you see any ID? No. Did she speak to you about where she was from? No. They kept shaking their heads. They were helpless, all those old people. Where was I to take you? To another home, they said. There was one nearby.

I have no time, I said. Please, they pleaded. We gathered at the crib and looked at you. The old people crowded around you, happy to have had your company and sad to see you go.'

'And then you found my mother?'

'Yes,' he said. 'I am a good cop, and she left clues.'

Two visitors arrived at Maya's studio, making an entrance. One was a guru, the other an industrialist, his premium chela. They mouthed niceties while their eyes roamed. Maya introduced them to Tara, who was left holding their umbrellas. One shook her hand while the other folded his and said, 'Hari Om.' He was quite a sight, the guru, and he circled the work on the easel, his step light, his eyes twinkling. A slight smile played around his lips.

'How art has changed,' he said, without saying how.

Some drops fell from his dreadlocks. A moment's silence elapsed. It was about to get awkward.

'We will take it,' said the industrialist.

It was that simple. Tara packed the work meticulously. Three layers of material, impeccable folds, big staples to secure it all, and a twisted rope handle they could hold; they watched her as she knew they would. She was quick, sure, and very precise. Once they left, mother and daughter collapsed on the sofa and whooped.

'I was so afraid that guru would touch me,' said Maya. 'I would have fainted.'

'I am surprised he bought it,' said Tara.

'Why?'

'Did you see Girish's review of your last show? Have you heard Anjana aunty bitch about your decline?'

'Don't be dramatic,' said Maya. 'Nobody reads Girish's columns and nobody pays any attention to Anjana's rants.'

She muttered something about fair-weather friends. She looked restless and that was a prelude to a habit. 'Do I scare people?' she said.

She was scared herself. Of what, Tara wondered? Of ageing? Many great artists never made it past thirty. Mentally, neither had Maya. The really good ones, the shining stars, took their own lives.

'I am scared of Inspector Pandey,' said Maya. 'He asked me if I suffered from AIDS. I said why would he ask me that? He said he had read somewhere that those who shared needles and poked each other suffered from AIDS.'

'Let's go to Unsocial,' Tara said. 'We have some money at long last.'

'No,' said Maya, gathering herself on her sofa.

'Come on. We can drink and diss your friend Anjana. Tell me, is she as narcissistic as you?'

'Am I narcissistic? Yes, and a lot more,' said Maya. 'But I am not like the other women. They are obsessed with their bodies, with ageing, with all this Mother Earth, fecund, receptacle shit. Some are obsessed with marriage, for God's sake!'

She said it with a lot of feeling – and she was just getting started. The thought of another evening alone with her was terrifying.

Tara called her friend Nupur and left for Unsocial on her own. Nupur arrived, sporting as ever. She ordered and they drank, happy to be together.

'Why are we drinking? You want to tell me something?'

'Yes,' said Tara, 'but I don't know what exactly.' A little later. 'My mother dominates my life. One part of me wants to get rid of her.'

Nupur laughed. 'You are trying too hard to be like her. What is bugging you?'

'I just learned from a policeman that I was an accidental pregnancy. And at the time of birth, I was an unwanted child.'

They raised their glasses to eye level, looked serious, and burst into laughter. Over the next couple of hours, days, and weeks Tara spoke to Nupur about herself. It came easily, the sharing, the unburdening.

Manicmind

I realize I like talking to others about myself. Few people listen; just one is sufficient. My mother is sensitive in her art, very insensitive otherwise. It's no secret: artists are like that, the real ones. They had an excuse, an age-old one that stars like Picasso and Lucian Freud had made official. 'Art gets made when you can live life on your terms. Norms are a hindrance.'

'Find your prism,' my mother said. Maya's advice was always cryptic and quite useless.

'Should I get stoned?' I said, half in jest.

'Either that, or marry your other,' she said.

Guess what, I got married. With a mother like Maya everything sucked. Looking at her and her procession of boyfriends was doing things to me. Watching her do drugs was making me insane. I needed a normal environment. A conservative family seemed just the prescription. And a boy who was inexperienced sounded just the companion I needed. I chose from a menu on a website and picked a traditional business family; they had a small business. The father was a simple man, and so his son turned out to be, in the end. Poor guy.

Imagine: I was a comely thirty and single. In India that's a confession, not a plea. People had knocked on my door, raided my bar, felt around, and asked to stay. I let them out. The next morning, I leaned out of my balcony, set my hands on the railing, sipped tea with pigeons for company. I looked to the skies and it rained. I remained clear-eyed, quick on my feet, with little to no money in the till. I was still single. Unfazed. Thirty was nothing.

In truth my floor is made of slag, the wall has a tribal squiggle; the sheen is gone, the tabletop lacks burnish. A brute of a man made it, hewed it off a solid trunk and worked it till the surface stopped hurting. One room is all I have and it holds my life, cups it like an intimate flame. The balcony helps me live; breath comes from breeze that filters through leaves, bringing a faint fragrance of frangipani. It sucks. The interior sucks. I know it but I get by, sleepwalking in here with my hands held out.

At least the music is amazing. Two rows of discs are lined up, wall to wall, the measure of four full steps: they hold my soul. Big headphones hang on hooks. They cover my ears. In bass I trust to break my stride; the treble challenges glass, and the anthems make me cry. Words can buy my kingdom. Often, I am found seated on the floor with headphones on, screaming them out loud.

My maid is more than a maid. She keeps me in line. She has a way of looking at me on days when I lie around, incapacitated. I still live the teenage dream, with clothes all over the place and a fridge full of expiry dates. She deals with the remains of my day (packets, ashtrays), my week (beer and medicine bottles), and my month (bulbs, newspapers, magazines). I don't trust my bai. She has confessed to giving wrong directions to people on the road.

'Think of how their life will change,' she tells me, tossing an omelette. 'Something surprising will happen to them, finally.'

She is noisy while washing vessels and talkative while cleaning the floor. 'Marry a South Indian boy,' she told me, on a week I stayed home for no reason.

'Why?'

'They are milder and they are more honest.' She let out a sly smile. 'It will suit your personality.'

After a year she knew me well enough to say, 'Don't have children, madam. Whatever you do, no children.' I did not ask her for a reason.

If you cannot find a boy in the city of Mumbai it means you are fixated on something. Am I old-fashioned, with quaint ideas like marriage before anything else? Yes, if you consider virginity a thingy. My body is a protectorate, a kshetra, whose ramparts preclude petting and oral designs. I am not a graduate spinster or a postgrad nun. I am just waiting.

I think I have an inability to let go. People remain strangers. Men want to hold my hands across a table over coffee. They want to sit beside me at a restaurant and examine my earrings and brush the hair from my cheek. They want to seat me in the corner of a dark cinema and search and squeeze. They want to shift closer, place an arm around my neck, and smooch in traffic. Every move has played out in my head. This cannot be. Which school do these men go to?

Talk to me, man. Speak of yourself, make me laugh, make me cry.

I cried last morning when I went to the tailor. The hip size was wrong again.

'Madam,' said Ansari. He looked cross-eyed. 'I cannot keep modifying your shirt. I have already opened it out fully. Shall I raise the cut on the side?'

That would show some flesh. He looked at me, taking care not to stare. We both knew my bustline had increased as well. He tapped the inch tape on the table where the garment lay.

'Madam…' he began.

I knew there was no place to hide. I did try though. Was this bulge an asset or a liability? 'Depends,' I said, turning sideways, holding my breath. 'Depends.' Up there was an asset, surely. Down below were me bums, balancing the books.

That night I dug deep and played *Sgt. Pepper's Lonely Hearts Club Band.* The album. And I stood before my mirror for my latest assessment. I mouthed it.

I have a fear of soiled sheets and blood in my knickers, a fear of sharing saliva. I cannot give up my sleeping space. I fear meeting someone who would insist on sleeping with me. I have twin beds far apart. I don't like spooning. You want to feel my tongue with yours? Why? It is not about taste. It is about taste.

Did you go to your parents out of desperation at the age of twenty-seven when your friends were changing nappies and discussing pre-school options that were cropping up in every neighbourhood?

Everybody expected you to get married, right? Your life was like a dry well in Rajasthan. Only freak weather could have saved it.

My extended family had given up and they all carried on with their domestic calendars in which I did not feature. And when I landed up after a huge gap, they cracked a desultory joke about marrying me to a farmhand before I left. When my protests were muted, they were taken by surprise. They rallied around and searched and found someone. A distant relative, he was young and like me in some sort of queue. He was from Delhi. How would this go?

After the formalities and song and dance, we would go to a place like Goa. There would be a room and there would be room service. And there would be hormones and the pent-up energy and curiosity of an unfulfilled porn surfer. Music would play in my head, a random selection of drumbeats. He would find the rhythm. I would find the view behind him, where the curtains flapped. I would find the fan on the ceiling. When he was done and flopped beside me, I would examine my human nature and family parampara and think about what comes next.

This could get ugly, I thought.

#bondage?

It happened, all of it, because I let it happen. From a distance I observed myself go through the rituals and this boy, who courted me with naivety in the short run-up to an awkward marriage, looked glazed whenever he saw me. I showed some flesh now and then beneath the finery and he was beside himself. He wanted to feel my heartbeat through my lehenga. He wanted to brush against me, catch the cup and the curve. I could see the week ahead would be beset with zabardasti, a state I had sworn off. Take it, Tara, sitting, standing, and lying down.

Am I asexual?

One week into my honeymoon in Goa I took to Facebook and Twitter, and they gave me a handle and a community. I was part of a small, incestuous group. We had a code: 'We will never meet in person.' You began with that and the rest was open season. That simple code helped loosen our tongues and our inhibitions. Very soon I was leading an intimate parallel life. Nothing was out of bounds and nobody sat in judgement. In so many ways the lack of physicality was a relief.

This was liberty for the huddled masses. We came out at night into the World Wide Web, each of us swathed in layers, hunched over a device, peering into a screen and at our expressive best. One hundred and forty characters could express love and hate. Hashtags could share a life.

My handle was @manicmind.

I posted a hooded black-and-white photograph as my profile picture. I wore a cape and my eyes seemed recessed. For some reason this was a turn-on for girls who loved girls.

I looked like a graffiti artist ready to work the underground. I was not an urban agent like Banksy, with a spray can in hand and irreverence to vent. My graffiti was online postings on virtual walls. They were not the 'Pay heed', 'World sucks', 'Why me?' variety. They were personal. 'Come, shoot me down. This is me in the velvet underground.' Why trawl the streets, smell the piss on the walls, and mingle with dwellers and their strung-up clothes? A virtual wall worked very well.

I had a blog as well and my posts on this blog helped me ventilate. No, to answer your unasked question, I was neither asthmatic nor arrhythmic. I was just complicated.

My first blog post got hit on. It was amazing to get hit online. Here I was, hunched over my netbook that night. The barrage happened. Two girls wanted to marry me, one thought I was cute, and some thought I was good for love. The post was a freewheeling muse that began like this:

> Mian, today I wore your pyjamas. I did not miss your Chote Nawab.

I was writing a post about my husband. He was a regular guy but he was not my type. My first graffiti series was on him. He was obsessed with sex and he passed that obsession on to me. Our life together was an intense two years and we discovered that we had nothing in common. His single-mindedness about sex and domination had me on my knees.

It hurt. I tried telling him.

'What hurts?' he asked finally. My crying turned him on for a while.

My back hurts, I said.

My eyes hurt when I looked at myself in the morning. I do not like you. My face had lips that I did not own, a mouth that was a crooked leer, and a nose that was smelling trouble.

I saw fear in his eyes. It happened one night. I had taken a red lipstick to the bathroom mirror and written something. He had gone to wash up and I saw him return. He turned me over and saw the look in my eyes. He slapped my cheeks and called my name.

'Say something,' he shouted.

'Elle,' I replied. I sounded manic.

'What Elle?'

'Lipstick, red lipstick.' I had seen it in *Elle*, a beautiful write-up on red lipsticks. I had used the one I liked: a Revlon, a lustrous red.

'Have you been drinking?' he asked.

I nodded. 'Not enough,' I mumbled.

Another year went by and our anniversary arrived. We were back in Goa to commemorate something. Nothing had changed. I went online. My handle still described my state of mind. This was my anniversary post from Goa:

> Dark night. Week without friends. Goodbye conversation. This has got to be the honeymoon vibe.

I received some likes and some 'Tell us more'. I was hallucinating.

In the morning I posted again.

> #digestedread. Shit happens.

That went viral and I got some laughs. And I got a reply from a girl who became my buddy. My closest online friend called herself banphool. I chatted with her right through the next year of my marriage. She was single and curious. I think she wanted to nibble my ears. This was our first conversation:

@banphool: Married life? Every morning I feel the nudge. He is ready. Relentless.
@manicmind: That isn't funny. I feel for you.
@banphool: I feel fine. Let it rain. I am a fucking #catchmentarea.
@manicmind: Talk to him.
@banphool: How?
@manicmind: Where did you find him?
@banphool: He is a delinquent. He has me, only me. #sob
@manicmind: Do you ever like it?
@banphool: Do I ever. Sometimes. Imagining.
@manicmind: Tell me more.
@banphool: Wait. Here comes the freight train.

Things changed rapidly in my marriage. Months of this relentless jousting and I was having out-of-body experiences. He was having fun running through postures and positions. He was well-read.

The first few weeks he had been tender, his manner attentive; he would do things himself, like fixing his own drink in the evening. Now I arrived with a tray that had a bottle of whisky, a helping of soda (cold), some ice, and two snacks (one hot). The day began at 7 p.m. The man sat with pillows propped up and remote in hand, looking like my perfect nightmare. He would watch serials. And he would drink and eat. I would watch him. His favourite was *Chhoti Bahu*. The women in this episodic disgrace were over the top; they dressed like mannequins and acted like cardboard cut-outs. But for him it was transformational.

I was losing it. I tried talking, discussing, and then considered pleading. No, I drew the line at pleading. How about biting? That would have been fearsome. That would have been a riot.

I went on a sex hartal, claiming an interminable bleed. After a couple of weeks, he tried subjugation. He ended up hurt. It was an injury that impeded his walk. He lost his voice. And he grew fearful when the covers were turned.

He was eight years older than me, and while eight years wasn't a long time, it was still a gap. My husband was rooted and had no pretence. But after a few months I felt the lack of connect. There was trouble looming; all the signs were there. He needed a creature for his habits and I needed a decent conversation about any one thing that did not directly concern us.

The trouble began soon enough. And it was a familiar trope that visits every family: children. I wasn't pregnant and it wasn't for lack of trying. In a family that believed in generations, this was an impasse. I knew birth control and I used it. It was my inserted device.

Imagine the scenario.

I am seated outside the puja room, on the floor, striking a pose. Inside, puja-path is on. I can see my husband's knee and his hand holding the bell. The monthly banishment has happened a day early for me. Mother-in-law gives me the look at that early hour. Her calendar has rung a bell. In the life she does not lead, she is a librarian, keeping an eye on people like me who borrow plot devices. She has my number, my menses calendar, and my due date. My husband has no such record. He did not hold back last night. In the morning after, he is ringing the bell and the agarbatti smell reaches me and I sneeze. Pujya Pativrata emerges, radiant, and smiles and I couldn't help smiling, at what I have no idea.

We did the yatras for a year, invoking blessings. Mostly we went to the Devis, the Shaktis, and the Matas, and prayed for a child. And my husband worked hard. I kept bleeding. My calendar refused to budge. The librarian pursed her lips – but nothing doing.

The family was relentless. Next would be the shaman. If black magic and fear didn't do the trick, then the test tube would. I dreamed of goings-on in fertility clinics. There was a clinic nearby. One night a sample broke loose from the deep freeze and spilled into the street outside. It knew where to go. I saw it coming. Speedy Gonzales, the Sperminator, squirmed across the street, gathered pace, and vaulted through my keyhole. The giant spermatozoa impaled me.

The next morning the family was in a sulk because I was back to bleeding. They needed an heir desperately. The in-laws were good souls but they had not foreseen this. There were two sons written in my horoscope. Horoscopes did not lie in their time.

I was losing sense of time. I had the feeling I was barrelling into a dark tunnel along with screaming teenagers in a theme park. I too was screaming my guts out. I came out of the roller coaster having aged. Where was I? I had passed out, it seemed. For a few minutes I searched my belongings.

'Tara,' I said. 'That's my name. I am married – have been, for four long years.'

What was I looking for? Who was I, really? A failed artist at best? I was looking for a significant life that would leave a footprint behind. The process of living could be hard and I was prepared for it but this married life made me tired. Eating, drinking, sleeping, waking: what on earth was this?

Painting kept me sane. I chose to do oils because the slow application and the waiting for it to dry helped me reflect, to retreat to another time, a time of impasto and layering. Oil painting can surprise you, even an amateur like me. I remember achieving tonality and the feeling that light fell and left its imprint behind.

'Why can't I make this marriage work?' I asked myself.

In my most desperate moments, banphool engaged with me.

@banphool: I am done.
@manicmind: Get away. Take a train to someplace. Pune?

Running away seemed like a good idea. If I did what I felt like, I could surprise him, bring some uncertainty into this whole marriage business.

@banphool: Done. Dining car, dark glasses, pot of tea with toast.
@manicmind: Wait for the men to arrive.
@banphool: Late forties. On a mission.
@manicmind: Word or Excel?
@banphool: Nerdy, should be Excel. Circling.
@manicmind: One fell swoop?
@banphool: Yes. Seat taken. #takeabreak. Tomorrow I spill.

@banphool: Turns out he was a planter. And he was a rice plate freak. Chicken curry rice for lunch, pandi curry for dinner. Pandi? Pork. Not bad for a thread-wearing Brahmin. He was a tea planter and stayed at around 5,000 feet above sea level. That sounded heady. He described rows of orderly green bushes and trees bearing cardamom. He said evenings were hard. He drank every day: rum and water. He chewed cardamom, one laung under his tongue at all times. He wanted to be a writer.

Dread that.

During the course of the train ride to Pune I got to know that a man who traversed the length and breadth of my attention had no agenda other than to talk. His eyes did not travel. His hands stayed on the table. And his manner was gentle. Around his eyes I saw weakness, a rheumy film, a glaze brought on perhaps by long evenings watching the clouds come into his veranda. He was worried that twenty years of tea plantation living had dulled him somewhat.

'I have reached that stage in life when I have started listening to old Hindi music,' he said. 'Kishore Kumar and Mohammed Rafi, Mukesh and Manna Dey.'

This is the end, I wanted to tell him.

'My wife paints to kill time. She started with landscapes.'

This *is* the end, my friend.

He was not looking to me for advice. I was tempted to tell him that I had seen worse. But he wasn't listening. Should I tell him my story? My life in three parts: one part litany, one part woe, and one part too many.

'Thanks. I don't know your name. I have no idea how time flew but we are in Pune.'

Curtains.

@manicmind: Then?

@banphool: I met a childhood friend at the hotel. The place I stayed in was near Koregaon Park and the proximity of the Rajneesh Ashram seemed to have set him free. He made a play, the snake.

@manicmind: Was he experienced?

@banphool: No. A leopard at a zebra crossing.

In the night I heard voices. My machine was on and viruses were feasting on my hard disk. In the morning my screen saver showed a chewed-up Apple. I painted my fingernails red, trimmed my eyebrows, and used a natural soap that had ginger and honey. I wore loose-fitting clothes that swayed when I walked. I caught an autorickshaw and went to the German Bakery. I sat alone and ate a sinful cheesecake and a croissant. I finished the crumbs and left a small tip. I had a bag with me that held a few clothes and a book that told me: 'Be realistic. Plan for a miracle.'

I walked, swinging my bag, my dress swirling, quite the picture for a matron in the hills that played *The Sound of Music*. I went to the Rajneesh Ashram near Koregaon Park. I gained admission and went for the first discourse.

'Be,' said Osho, speaking to me from a large screen. 'Don't try to become.'

I looked around. There were others like me.

I joined the Osho Ashram and nobody knew. This was a quiet period, one I would recommend. The quietest you can become is when you are learning to forget. Can you do that: just forget? In the ashram I could, for a while; in that commune I was living out what has become a cliché, which is 'Be in the now'.

Anjana aunty says remembering is noise. Why? Because it colours your thoughts with sepia. She says sepia is ugly, a tint that is unforgivable. 'Triggering memories in the viewer of a place and a time, invoking in them a sense of loss or yearning is cheap; it is not art, it is pandering.'

My mother said, 'I know people who ask artists to paint happy pictures that remind them of better times. Some of them are my friends. I am quite fond of them. I don't have the heart to tell them to fuck off.'

Here I am having painted a picture of a past that I would like to forget. It is hard. It helps that I stay in Mumbai. Mumbai keeps me grounded; you can be busy in Mumbai just being. I am done with my excavation. My fridge has a magnet expressing a view that I would commend. Memory, it says, is your enemy.

Tara and Nupur

Ardeshir asked Nupur to help him sift through the ton of material they had received from young artists hoping for a debut at TG. They went through slides for a couple of hours. One particular set was giving Ardeshir some grief. He went through the images twice and finally threw up his hands.

'These are from Maya's daughter. Her name is Tara.' He clucked and marked a red X across her CV. 'She will never be an artist.'

'Oh,' said Nupur.

'I cannot send her a form email. And I don't have the heart to call Maya's daughter with this news.' He tapped the résumé with his red marker. 'She is such a lovely girl.' Nupur knew what was coming. 'Can you handle it, love?'

It was a delicate task as TG handled Maya's work. Nupur decided to meet Tara in person. They met for coffee in a cute place on the Causeway. Tara looked nervous, perhaps sensing what was coming.

'You know what, I like you enough not to prolong this,' said Nupur. 'TG is unable to take on your work. I was asked to send you an email or something but I didn't have the heart to do it that way.'

It hurt, visibly. 'I need something stronger,' said Tara, staring into her cup.

'Listen,' said Nupur, 'the art world is probably the right place for you. But perhaps not as an artist.'

'What do you mean?'

'I have firmed up my plans,' said Nupur. 'Let us stay in touch. I could have something interesting on which we could work together.' She placed her hand on Tara's. 'I am serious,' she said. 'You did well in your filmmaking courses, I am told.'

They kept bumping into each other at art openings and the conversation continued.

'Hey, listen,' said Nupur.

'No, no, it's fine,' said Tara.

'Please talk to me,' said Nupur.

Tara took a deep breath. 'You know I won't give up. I too have a story to tell.'

'Of course,' said Nupur.

'I think my story is more important than the ozone layer.'

'What?' Nupur giggled.

'It is my world, you understand, as much as it is yours.'

'What are you waiting for then?' said Nupur. 'Begin now, shake the rafters!'

Tara laughed. 'I will, just you wait.'

She recovered slowly. She needed to get away and she reminded Nupur about their grand plans to visit overseas museums and shows.

They applied for and received Schengen visas that gave them access to the European heartland, where their imaginary heartbeat resided. They bought backpacks, dark glasses, shorts, and walking shoes. And they left, breathless with anticipation. They spent a blissful week in coffee shops, resto-bars, museums, and promenades. They fought now and then. Nupur liked the Impressionists, the romance of that period, the dated look, the men and women with their elaborate turnouts, the salons they lounged in. Everything was well-rounded, soft focus, in rouge, white, and pink. Tara liked angst, expressionism, Bauhaus, grunge, urban noir, graffiti, espresso, and coarse bread.

They endlessly discussed their shared dream of setting up a salon that would encompass painters, writers, poets, and filmmakers. They would serve coffee, brandy, and quiet. It would be near a dead-end road, on a grassy rise, overlooking a disused railway track. Nearby would be a maidan, cordoned and under dispute. There would be shade from a single tree, a dog, and a cat. And the watchful eyes of neighbours itching to complain. The place would be full but the till would be empty. After a year of this they would be broke and the landlord would drop by to see what was happening. He would give them advice and leave. The customers would overhear and leave change in the till.

There was a romance in this setting, a tale of trying to make ends meet.

Nupur left for London and Tara returned to India. Nupur sent postcards. Her writing was always interesting, a running hand interspersed with squiggles and small visual footnotes. London was exciting and her visit helped her clarify what she wanted to do next.

'I feel alone out here,' messaged Tara. 'I have to deal with my mother's neurosis. She is at a flashpoint because Anjana the great, who she thought was her friend, has panned her recent show. I wonder what Anjana aunty eats for breakfast. Nails, I guess.'

'It will blow over,' said Nupur. 'Find something to distract her.'

Tara needed something to distract herself. She watched films; cinema, she called it.

'And you? Are you cooking up something?'

'It was all building up,' wrote Nupur. 'I was sure it was. But it has come crashing down. I had a showdown with Ardeshir before we left. I should have told you but the wound was too fresh, too raw. He asked me to curate a show, not a real one but a virtual presentation. I said I would mount a real one, picking from the stockroom. And over a weekend I did just that. God, how I slaved putting up that show. I even wrote a curatorial statement. And he came like he does, smoke billowing, the unsubtle smell of weed, looking his languorous self, and he strolled through the show, sat, and groaned. No, he said, not happening.

'He trashed it. He said I lack the eye, the eye of a gallerist, which he has been blessed with. I said I wanted a second opinion. I think he was shocked by my request. He complied. The bastard was gracious enough to call Anjana aunty and she strolled in like she was royalty, with no idea who had curated it. She dissed the show. So, to answer your question, am I cooking something? Poison, maybe.'

Anjana

Anjana's father wanted to witness her birth. Enthused by a film he had seen on television, he had made a pact with his wife to be at her side for the firstborn. He visualized holding his wife's hand and helping her in some way.

He was a musician by profession; he played three instruments in a band that recorded music for film songs. Culturally, he was stuck in an America that had Cary Grant, saucy heroines, film soundtracks, costumes, and set designs.

One day he brought a second-hand jukebox home, one that had tracks from films he had seen.

'In for a dime,' he told his bewildered wife, 'in for a dollar.'

There was one track that he favoured over others. It was 'Sarabande', a martial number from a Stanley Kubrick film. It gave him goosebumps. He decided that his daughter's arrival in this world would be heralded by 'Sarabande'.

When the moment arrived and the contractions began, the way to Bombay Hospital was blocked by a marriage procession. The groom was a slight boy on a white horse, there was a brass band playing, and the dancing baraatis had taken over the road.

Anjana's mother, stuck in a taxi, screamed. The piercing sound reached the ear of the groom's brother. He was in the midst of an energetic display, but the primordial cry got through. He was at the window in a flash. He thought somebody was dying inside the dark Fiat. Anjana's mother, splayed in the rear, had one leg over the front seat, which was acting as a stirrup. Sweat poured down her face. The drumbeat reached a crescendo when Anjana arrived in this world inside a Mumbai taxi, heralded by a Bollywood brass band. Kubrick and Handel had been upstaged.

Every once in a while, Anjana stood near the place of her birth. This Mumbai was daunting. No time, never still, people brushed past her. 'Baaju,' said someone for the umpteenth time. 'Side,' shouted another. She moved from side to side, sidestepping a wheelbarrow carrying garbage. A call from a mosque, a hoot from a suburban train, a flurry of pigeons amongst scattered grain. The ground beneath her feet had been described by Salman Rushdie, but the words that came to mind were from the poet Nida Fazli. 'Muqammal jahan' – a complete world – was what she sought but could never grasp. Two square feet was all Bombay granted her. The rest was poetry.

'How can I respect this Mumbai where small is cosy and cramped is intimate?' she asked someone. 'We travel like sardines and sleep like spoons. We learn how to subsist. The city does not trust silence or value subtlety. It is a sweet spot for extremes. On the one hand, it excites your imagination; on the other, it deadens your senses. It is a hungry city, a giant Pac-Man that munches the old, the weak, and the distracted. Today, it looks like an engorged widget at the end of its game.'

In Mumbai film parlance, Anjana was 'hatke'. Different. In her case a day promised a night. She grew up a nocturnal spirit in a small thicket called the art world. The art world admired her, describing her as a femme fatale. A Mata Hari. Hers was a pincer gaze that viewed the creative commons as a petri dish.

Her first takedown as an art critic was in a debut group show.

In the beginning artists from Baroda paint like each other and think like each other. The foreshortened figures, the landscape with its anthill obelisks, the homage to Kitaj, the trap of narrative art. The school for unlearning began today at a gallery in Mumbai where they experienced the veiled derision of critics and the summary rejection of the market.

'What is the art you like?' an artist asked her.

'Art that is a slow and gradual unravelling,' she said. 'What slips to the floor is camouflage.'

She was a private person, happy in the company of her cat, Awara, in her sunlit library. Her daily come down was a bloke, a journalist called Girish.

Girish admired her from afar and up close. She was a mistress of her own being. She wasn't overly concerned that time was passing by and that the life she was leading was incomplete in normal terms. What animated her was art. She thought long and hard in academic terms, and while doing so she listened to music that bore repetition. She had her addictions, her human side. Red wine, a sweet called motichoor ladoo, a savoury called hing kachori. Her nights belonged to all of these, and long, slow-unfolding ragas like Malkauns.

'Can I meet your parents?' asked Girish.

'Why?'

'What did they give you, each of them? I want to know.'

Anjana was nonplussed. 'Let me see. My father practised at night, each instrument in turn. He was after perfection. My mother was a mathematician. Her life was abstract; she was full of proofs and theorems and unsolved riddles that haunted her. She wore specs, she had thick hair, and she was so good-looking. Home for me was a fog, a haze, a coming together of rhythms and notations. Have I answered your question?'

There is a Baroda of old where encroachment, the plague of daily life, impedes your movement. Wires crisscross and tangle with poles, like braces on crooked teeth. There is a cantonment in Baroda, a palace, and a station. And there is MS University, home to Indian contemporary art. In the state of Gujarat, Ahmedabad has a textile legacy; Baroda has paintings and a monarch as patron. Legacy was a serious business in Baroda – a satisfactory one took decades. It is fair to say that in the history of Indian art the Baroda School exists, and while people may differ on what that school represents, they will agree it cannot be ignored.

Anjana's shoes clacked as she entered the art department of MS University. The rest of the new batch walked gingerly, like it was hallowed turf. The surface was calm but she wasn't fooled. It was an unruly quiet. It wasn't just grains of sand that separated departments.

'Art is death by department,' said a young professor, staring at her clean fingers. 'Before you get those hands dirty, go to the library and read. There is a language there waiting for you.'

She entered the zoo. She walked past carrels that had rows upon rows of hardbound tomes; they had glossy reproductions and were full of orderly lines typeset to perfection. She went to the carrels that held stacked catalogues, dusty doctrines, and shaky philosophies. No toying with Walter Benjamin, beating herself up with postmodernism, or grinding through a 1,000-page tome by Hans Ulrich Obrist.

She found her epiphany in the restroom where the class charsi had used a felt pen and wanked out a private manifesto.

In her first group project she passed some caustic comments. She got her first nickname.

Gujarat was thought to be a mercantile state by the rest of the country. An average citizen in Gujarat was a happy merchant, governed by pragmatism. If the pursuit of profit led to wealth, he or she bought a larger house, an imported car, diamonds, and business-class tickets. At home a Kashmiri carpet, a brass lamp, a bronze God. Very few bought art. Few in Baroda knew what went on in the fine arts campus in their city. Some of them attended the annual exhibition where graduating students showcased their work. Anjana was there in her third year and she could sense the excitement and anxiety. 'Bitch,' said someone, 'why have you brought your smart ass here?'

Students of art history and criticism like Anjana lurked in the corners of galleries, observing the commerce. They were on the way to becoming critical thinkers, the new creed. They knew their time would come. Outside the campus cloister, in the real art world, their discourse was spreading, their will was prevailing.

Discourse was a recent invasion of the art world, practised by new sages who honed their skills in liberal arts colleges. Under their watch art became thoughtful, oftentimes a clever confection. Just like food broke down and became molecular gastronomy.

Years ago, Tara was home for the summer holidays.

'Anjana aunty is coming,' said Maya. 'Spend some time with her.'

'Why?'

Aunty took her shopping. Tara needed to buy a bra for the first time. It should have been a simple exercise but people like Anjana were complicated. They went to Marks & Spencer. They left Girish in the men's section. Tara looked around the undergarments section with a mixture of curiosity and awe.

'Of all the clichés that have lost their power to surprise, the one that got resurrected is an everyday one: "The cup is half full."'

This was how Anjana spoke.

'Will I find a size that fits?' asked Tara.

She looked into the mirror, standing sideways. As did Aunty. 'I am still growing up here,' said Anjana, holding her ample breasts. 'I mean, come on, this has to stop sometime.'

Tara giggled.

'I will topple over one day. Should I try homoeopathy?'

Girish called, sounding impatient. 'Are you done? Can I come?'

'No,' said Anjana.

She smiled at Tara. 'Men are such babies. Girish is no exception. Sometimes I have to tell him to stop the squeezing and the pinching. I am planning to buy a bus horn.'

She led Tara to the padded section.

'You are your mother's daughter,' she said. 'May I present the cup half full?'

Tara wasn't sure.

'Up to you, sweetheart,' said Aunty. 'The padded bra has worked wonders.'

The cashier removed the protection tags at the billing counter. He swiped their cards, looking down intently at the machine.

'Do they pay you to sit here?' Anjana asked him as she leaned over, resting her breasts on the counter.

For that summer holiday Tara was placed under Anjana's tutelage. It was life-changing. She paid attention to Anjana's every word and found many of her throwaway lines worth recounting. She browsed her vast book collection and her music. There was a lot of poetry in her shelves, most of it melancholic. They sat together, drank dark wine, and listened to classical music. The pieces sounded melancholic. They were night ragas and each had a prolonged opening. Anjana stayed the distance, her eyes closed, seated in a posture of complete surrender.

'There is something sad about her,' said Tara to her mother. 'Her sadness is special. Like everything else about her.'

Years later, Anjana held Tara's hand and traced the lines in her right palm. 'So much of your mother is in you,' she said. 'Do you resent that?'

Tara nodded. 'I do. I resent the fact that in public functions my mother is refined and elegant. On a podium she is articulate. It isn't her. Only I know what lies behind the mask. I live with the stripped-down version.'

'Maya is bohemian,' said Anjana, looking at the framed jacket covers of bands near Maya's bedroom door: the Rolling Stones, the Doors. 'She belongs to that era. The style is out of fashion.'

'You mean the Woodstock crap?' said Tara. 'The swinging sixties bullshit? She can try all she wants but she is not hip. She is just… confused.'

'Well, she draws blood. She is mercenary, mind you. For her, art is prey. She braves the dark and lies in wait.'

'Then why did you write that harsh review, Aunty?'

Anjana took a deep breath, relieved that the question had been asked. 'I knew you would ask. I have dreaded it, all this time that you didn't ask me.'

'Why did you do it? My mother is your friend.'

'She is more than a friend,' said Anjana, twisting a tendril from her long tresses. 'Maybe that's why. Does that make sense?'

The magazine copy lay between them. Anjana flipped it and the offending page appeared, the one Tara had gone to again and again.

'I read the review carefully, many times. It is a personal attack. Why would you do that?'

Tara waited, fearing she would get a prepared answer.

'Set against my friendship, my sense of discernment prevails,' said Anjana. 'Her work has deteriorated. You can take my word for it. I think Maya's health has too, and the two are related. Her drug habit is beginning to worry us all. For some reason she seems to think that punishing herself, which is what she is doing, is necessary for her art. I ticked your mother off once when I walked into her studio and found it filthy. She tried to justify the squalor. Art gets made in trenches, she said. I told her, trenches are fair enough, but you are in the gutter, my dear.'

'Is it a compulsion, Aunty?' asked Tara. 'For you to be so brutal and honest?'

'Call it what you will.'

'Do you sleep well, Aunty?' asked Tara.

'I dream a lot lately,' said Anjana. 'Maybe I should see an analyst.'

'Maybe,' said Tara. 'Maybe you should allow people their failures. Maybe failure needs a private space and not a public trial?'

'You think all this is easy for me?' asked Anjana. 'You have any idea what I go through? Even a simple trip to the art district in Colaba and Kala Ghoda, and I get a fever.'

'You are joking?'

'No,' said Anjana, her face deadpan. 'My eyes turn yellow.'

'Because jaundice?'

Anjana laughed. 'Yes, a jaundiced eye. You see, after years in this calling, I have developed an allergy.'

'Against?'

'I am allergic to the gallery as a sacred space, to artwork being treated as a deity. I am also allergic to collectors. Buggers. For them art collection is like a Holy Crusade, and look how they display their prized possessions, like some sort of trophy display.'

Girish

Every year the spirit of Mumbai is tested by rain. Some days the clouds don't listen, neither does the tide. The brave in Mumbai are foolish; they heed the urge to get to work. For a brief while I was like them, in a nameless hurry to get from place to place. To cope I pilfered moments in the shower, singing till the water ran out. In the train I missed stops and made friends. I was thirty years old. My family said I lacked a relevant life. The fuck was I doing, wasting time placating them and my poorly phrased well-wishers? They kept hounding me; they thought I was meant for something more. I was a page in Everyman's Guide to Whiling Away Your Best Years.

My family name was on posters on every station wall in the city, advertising classes for entrance exams. Engineering and medical entrance exams were a competitive nightmare. Bhatkande Classes gave tuitions in cheap premises equipped with a tube light, a blackboard, and sheaves of sample test papers. My uncles were good businessmen; they had faith in me, and I had shown no signs of rebellion. But things turned when I applied for an arts course in Baroda. I gained admission without their assistance.

'What will you do in an arts college?' asked an uncle. 'It is full of useless people. They teach you how to draw?'

'Yes,' I said. I showed him some naked people.

'Where do you find them?'

'They are regulars; they come every year and pose,' I told him.

'Women?'

'Yes.'

'You pay them to pose naked?'

'The college does, I think.'

'Have you sold a painting?'

I was an arts graduate but I was yet to find my voice; my work lacked that important something. Back in Mumbai I stood on my two feet; they led me to a cheap suburb, to a one-bed space that was tight, barely enough room for me and my pride. I used every corner, sliding doors; the bed was four feet wide, the dining table was three-sided, and three stools of graded sizes slid into each other. I did my morning yoga, stretching my arms and legs out in slow motion, holding my breath. When my luck ran out, I knocked on wood. At night I had a distinct feeling of a tortoise retreating into its shell.

In this hopeful pad I painted till I ran out of material. I stacked the work, luckless stuff really; I knew it would never sell. I passed time reading books, tried my hand at writing, and ran out of money. The Bhatkande clan assigned an uncle to handle me.

'I will come with you for a day,' he said. 'Do what you normally do.'

I stood before landmarks, walked through lanes and down alleys. I stood before a retail outlet that had spice powders, dried fruits, pickles, and grain sacks that were open on top. The shop was cramped; the shopkeeper sat on a cushion, he had a calculator for a brain. His son did deliveries, his old man at the rear made useless suggestions. Transactions were noted on one-side printed paper, a pencil hung from a string. A fire extinguisher hung below an exposed switchboard where wires occasionally sparked.

'Are you hungry?' asked Uncle. 'What are you looking for?'

'I had no idea. Inspiration,' I said.

There were murmurs in my family that night. It was a peculiar sound.

'I have an idea,' said Uncle. 'You will teach English in our coaching centre. We pay well.'

I taught English in Bhatkande Classes for three years. I moved into a flat that had two rooms and an enclosed balcony. There was a small corridor where clothes on a rack rose to the ceiling and dripped on my head. The building had a provision store, a milk vendor, and a yoga teacher. The yoga teacher stretched before me, his limbs elongating like India rubber. He contorted into a knot and emitted a sonorous OM that made my hair stand. I loved the ending: profound idleness lying on a mat.

'Can you teach anything else?' asked my uncle. 'You have spare time.'

'No, sorry.'

'Doesn't matter. Don't worry.'

My family thought I was on the road to recovery. My uncle turned his beady eyes away and everybody relaxed. Things were quiet. But then I met Anjana again.

Anjana and I is an accident that happened in Baroda. What on earth did she see in me? It seems I belonged to a lost Bombay. I reminded her of characters from movies she loved which were directed by Saeed Mirza. He was a master of parallel cinema; his films did not pander, they did not paper over cracks. Bombay showed up in them through flawed characters like Albert Pinto, Salim Langda, and Mohan Joshi. Each was searching for identity; each was battling the system.

That explained only so much. Anjana liked me because early on in our first year she asked what was the one thing I wanted to do in life. I said, 'Swim with dolphins.'

Anjana indulges me. She is an art critic; some say a life critic. She is a blood-soaked, marrow-of-life type that Mumbai takes to heart. She comes alive in the evening, visiting galleries and ateliers. People love her: her throwaway lines, her casual meter. At her best she is deep, poetic without meaning to be. At her worst, she is savage. She speaks truth in art and it hurts the art community.

She found me a job in a newspaper; she knew the editor. 'You should join. It will suit you more.' I did what she asked me to; I joined: it was what it was, a capitulation. I struggled with the assignment; some days I wished people harm. She looked so happy; I was doing something she thought I should be.

She is a life force, my Anjana; she has a different energy. She will never change, I will have to adjust. Everybody adjusts, I told myself. Just look at Mumbai people surviving in chawls, making love in rickety kolis. The weather beat down their windows, water invaded the roads, and yet the struggle continued.

I boarded a train every day because I had to. I pushed and shoved but I didn't make enemies; I breathed carefully because my nose was stuck in an armpit. Now and then I chose to hang precariously out of the moving compartment to breathe fresh air; it would rain and for a while I would be laughing for no reason, relishing the raindrops, even as the rest of the people struggled to stay dry.

In my spare time I struggled with a manuscript that began every month. In a year's time I had twelve beginnings; each was a local train that left Churchgate and gave up at Dadar. I wrestled with my day job.

'What are you capable of besides growing a beard?' the editor asked on the first day.

'I can review art shows,' I said.

His lip curled. 'Newspapers do not waste columns on art reviews,' he said. 'But I will make an exception. Because of Anjana.'

I was assigned a desk that was a shaking distance from the toilet. The office atmosphere was rough; my colleagues bawdy. They had convinced themselves it was hard work to write, edit, proofread, and produce a daily. We produced a broadsheet; it was a marvel to hold when it came off the press smelling of ink.

'Don't talk to me early in the morning,' said my boss. A born pessimist, he always had his head in his hands; his bald head was smooth and pink. Scanning what he had approved the previous day, it took an hour in the morning for his gloom to lift, for his gin breath to dissipate. Nobody really knew why he was the way he was.

'Bring your piece,' he shouted.

He began his day with me because I was easy meat hung on a rack called trainee; my nape was under a sword that had killed.

'Make it shorter,' he said. He hadn't bothered reading it.

'Sir, I need to discuss something with you.'

'Now? No chance. Later.'

'Now, sir? Please.'

'You are in my face, young man. Please go. Shut the door softly when you go; the hinge is not working properly.'

I should have instigated a transfer to a safe harbour like City Happenings. Instead, I persisted in trying to interest my boss in my pet project. I must have been pitiful in my earnest foolishness. I was a dreamer; on weekends I imagined a new day, a new dawn, away from Mumbai on a writing sabbatical. An Apple laptop, MS Word, and Times New Roman, 12-bore.

Back in my small pad I let go of all that had built up during the day. I listened to my new love, Bhimsen Joshi. I was awestruck as the maestro lost control over his body, launching his being into vigorous riffs. I wrote in that spirit, without containment. I had this uncontrollable urge to write. I had no idea of its worth. Its time would come; the rush to judgement would come: till then I was safe. Anjana in her wisdom called it the 'Universality of the Artistic Impulse'.

'Why does art get made in nooks and corners all over the world?' she asked. 'Is it a primordial impulse?'

I had asked these questions of artists. Artists loved to talk about themselves, their practice, their difficulties in living. Living, they were at pains to point out, was a subservient activity to art making.

'Imagine us, having to fix the flush, cook meals, stand in queues, and pay the electricity bill.'

So said my friend Krishna Kumar, another Mumbai accident, a six-foot Malayali drama queen with a moustache and black beard. He was a performance artist. Krishna was from Alappuzha, a backwater where fresh and salt water met in equal measure and traded places. We went back longer than we cared to remember, to days when we shared a room and a toilet seat.

'Girish, you are full of foolish questions. Don't take everything seriously.'

'No, but seriously, tell me, I am recording this.'

I showed him a small device that looked like a cigarette case.

'Can I smoke here?'

'Wait, let me open the window. Can you sit near the railing?'

Krishna lit his cigarette. 'Do you have rum? I left some last time.'

I rummaged through my cupboard, which had many bottles; some had dregs. I poured an inch into two glasses, added some water, and we sat near the balcony.

'Do you remember our years on campus?'

'Of course,' I said. They weren't memorable but who forgets?

'Why do I make art, you ask? What else is there to do?'

There are times when Anjana speaks in her sleep. She is alone, no family to speak of. Art is the enduring passion that she lives by; she places that in the centre of her vision and she expresses her thoughts on it like nobody else. I have witnessed what she is famous for: brutal takedowns.

'An art that is meant to please,' she told a senior artist, he was popular with corporate chieftains for a kind of landscape. 'A practice that seeks to seduce.'

'I see. What does that make me?' He shouldn't have asked.

'An artist who tears down nothing, who cannot pierce through fog; you collect raindrops in a teacup outside your window. Your idea of beauty is a vanishing point behind my head.'

We left in a hurry. We sat in a café in Kala Ghoda where the beer was cold.

'That was unnecessary,' I said.

She wouldn't listen; she didn't care. 'It doesn't matter,' she said. 'I don't think he understood.'

I wondered again if we were meant to last as a couple; there was only so much that I could handle. Krishna and I discussed it at times.

'There is a class difference,' he said.

'Class?'

'She is classy, you are not,' said my good friend.

'Three days ago she asked me to help her buy drapes,' I said. 'I didn't know what a drape was.'

'People like her buy drapes. You and I buy curtains. She will use an elevator; you will be stuck in a lift.'

It was irritating. 'She says her living room has a diwan and a settee. Even her sofa has a name. Chester something.'

'Do you have a living room? I don't remember one.'

'Krishna, I am not poor and she is not rich.'

'It is a matter of upbringing,' said Krishna.

Anjana has a calf muscle that cramps in the night. In a sleep beyond pain the first sign of the cramp is a twitch; the second is the knowledge. She surfaces and sits bolt upright, grabs at her leg as the knot forms, and then remembers to lie down and stretch it to the fullest. The knot loosens and the pain subsides. She looks around in the dark; I think she misses her mother. In sleep her shrouded form looks smaller. Outside the window a streetlight is flickering and it shows up in the drawn curtain as a dull landing light. I am awake and sneaking looks at her through half-open eyes. I like watching her unawares.

'Reminds me of the window in my house in Vile Parle as the big birds came in to land.'

Damn, she knows I am awake.

'In school in Mumbai I was asked to eat bananas and drink lots of water.'

'For cramps?'

'Yes. I was also told the mind would cramp. It needed to be tested every now and then to keep it in shape. It is a muscle like your calf.'

'I see.'

'Yes. While sitting and eating bananas I would do the crossword.'

The daily crossword keeps Mumbai busy on the long train rides. The newspaper is folded twice to a quarter page, held by the left hand while the right held onto a bar, warding off evil spirits and sudden jerks. Between Vile Parle and Mahim, Anjana would have finished the two-word and three-word combinations and the anagrams and all the words that started with letters she knew. The difficult ones would come to her as revelations between Bombay Central and Marine Lines, just like glimpses of the ocean.

She is a mental gymnast. Sometime in the afternoon she plays a complex online word game, pitting her mind against a secretary from Bandra who works in a legal firm and a reporter who covers the daily beat and makes sense of minor crimes in the suburbs.

I was tasked with saving the arts page by the art community. 'Think of it like saving the city.' Galleries encouraged me, made big promises, offered incentives. They said, please work on your boss. I said I would try. In a heroic moment I took my boss Sastri for an art show. Sastri sir, the editor of the arts and culture pages, was a misfit. He thought modern art was pretentious and a plaything of the wealthy. Sastri had other stereotypes in his head, all of which had come from years of indifferent journalism. To steer the man away from his shallow end I chose a show that was different. We walked from Horniman Circle; traffic clipped our elbows as we passed the Asiatic Library. We neared the Max Mueller Bhavan, opposite which was the Experimental Gallery.

'Who is the artist?'

'It is called the Collective.'

'Why?'

'Two of them work together. Think of it as a duo, a jugalbandi.'

'Paintings, I hope.'

I shook my head and said nothing. The Collective used new media like LED screens, video, assemblages of still photographs, and sound pieces.

The gallery had been transformed into small alcoves and each of the alcoves had a work.

Sastri was patient: he looked into each alcove, he sat through the videos, he stood before stills, and he cocked an ear when sound emanated from corners and from the ceiling.

'Are they Indian?' he asked.

They were; this was the New Wave of art that came from the worldwide ether, that had no visible roots in country or region.

'What is this strange sound?' he complained.

He had a right to complain. The soundtrack seemed to come from the bowels of the Earth. I referred to a handout.

'They are mating calls of the blue whale.'

We listened for a while.

'Very moving,' said Sastri.

One of the alcoves had a video projected onto the wall. There were birds at rest on windowsills and trees. As we entered the birds sensed our presence and flew away, one by one.

'Motion sensors,' I mumbled.

The birds returned and Sastri revisited his childhood. He jumped, waved his arms, and freewheeled around the room. The birds went into a tizzy. I looked at my boss with a degree of compassion.

The last alcove had a gritty video that was shot with a handheld camera. It was a street scene and it ended in mayhem and chaos. Sastri stood, rooted.

'This is like breaking news,' he said. 'Who is the reporter?'

'The artist is a friend of mine,' I said.

'Is this what art is these days?' asked my boss. 'I didn't know.'

'Yes,' I said, not knowing if I should be proud or apologetic.

'The audience is shrinking, the pages reporting art are shrinking. In the face of difficulties these artists are doing all this?' He waved his arms accusingly. 'What do you think, Girish? Is this art?'

I hummed. 'Someone important said if you house something in a gallery it is art.'

'Explain it to me,' said Sastri. 'If I can understand art, I am sure our readers will.'

This wasn't going well. Explaining art, making my boss understand art: these were impossible tasks.

Every time I wake up in Mumbai, I worry about what time it is. On weekends I want things to slow down. The sun is up, I am half awake, and I am slurring. There is a pair of pincers at the back of my throat and my tongue is coated white. Anjana is travelling and there is nobody to talk to.

I am hungry. If I drag myself out of bed and get to the fridge without falling, I will find some yoghurt. Low cream, low fat, with some fruit pieces in a small cup. No, I will not be able to. I will trip on my sheet and fall. Beautiful people were partying last evening.

Celebrities who seemed oblivious to envy and hate. They had no idea how vulnerable they were. It was a matter of time. Harm would befall them; a pity they would be blissful till the bloody end.

I drag myself up and spot myself in the mirror. I have seen some sad people in my life. That's what the mirror tells me. I have officially succumbed to a state called melancholy. It has a seductive embrace and it won't let go. Not that it matters; I am not fighting.

My maid comes and goes; she talks as she works. She sweeps, swabs, dusts; she dries the clothes, irons a couple on request. She has seven places to go in a day. She doesn't express an opinion, she has no advice, questions do not torment her; the price of a few things troubles her. Salary is accepted in cash, bonus with a small murmur, surprises evoke a smile. When Anjana is around, her workload increases, she spends a little more time, she even finds time to sit with Anjana and chat. I am not privy to what they speak about but the exchange has its place. It is oddly comforting to see them seated close for a few minutes.

'Madam will come back,' she says before leaving. 'She told me she would.'

Anjana returned after many days; I thought she never would. We spent a day together pretending things were the same. I had to ask her, and I did, the one question that was fighting against my being. 'Why, Anjana, why are we together?'

'Together till we part,' she said and laughed.

I laughed as well, a little awkwardly.

'What were you up to? Missed me?'

I should have asked her where she went and why. I was afraid. She wanted me to ask but would be angry if I did.

Two days later we fought and she went away again. She left some things behind and that gave me hope. I decided to shake off my melancholy by going out. I spent a day walking around. I sat in a café till they chased me out. I had my ears cleaned and my beard trimmed on a pavement chair. Leaves fell on my head, a crow shat nearby, a boy stood and watched. It was hard to be enthused by anything, hard to peel off the Mumbai mask, hard to see optimism in its dirt.

After a couple of days waiting for Anjana, I was sleep-deprived. I had nothing interesting to say. The weather was turning; summer was due and the nip was gone. The morning walkers breathed heavily in the marinas. A cocktail of smells hung over the city. In the trains, in the building lifts, and in taxis, sweat made ugly patches.

I decided to catch a flight to Goa, a place that never failed to revive me. I called the office and said I wasn't well. The airport was crowded. I checked in early and sat in the large, soundproof, glass-walled terminal. I saw planes arrive and depart; small people emerged, heads bowed, bearing luggage, holding private possessions, and they lined up silently and stepped onto an escalator that ascended quietly into the heavens. I walked to a kiosk and bought an expensive coffee. It tasted like tea that had curdled. There was a bar with stools where a lone figure sat with what looked like a margarita. I licked my lips and checked my watch.

Announcements on the PA system rang in my ears. Passengers; the very name spoke of their status. They arose and were herded away. Some stragglers waited but they had no choice. They had to go. Soon it would be my turn. I fell asleep. I awoke when someone tapped me on the shoulder. I picked up my bag and walked slowly down a corridor, through a gate into a white aerobridge at the end of which was an oval nothingness.

My incredible sadness stayed with me. When the lunch was served on a tray I eyed the packed contents, poked a soggy sandwich, and almost wept.

I returned after a couple of days because Anjana was back. This time I had no questions for her. I would have to get used to her disappearances.

Sastri kept calling me. I was groggy when I met him the next evening – outside the office because he insisted. He looked grim and a little relieved. I knew bad news; I knew its cadence. Here it was in my face. 'Your column has been scrapped,' he said.

'Why?'

'Not important,' he said.

I sat there waiting for him to say it; his eyes were on his coffee. 'What will you do? Do you have options?'

'Only part-time teaching,' I said. 'Nothing permanent.'

'What is permanent?' said Sastri, still staring into his coffee. 'Tell me?'

'Regret,' I said. I don't think he heard.

'You have made me curious about art,' he said. He looked up. 'I thought I should tell you.'

I was sacked that day. I left behind a curious boss, genuinely stumped by the art he had seen. I felt I had sown a seed, a small victory in the gathering gloom, the kind that got Saeed Mirza started on another film.

I stepped out into the road. It was hot, cramped, late, and lonely. My eyes took some time to adjust; when they did, I applied to another newspaper.

I waited and waited for a response. In the meanwhile, I continued to live in Anjana's shadow, hating it now and then. Jobless, I moulted, needing help, a leg up perhaps in my career, or just a friendly shoulder. A while ago I had stepped down from my imagined perch of art critic. My career thesis, 'Time Has Turned into a Clock', a takedown on objectification in the art world, gathered dust in my cupboard.

I wasn't fazed. I wasn't despondent, though I would have been happier with some recognition and some hard cash to feed my habits. One fine day I received a reply. It said, when can you join?

I bought myself a second-hand bike. On the morning journey to the office I plugged into earphones for the hour and a half it took to reach South Mumbai. My bike sputtered its way through traffic. Trolled by bitty, smarmy four-wheeler owners, I became aggressive myself, darting in and out of traffic, cutting lanes and scraping fenders.

Occasionally Anjana rode pillion with me. She wrapped her hands around my middle, rested her head in the crook of my neck, and played with my belt buckle.

In our social circle her considerable intellect and aesthetic sense excited the nerds. They looked up to her. They sent her friend requests. There were others who were turned on by her for more obvious reasons. In pole position was Krishna Kumar. The lowly bastard dreamed of sharing a lungi with her.

Most evenings I halted at a couple of stores on the way home. I would buy a bottle of wine and ribbed condoms that showed a couple in great nick and fine fettle. And I would head to Anjana's place, having washed my face and brushed my hair.

The building watchman smiles; we wink at each other. He is excited by the idea of an affair.

'Kya, boss?'

I share the lift with the comely Mrs Sinha. She is in a yoga T-shirt, wearing pink shoes, her deo hard at work. She mops her face and smiles. 'Which floor?' she asks playfully. We stare at the numbers as the lift climbs.

'Same floor as me?' I ask her.

'Simply you ask,' she says.

The lift shudders.

'Bye then.'

'What, no tea invitation?'

'Simply you ask,' she says again.

Anjana opens the door before I can ring the bell. She is wearing a frown.

'Did you get the catalogues?'

I had done the rounds of the galleries and picked up whatever was printed. Some days Anjana feels infirm and refuses to trek downtown. She sits at home and reads. Somewhere in a bank there is an annuity at work that pays for her indolent life and expensive tastes: her hardback books, imported DVDs, and air tickets to culture capitals.

'Did you go for a walk, lazybones?' I hear myself say. Fuck, that sounded domestic. She throws a pillow at me.

We discuss the shows that were on currently. It feels like an inquisition. Anjana has no respect for my ways of seeing when it comes to art. I am still a known lightweight in art circles, the type who would never 'get' Gaitonde or Mark Rothko.

'Are you colour blind, do you lack soul?'

'You could pretend to like them,' she tells me. 'Lots of people do that.'

I have tried; I can't pretend. Piet Mondrian constructions do not excite me. And Picasso and his cross-eyed Marys gave me a migraine.

'What do you like?'

I like Paul Klee and I like Frida Kahlo. I also like Francis Bacon, especially his popes and his contorted men fighting constipation on toilet seats.

'Are they low-hanging fruit?'

I have been told in no uncertain terms that there is a higher plane in fine art, a summit where lesser mortals like me struggle to breathe.

'Try telling me my experience is less valuable.'

'It is,' says Anjana.

I show her a press cutting about a work by Francis Bacon fetching more than 140 million dollars at an auction.

'This is your vindication?' Anjana laughs in my face. 'The market is the arbiter of value because it sets the price?'

She has questions like these that blight every possible answer.

'Imagine my plight stuck with this heavyweight,' I told Krishna Kumar. 'She can throw lines at will, she can conjure a putdown from thin air. She makes me feel inadequate.'

'Write something profound,' KK said. 'Impress Anjana.'

I tried impressing my new editor. It had become a habit.

My new boss was more of the same; he represented readers who flipped channels and skimmed newspapers. He tried teaching me life lessons. 'You are a journalist for a daily. My readers are day-to-day people. Do I have to teach you dumbing down?'

'No literary flourishes, sir?'

'Do you notice anything at all?' he said. 'You come from the suburbs, right?'

After a few days I was summoned. 'So far you have written nothing worth publishing.'

He tapped the pencil on the table – an ominous sign. 'What should I do?'

'Give me another chance?'

He smiled. The sword dangled, and I shut my eyes. I got a second chance. I was tasked to cover art. It was a safe option because hardly anybody read the art column.

My first column was two pages long. I was interpreting and explaining. There were two visuals in the piece. The editor took a red pen and marked a large X over my efforts.

'Can you be brief, Girish? This is a newspaper, not a magazine.'

I tried again.

The Jehangir Art Gallery is a public space that is available to all comers. Just book well in advance. There is no quality control and it shows. Visitor count has increased year on year, but business is poor. The number of red dots that mark a sale has declined.

Commerce and a public gallery are poor bedfellows – a hard taskmaster in the company of a lazy servant. The traditions of the art salon are best carried on by private galleries. Daily footfall in these forbidding spaces is in single digits. The salons are run by impresarios and divas. They are tastemakers. To exhibit poor taste in their presence is like picking your nose or scratching your crotch.

In the Jehangir Gallery these latter activities go hand in hand.

This piece drew the ire of many. I thought the editor would be upset but he was pleased. Be more critical, I was told; go out and pan a show, let there be an outcry. I tried.

I have been to art exhibitions where all I could see were people. Some were lighting lamps, some were posing for photographs, some had this look that said, when can I leave? Such exhibitions usually have too much work, they aren't hung very well, and the artist is present in person and not in the art. There is a category that exhibitions like these belong to. It is called 'Kuch Bhi'.

The outcry happened. I was placed on mute for a fortnight.

My next piece was on a soiree.

Yesterday there was a soiree in Mumbai. I was invited. In preparation I visited the Palladium Mall, where I bought brick-red trousers, a white full-sleeved shirt, a short-diameter hat that had blue trim, and a pair of pointed shoes. I could not afford the jacket on display at Zara. I went to a salon, asked for the senior hairdresser, and told her to try something different. She confused my parting.

I arrived at the event, well-scrubbed, smelling of what I could afford. I nodded in one direction, smiled in another, catching people by surprise. A few glasses of red wine, a catalogue under my arm, and a few hugs later, I had an animated conversation with a realtor, a diamond merchant, and a car dealer.

The next day I opened the catalogue and realized I had forgotten to see the work. Most serious collectors come into a gallery a day before a show. Some buyers revisit the day after. I met two of them when I returned to the gallery. One was a realtor and the other was a car dealer. They ignored me. It was as if we had never met.

This is New India, it had hit middle age when I was born. I was twenty-nine years old then, a late bloomer. The eight-storey building I stayed in skirted a slum. The entrance skirted an open drain, and a rubbish dump brought up the rear. People paid money for a higher floor because it kept the smells at bay.

As a late bloomer I had a few phobias. Principally I feared good-looking, confident twenty-five-year-olds who had declared themselves writers.

'Why can't they be DJs or bartenders?' was my question.

Was twenty-nine a good age for becoming a writer?

Anjana had answered this question in her trademark style in her column.

Write when the age of reason is behind you. Write in the age of uncertainty, when you have figured that reality is not what you dream, it is what bites your shins. You will know it is time to write when you experience a calm melancholy. By then you will be perched between penury and madness.

I sought refuge with my friend Krishna Kumar. 'She told me it is not enough that I exist,' I complained. 'She says I need a reason to wake up every day. She is a pain in the ass. But we are still together.'

'I know why, you lucky bastard,' said Krishna Kumar. 'Because you are joined at the hip.'

'She has this superior air which irritates me. But I love her, man.'

'You are in love with her perfect body,' said Krishna Kumar.

'Don't be cheap,' I said. 'What do you know about love?'

'Why don't you say it? What are you in love with?'

I asked that question of myself. Often.

'Anjana is a reason for art, she is a motive force that drives my distraction. She sits before me like some women do: legs tightly together, a breast on the table, a hand that brushes hair, eyes that light up before thought is expressed.'

'I like your aforesaid,' said Krishna Kumar, smiling, 'but I dread your bloody hereafter.'

'Yes, one day she will tire of me,' I said. 'And frankly I will tire of her, her fine wines, and her rare whiskies.'

'The best women I know are not picky about their booze,' said KK, 'or mating positions.'

Anjana has such a different trajectory. For her, dance means Pina Bausch and Merce Cunningham, music means the Bauls or the Manganiyar Seduction. A film library has to have Tarkovsky and all the Ozu films. Poetry has more space on her bookshelf than fiction.

'She is nibbling away at your soul,' said KK, 'and what are you doing? She is not meant for you. You will never measure up. You will never be good enough.'

I suffered; my columns suffered. One attempt earned a strong reprimand.

India is anchored in the wrong place. The country is a vast humidor, peopled by mosquitoes and buffaloes. We are squatting near the Equator and have turned into a haven for pestilence. The bigger tragedy is that we have been denied a whole season, one that offers vistas for reflection. We should be resting on window sills and reflecting on autumn. Autumn is a time for classical music, for exalted wines, and Balkan languor. There is no autumn in Mumbai. Which is why there is no art worth its name in Mumbai.

We decided to get away to Panvel on the weekend. There was a small cottage by the riverside. We left on my bike, joined at the waist. We chose the 'pipe roads' of Mumbai, bypasses where a currency note fetched a greener route, better air, the odd stream, and a view of children at play. A large black water pipe that looked like a giant centipede kept pace with us till we broke off, short of Panvel. We checked in; we had no luggage.

'Mr and Mrs?'

We made love and fell asleep. Somewhere near a river I dreamed of drowning.

'Call the desk!' I shouted. I couldn't breathe.

'Sleep on your side,' was her retort. 'Take your hand off me, right now.'

I scowled into my pillow. Anjana had her back to me. The sound of birds through the open window heralded the morning.

'The sun is out, Madhubala.'

'But the sky hasn't slept, Salim.'

A little later she said, 'Could you play some music, Girish?'

I dragged myself up and played her music.

'What raga is this?'

'Gurjari Todi. Do you know it is the raga that stilled the feet of a dancer and killed a competitor? It gives me a high to think about its history.'

I lit a joint and smoked for a while.

'Dude, why do you dope?'

'Why do you drink, Madhubala?'

'What do I drink, Salim?'

'Wine mostly.'

'Exactly. But only Italian. I have found my terroir. Do you know that in Italy if the land pouts you get grapes?'

'Funny.'

'A good wine fights for my affection.'

'I do too.'

'Right,' she said. 'Just use a condom every time.'

Back in Mumbai, the first glass of wine was savoured while I cooked. She stood at the kitchen counter, leaning on the microwave, looking out of the window. She inhaled each aroma.

'Why do you tolerate me?' I asked her.

'Because you use an apricot dressing. You flambé fish. You make a heavenly cold soup, and I never ever need to order pasta.'

The second glass of wine evoked an 'aah'. It was a good varietal. The flavours opened out in a glass decanter that tapered gracefully. She was fond of full-bodied reds. She always read the tasting notes aloud.

'Today is a day for a sauce-less pasta that will live on oil alone,' I said. 'Perhaps a hint of pesto, a sprinkle of ground red chilli, a treasure-hunt serving of garlic. I have to get it off the flame at the right moment – like now.'

The third glass of wine went with the pasta.

Our lovemaking was unpredictable. I have to say it, we fucked without finesse. Everywhere she went, she went with gusto. She was stormy, a flamed terroir, tannins on her tongue, a red-bruised aftertaste on her lips. We shook up the bed. It didn't matter if the mattress moved, the sheets had been thrown off, or in the final moment a glass shattered.

'I have no bones left,' she moaned, smiling.

'I feel like I am dying,' I said.

'Get off me!'

I landed on my side.

An hour later I padded up to the fridge and pulled out a coffee-infused dessert that had an orange twist. I smoked a joint while she tasted it.

'Mmmm,' she said, looking at me. I knew that look so well.

'No,' I said, 'not again.'

'Why?'

'Because I have to write.'

I was inspired. I sat naked at my computer and hammered out my next piece. I remembered Krishna Kumar urging me. 'Write when you are angry,' he had said.

You want to know what is art? Art is this very same fuckwit question.

Was that enough?

Art is stuff that gets made that raises this very question. The lack of a satisfactory answer ensures you stay the course.

That wasn't hard-hitting enough. I had to do better.

Art is a hydra-headed monster, a Medusa with snakes in her hair and sting in her tentacles, a monster Gorgon that transfixes people, turning some into jelly and others into stone. Art is an exotic courtesan, the original Mata Hari, a black widow that brings artists to their knees, that spares no one in its hungry quest to take over this world, its many riches, its wealth, and its soul.

Krishna Kumar

Girish went looking for his friend, Krishna Kumar. He had in the past gone looking for the Great Indian bustard with better results. Kumar's gallery was vague; they told him their artist was busy.

'He is performing.'

'Where?'

'On the streets of Mumbai.' They had no clue which suburb he would be in. 'Ask the police,' they said.

'Seriously?' The gallery assistant looked serious. 'Crime Branch?'

'Traffic police. I am not joking.'

Girish asked a senior cop in a police jeep that was parked near the Taj Hotel. Hordes of people thronged the Gateway of India; some of them were peering into the jeep. The cop was seated, half asleep, his legs spread out below the steering wheel.

'Krishna Kumar?' He picked his nostril. 'Is he a regular nuisance maker?'

He rubbed his eyes and looked at his walkie-talkie, a black handset that was twice the size of a cell phone. He fiddled with it and it came to life.

'Laukar. Go to Worli Naka,' he said.

It seemed KK was being discussed by cops on their walkie-talkies. They were calling him a bawaal.

Getting to Worli Naka took an hour but it was worthwhile. Girish found KK and saw his bravura performance. It had to do with statues.

Mumbai had very many statues. Viceroys Cornwallis and Hardinge were still lording it outside foreign banks. Near a traffic signal there was Jawaharlal Nehru wearing his trademark jacket, smelling a stone rose. Inside an island near Cooperage there was

Baba Ambedkar in his characteristic suit, pointing at a passing airplane. Adjacent to Regal Cinema, a diminutive Lal Bahadur Shastri was midstride. All around the city there was Bapu, marching bareheaded. And museums and libraries in Kala Ghoda had room for their Parsi benefactors; in stairwells were Nowrozji and Cowasji, austere in white marble.

During his performance, Krishna Kumar was gesticulating. It was a busy road and a working day, and KK was aloft, seemingly, but actually secure on a raised pedestal where a statue should have been.

Which begged the question: where was the statue?

It was missing.

Krishna Kumar from Kerala missed the trade union movement by a few decades. He missed the hammer and sickle signs and the red flags of protest. He missed the industrial hartals, the passionate street addresses, the tool-down go-slows, the traffic jams, and the public commotion. He missed the attention of gathered crowds. When he looked at statues in the cities of his country, he felt sorry. Venerable folk, from their pedestal perches, had had to witness the decline of the Republic. These noble men (yes, mostly men) had lost their voice.

Making bystanders of people defined most people's art. KK wished to achieve that on the streets of Mumbai. And he did so by replacing outdoor statues with a live performance.

Antony Gormley did something similar in Trafalgar Square. He called the public art intervention 'Fourth Plinth' and he gave members of the public one hour in which they could get onto the empty fourth plinth in the north-west corner of Trafalgar Square, occupy it, and do pretty much what they wished. A camera recorded and broadcast the performances as a live feed. KK was a little disappointed with the Gormley project because nobody got arrested.

KK couldn't dance to save his life. A purist might describe his movements as an attempt to destroy the air in his vicinity. Was he exorcising the Devil? Each attempt of his was a virtuoso performance. The police usually got to him within half an hour. They were on course this time, ladder ready.

In the half hour that Girish watched, the police climbed a ladder; as it came up short, they stretched manfully and tried to remove KK. A cop latched onto his leg but KK shook him loose. A second cop made a grab and got hold of a shoe. A purple sock came into view. The cops gained traction and had KK pinned by the leg. Reinforcements arrived on a motorcycle: a sub-inspector, a portly senior who wasn't amused at the commotion in his precinct.

'Marathi manoos kute aahe?' asked KK, speaking Marathi with a Malayali accent. A few in the crowd sniggered.

'Thamba!' said the sub-inspector. He looked at his juniors. 'What is the problem?'

'Statue is moving,' said one constable.

'Where is the real one?'

The senior cop looked at where the constable was pointing.

By the side of the road it leaned against a lamp post. Baba Ambedkar placed respectfully, at an angle, pointing to a balcony where a maidservant stood under a clothesline holding a cleaning cloth.

'Replace!' shouted the sub-inspector. He was a man of few verbs.

A smiling KK was held aloft. His tandav was over. He was hustled into a cop van. The crowd dispersed. The next day a crane arrived, as did the pigeons.

'Waiting for the signal?' asked the cop.

KK had pressed the phone to the tightly meshed grill. It was dark inside the police van, like a cave, and he was having difficulty breathing. The air seemed to have expired. He tried calling again. The police van was parked in a cramped by-lane, with buildings pressing on it from both sides.

'Who are you calling?' asked the cop. His body odour seeped out of every pore and suffused the space. After the initial animosity the constable was showing signs of relenting.

'My friend,' replied KK. 'His name is Girish.'

Where the fuck was he? He was supposed to have come and recorded the incident live.

KK got through, finally. 'Where are you, bugger?'

Girish was nervous.

'Why are you mumbling?' said KK. 'I can't hear you, man.'

'I am just outside,' said Girish. 'I can see the van but can't see you.'

He had recorded the whole thing but was now reluctant to get involved with this brush with the cops. Where he came from, cops meant the law.

A week later the two of them were back on the streets of Mumbai. The day was to be spent with a threatened tree in Khar, a grand, fully grown one, a rare sight in Mumbai. Growing up in Mumbai was hard for a sapling. Soil eroded, roots were exposed, tar accumulated around the base of the trunk, branches were lopped off indiscriminately. When it rained hard most of the leaves fell.

KK and Girish arrived at 16th Road and stood next to a board that said, 'Road Widening'.

The road had turned busy and the cops couldn't handle the traffic that plied through it. The pavements had already been shrunk. The grand tree stood in the way. Citizens were protesting and things were at a standstill. A week ago, a car had rammed into the tree and a child was badly hurt. Who was to blame? A cartoonist blamed the tree, suggesting a case be filed against the offending species.

Girish filmed the tree and he filmed KK hugging it. Seeing this, passers-by congregated and took turns hugging the tree. It was done in silence. A corporation truck arrived carrying a buzz saw. Workers alighted and dragged KK away. Others took his place. They dragged them away. A police van arrived and the tamasha grew into a protest. Slogans were raised. The area was cordoned and gradually the protesters were dispersed. The tree stood defenceless. The corporation staff strung ropes on its branches and lopped them one by one, starting from the higher reaches. In the end they took out the buzz saw. There was a high-pitched whine that turned into a grating sound when the blade cut through the wood.

'Tree is weeping,' shouted KK.

They cut through the base of the tree. A dull thud and the tree, or what was left of it, came down. People shed a few tears, people who had never looked at the old fellow, ever.

'It was fifty years old,' said an overwrought KK. 'Do something.'

'What?' said Girish.

'Write about it, bugger.'

'Nobody reads,' said Girish. 'Hopefully the film will move people.'

When asked what drove him to do what he did, Krishna Kumar said, 'Apathy. It is a new condition. In this online world people have forgotten how to protest. They file online petitions, they post opinions, and when everything fails they move on to something else.'

'And you?'

'I take everything personally. I get physical, I brush against the law in ways they don't expect.'

That wasn't new in Kerala, a verdant state the size of a communist country. It has ancient trading ports like Kollam and Calicut. You can feel an undercurrent in its tea shops and its colleges. Discussion runs around with its tail on fire and differences are deep-rooted. People hold their ground; they meet you halfway, like the local language does – a palindrome called Malayalam.

Krishna Kumar did his Bachelor of Fine Arts in Trivandrum. Where he grew up there were images of Che Guevara etched on walls, T-shirts, and trees. He broke rank when he signed up for a postgraduate arts course in the faraway city of Baroda.

He arrived in Baroda in a haze, dragged his suitcase past two-wheelers and cows, and asked for directions from a stranger, a fellow student called Girish. Girish, an earnest wordsmith from Mumbai, came from a family that ran coaching classes for hapless students. They shared a chai at a tea shop and got talking. They ended up sharing a room in an apartment. Kumar remembered the date and the time. He remembered the few words they spoke.

His first class in college, though... The effects of the long journey hadn't subsided, and he somehow managed the whole of the first day, sitting erect. But he could have sworn the doyen K.G. Subramanyan delivered that first lecture.

'Where did you do your bachelor's?' KGS had asked, according to Kumar's memory.

He had looked hard at Kumar's unkempt beard, his sweat-stained shirt, and his ragged sandals.

'Trivandrum, sir,' Kumar said.

'Thiruvananthapuram?' The professor looked at him kindly. 'Don't worry. Baroda will save you.'

Later that evening a masala chai woke Kumar up. 'Did KGS take our class today?' he asked Girish.

'My dear Malayali, KGS retired from teaching while you were still a sperm.'

'Is it?' said Kumar, spitting out some tea leaves. 'By the way, I was a sperm given to reflection.'

'You are certain?'

'Yes. A sperm that asked of itself: why me, what is my existential purpose?'

'Of course. A respectable Malayali question.'

They walked towards the room they had rented.

'I can hear you thinking, comrade,' said Girish.

'They say that when I was born, I looked surprised.'

Their landlord was Mr Varadarajan. He had two spare rooms, one of which was occupied by Kumar and Girish; the other had Maya and Anjana. The foursome came from middle India, from families that were careful with their fixed income. They knew how to wash their clothes and cook survival rations.

True to form, Krishna Kumar had political ambitions. The campus was an arena rife with possibilities. He imagined himself as student leader in their senior year. He wanted his flatmates on his team.

'You have the arrogance,' said Anjana.

'And the required scruffiness,' said Maya.

'But you lack the credentials.'

'Why, who is good enough to be your hero?'

Anjana had high standards. In her pantheon were Walter Benjamin, Borges, Andrei Tarkovsky, and Louise Bourgeois. Krishna Kumar wasn't going to fill in for them in a hurry.

'And who is your hero, madam?' Kumar asked Maya.

'My hero has a bath every day,' she said.

Girish thought himself a dude; after all, he was from Mumbai. He often gawked at Kumar, fascinated by his quaintness and rusticity, his rapacious need to prove himself. Kumar was a subject who could help hone his skills as a writer.

'I will support you,' he said. 'We will have banners, slogans, and rallies. The student election could be our senior-year project.'

A few months elapsed; time hung heavy on campus. Kumar cut a forlorn figure. He was visibly restless.

'I can't,' he said.

'Can't what?'

'I can't paint like you can, Maya.'

'Even your drawing is terrible,' she said.

Kumar's line was an uncertain one, a rat in the dark that had sniffed a cat in the air and was seeking an escape route.

'I lack fluency. I don't know where to begin. I keep over-painting.'

'You are in luck,' said Anjana. 'Contemporary art is more than just drawing and painting. You can be poor in both and get away.'

'I can carve,' said Krishna Kumar.

'Really? What will you carve? Stone?'

'No. I meant air. I can perform. That is what I am meant to be: a performer.'

He began cutting classes and spent more and more time in his room, smoking up a storm. This had happened before. Students who were unable to stay the course gradually dropped out.

Anjana disliked him and his gaze, directed as it was at her bosom. She never said anything harsh to him; someday she would. She spoke of him in the third person in his presence.

'A man who never paused, who never watched a garden grow, what will he take away from this world?'

'Nothing?' said Girish.

'Yes, nothing.'

'Are you talking about me?' Kumar said.

She continued to ignore him. 'There is something futile about Krishna Kumar,' she said. 'He thinks he is meant for bigger things and a larger life than a mere artist's existence.'

Smoking came naturally to Kumar. He ran through two packs of twenty every day; each cigarette lit another. His bed sagged in the middle; his pillow was permanently propped. The wall that faced him had a poster from the Cuban revolution and a still from the film *The Year of Living Dangerously*.

Kumar did not complete the course requirements. He was glad when the academic year came to an end. His grades were terrible, his teachers frustrated by his lack of application.

'Go back to Trivandrum and do your course again,' said one of his teachers.

He left for his home state the way he had come, catching trains in sequence.

'What will I tell my family?'

The further south he went, the more unpredictable his journey became. He was tempted to get off somewhere in the middle, in a strange town where he could lose himself for a while. He called Girish from a remote station.

'Baroda taught me nothing!'

'Nobody can teach you anything.'

Within hours of arriving in Alapuzha he was missing his three friends in Baroda. He wanted to meet them again but had no wish to return and complete the course. Days passed by, weeks added up, and he stayed on in Kerala.

Girish called. 'Where are you? College just opened.'

Kumar was incoherent. 'I am not well.'

'Call me back when you are well. Will you?'

He did not. But a few months later he wrote them letters by hand, stamped the covers, and dropped them into the red postbox near his house. When he did not receive a reply, he returned to Baroda.

'Welcome back, comrade,' said Girish.

'Look at you!' said Kumar. 'You are not half the rebel you used to be.'

'I am now part of the establishment.'

They looked intently at each other, stifling other things they wanted to say and do. Both realized how much they had missed being together.

They went off to their familiar laari for a glass of chai.

'Everything has changed,' said Girish.

'Maya?'

'She has moved to Mumbai. Two years from now she will unveil her first solo show.'

'Anjana?'

'She has moved to Mumbai as well.'

'I hope you will be staying on?'

Girish shrugged. 'There isn't much to do here. I have tried the academic option. It is exciting but it doesn't pay very well.'

'So?'

'I might move to Mumbai as well. I have a job offer from a newspaper.'

Kumar realized he had returned far too late and was likely to be alone in Baroda.

'What kept you in Alapuzha?' asked Girish.

'I don't know,' said Kumar. 'I was confused. I still am.'

'Did you learn anything?'

'Kathakali,' said Kumar. 'I tried. In Kalamandalam, the best school.'

'Did you qualify?'

'No. It is still a work in progress.'

'And why have you returned?'

'I don't know,' said Kumar. 'I am just wandering, trying to find myself.'

The year Kumar returned to Baroda it rained without let-up. It was a bad time for the boy from Kerala. He stood alone, far from his home state. Water lapped his feet.

The phone rang; he waited. It kept ringing. He removed the device carefully from his pocket and answered. It was Maya.

'Thanks for calling back,' he said. He was close to tears. He spoke to her about this and that, about failure, about stepping stones to nowhere. Maya listened patiently.

'You are beginning to remind me of men who grow old, turn bitter, and die young,' she said.

Kumar looked at the phone in his hand. He dropped it into a puddle of water. He walked to the railway station and forced his way into an unreserved compartment. When the train reached its destination, he caught another. He arrived in Kerala a week later, with lice in his hair, dirt in his fingernails, and blood in his spit.

A few weeks later he visited the Art Biennale in the nearby city of Kochi. His face was mottled, his hair was matted. He looked like an old free-range country chicken, an aged naatu kozhi, full of protein but too ugly for the knife.

He spent three days wandering through the sites and installations in the Fort Kochi area. On offer were poetry, video, sculpture, and site-specific installations. A few paintings as well. The weather was uncomfortable: warm and muggy. He wore himself out those three days, looping around the various sites; in the evenings he drank himself into a stupor.

He couldn't leave the place. He found himself returning to a particular work. It was by the well-known artist Atul Dodiya. It was a life-size work; it had what looked like a usable noose made of thick rope that hung from a single upright scaffolding. Next to it was a large stretched canvas on which the artist had drawn a poem. On his third visit to the 'gallows' he gathered courage to get up close to the work. It was macabre in how it called out to him, he felt. The noose looked ready for use; the scaffolding would easily bear his weight. It was a performance piece, he thought. All it needed was him and a stool.

For some reason he could not fathom, he was profoundly moved. He sat before the installation, his legs folded under him, and wept like a child.

IV

VI

Ways and Means

Salil Gupta hosted a series of parties during the art season in his newly rented apartment in Mumbai. Over two weeks in November, the Mumbai that mattered to the art world enjoyed his hospitality. Prominent at each gathering was Nupur, a study in quiet elegance.

It was obvious an announcement would be made soon. Most people expected a private museum that would house Salil's collection. Some expected a gallery. A rumour doing the rounds was that it was likely to be an auction house. There were three active auction houses in Mumbai and two overseas giants who operated through local offices. They served a minuscule percentage of the affluent in the metros and none in the smaller cities.

A company was floated with Salil and Nupur as principal shareholders. The advisory board had a couple of senior artists, some industrialists, an ex-bureaucrat, and a prominent lawyer. Tara was part of the management team. Immersive, Salil's tech company, was to set up the infrastructure.

To attract investment for this business Salil invited money home. It was a powerful display. His reach in the investment community and their faith in his business acumen were proven.

Tara and Anjana entered together, the latter reluctant, suspicious, and disdainful. She looked at a version of Krishna near the entrance, angelic in white ceramic.

'Kanhaiya by Lladro,' said Tara.

'Nudge it,' said Anjana. 'Push it over the edge while I watch it shatter.'

In the foyer, craft items from state emporiums rubbed shoulders with decorative objects made from Swarovski crystal.

'I hope Salil Gupta isn't setting up a museum,' said Anjana. 'That would be a travesty.'

There was a dressing table in the living room. It looked like someone had spattered it with paint. A closer examination revealed hundreds of bindis that had been pasted on it. Each had a tail; each looked like sperm. Next to this artwork was a steel bucket, six feet high, which looked like, well, a large bucket. On the wall and the floor were blank canvases that were titled 'Untitled'. It seemed it was a sculpture made of fibreglass.

'How come he is buying contemporary art?' asked Anjana.

'This is Nupur's doing,' said Tara. 'Catch Salil buying New Art!'

It was a large living room, an untidy one where nothing was what it seemed. The host welcomed them with a hug, a peck on each cheek, and a comment.

'Look who's here,' said Salil, welcoming Anjana. 'Theory has come to bite.'

'Art theory is a provocative practice,' said Anjana, 'as much as art. Sorry, who am I telling?'

Salil smiled. 'Come, meet people.'

He sat them down, ordered their cocktails, and introduced them to the power set. Most of them were members of the World Presidents' Organization.

Anjana grabbed some pistachios from a bowl. She was staring at the bucket. She placed the pistachio shells in a nearby ashtray. An ashtray that showed a young girl smoking, with the words 'Too young to die' etched on it. Tara removed the shells and used her hanky to clean the Yoshitomo Nara sculpture.

The money gang welcomed them heartily, raising their whisky glasses.

'We are not arty types,' said one of them.

'Yes,' said another. 'In my house buckets are in the washroom. Where they should be. And the dressing table is in the bedroom.'

'But we understand money. Do you?'

Anjana was startled. 'Money? What is there to understand? Money is what money does.'

'More good than harm,' said Tara quickly.

'You know what we have learnt today at Salil bhai's house?' said an investment banker. 'Never take art at face value.'

'And what does that mean?' asked Anjana, spoiling for a fight.

'There is nothing called face value in art,' said a real estate tycoon. 'Even I know that.'

'What is the price of a Gupta these days?' asked a grey-haired venture capitalist.

'Subodh Gupta?' asked Tara. 'Or Salil Gupta?'

They laughed.

'And Gupta period?' asked a share broker. He smelled of Emporio by Armani.

Price was discussed threadbare that evening. Art, especially New Art, was taken to the cleaners. The discussion wore off as the evening progressed. Anjana and Tara retreated to a quiet corner.

'This is the blind leading the blind,' said Anjana, looking up to the heavens. She noticed some squiggles of paint on the ceiling and raised an eyebrow.

Tara smiled. 'Ceiling art,' she said. 'Takes after a famous cathedral?'

'Look at these people,' said Anjana. 'None of them can parse a sentence. Yet they are wealthy. It seems dishonest, somehow.'

'Nupur says there is a new currency in town,' said Tara. 'It is called smart money. Right now, the smart money is on Salil Gupta. That is the good news.'

'And the bad news?'

Tara smiled. 'Don't quote me, Aunty. I am now part of the team. But honestly, the project is very hare-brained. It rides on an untutored vision.'

Smart money was dressed in smart casuals. The wine was Malbec, aged in oak. The chatter was heady. Groups formed and disbanded minute by minute.

'Shapeshifting,' remarked Tara, watching the ritual.

The brackets took shape; billionaires stood in the balcony where there was privacy and a view, the multi-millionaires gathered below a Raza painting and looked each other up. Tara and Anjana were in their corner twirling the umbrellas in their cocktails.

'I wish the art world had a different currency,' said Anjana. 'More generous, less accountable. And with no strings attached.'

Tara smiled. 'Good one, Aunty,' she said. 'Never relinquish your private utopia.'

At that moment Bharat Singh came up to them. Bharat Singh was landed gentry with more assets than income. His family had a jagir, a hamlet in Rajasthan where he had a haveli. He had turned it into a hotel; the earnings from that paid for his art collection, entirely of the established Progressive group. He stood in the midst of Salil's contemporary works with a gathering sneer. His moustache, a wind vane of his prevailing mood, drooped. Tara had spotted him in auction rooms. He came alive at their previews. He would stride up and about the posh five-star halls where the moderns were displayed in their restored glory, exclaiming, 'This is art. This is art.'

Tara had chided him once. 'But surely, Your Eminence, you mean this is the essential art of your time?' she said.

Ever the gentleman, he had smiled and mouthed, 'Touché.'

In Salil's house he was happy to look down at the contemporary pretensions on display. He sought Anjana's views on them.

'What school do these works belong to?' he asked her.

Anjana was waiting for this. 'This is the mar mit jaave school of art,' she said.

Bharat laughed till his eyes watered. 'I was told this was the dil aur dimag choone wali school,' he said.

Anjana shrugged. 'Depends,' she said, 'on where your dil and dimag are located.'

Nupur waved at them from across the room, busy and happy. She was working the crowd, using skills that the hospitality industry had imparted. She caught hold of her father and dragged him towards them. Salil raised his glass of whisky. 'Prost,' he said.

Anjana had questions, as always. 'Who are you in all this, Salil?'

'I am the knave,' he replied.

'He means naive,' said Nupur.

'Yes,' said Salil. 'I am the one with silly questions about art. Why so painful, why so sad? Why so bare and empty? Why so full of words when you could have used pictures?'

'We all have such questions,' said his daughter.

'Yes, but I ask them in public and get caught out, as usual. But there is one question that I ask myself only in private. An important one for business, which I learned is never asked in the art world. In fact, they have passed an ordinance against that question.'

'I see,' said Anjana. 'And that is?'

'I am not saying,' he said.

Salil raised his glass again and retreated to the centre of the room.

Anjana sniffed her wine. 'Does he really have an opinion on art, one that is worth restating?'

'Aunty, he does not say much,' said Nupur. 'But contemporary works get his goat, especially the ones that you need to read about to be able to understand and appreciate. He calls such work Art on Crutches.'

'I don't get it.'

'Oh, I think he means much of contemporary art needs an intellectual prosthetic to stand scrutiny.'

'Ah! That language I understand.'

Anjana smiled at Nupur. 'You have such a way with words, even if you lack the qualifications. You told me you took him to Jaipur House to see the three shows. What happened there?'

'Tara was with me,' said Nupur. 'Maybe you should ask her.'

They drifted towards an anteroom where a work caught Anjana's attention. She stood long and looked hard at a wonderful etching by Zarina Hashmi.

'This looks out of place,' she said, 'in the company of Salil's best mistakes.'

'A gift,' said Nupur.

'An error of judgement?'

'An accident,' said Nupur, laughing.

Later that night, after the others had left, Salil, Nupur, and Tara sat on the balcony and chatted for a while.

'Who invited Anjana?' asked Salil.

'I did,' said Nupur. 'She is an important person.'

'Maybe,' said Salil. 'I don't like her. I find her…'

'Petulant?'

'Yes, exactly. She thinks she is the only one who reads. Some months ago, we met by chance and she gave me a typed list. Prescribed reading, she said. And she looked at what I was buying and made a face. Like today.'

'She is a critic and a curator,' said Tara. 'What do you expect?'

'She is an intellectual puff piece,' said Salil. 'She is also so…'

'Obtuse?'

'Exactly, obtuse. Like your New Age artists. They stand around at the entrance and...'

'Accost?'

'Yes, accost you, pretending they are there just by chance, and then they insist on conducting a walkthrough, as if we are incapable of understanding their art. And if you have a question, they ignore it with such…'

'Impunity?'

Salil paused. 'Are you by any chance...?'

'Leading you on?' Nupur shook her head vigorously, pinching Tara's arm, quelling her barely hidden mirth.

'Do you feel the same way as I do?' asked Salil finally.

'What do you feel, Dad?'

'I feel intellectuals are dangerous. They will ruin free enterprise.'

'Whoa! Does she scare you?'

'It is scary,' said Salil. 'The power these people have. I am not an idiot. It is us versus them. Make no mistake.'

Gavel

The two sat at a bar that had soft lighting and muted colours. It served a good whisky sour and a decent old-fashioned. The place was empty at seven in the evening.

'Goodbye, salon,' said Tara, sniffing into a coloured napkin. 'Goodbye, sweet soiree.'

'Spare me the senti nonsense,' said Nupur. 'The age of such romanticism is past.'

Tara clutched a cushion. 'Gupta, you said one day it would surely happen. Art will talk to power, you told me.'

Nupur picked the orange peel from her drink and squeezed it. Her eyes smarted.

'It will,' she said.

'We will be old by then, Gupta. Infirm. Selling T-shirts bearing slogans. You have sold your soul.'

'Maybe.'

'Shall we blame your father?'

Nupur shook her head. 'Ardeshir is the villain. I would have set up a small salon. I might have failed. So?'

The two stared into their drinks.

'I will never run a gallery.'

'You don't have to believe everything Ardeshir says,' said Tara.

'I believe him,' Nupur said, without rancour.

'So that's why you are—'

'Yes. He advised me to go the auction route. He said, you are your father's daughter. Go to the market, love, be savvy.'

'And Daddy dear?'

'He met Ardeshir. I insisted. They spent an evening together. Both got high and talked rubbish.'

The drink meter had run high when they met. Salil was flying, high as a proverbial kite, powered by a malt that had been smoked out of a watery cinder. Ardeshir was supine, in the hands of angels.

'Ultimately, starting a business is a rush of blood,' said Salil. 'An irrational phenomenon. The first time I was a victim. Then the payoff happened. Now I am an addict.'

'Mr Gupta,' said Ardeshir, 'what do you want from me?'

Salil spoke softly. 'A perfectly reasoned response.'

Ardeshir sat up. 'Your daughter doesn't have the eye and you, my dear sir, don't have taste,' he said.

'Why don't I have taste?'

'I am not sure,' said Ardeshir. 'I think taste is in some ways an inheritance, what you grow up with. You, sir, have self-professed baniya origins. What have you missed out?'

'You tell me.'

'Literature, cinema, theatre, opera. I don't know what else. Do baniyas do weed, do they drink Rhone reds?'

'Bunkum,' said Salil. 'Our ancestors had good taste.'

'They mostly had samosas and kheer,' said Ardeshir.

'I see,' said Salil. He was visibly seeing red.

'Sir,' said Ardeshir, 'you are in good company. Most people are like tourists; they don't dive deep into anything. Their attention span is that of a butterfly.'

'Let us not labour over this,' said Salil. 'If I stick around in the art world long enough, taste will come.'

'You are getting defensive.'

'Right now, I feel like putting you in your place. Your superior air gets to me. I cannot act superior like you can.'

Ardeshir poked his finger into Salil's chest. 'Art is a good place if you have money to burn. You seem to have it. And why not burn it all? You have made it yourself. It is yours.'

'I see,' said Salil.

'Enjoy the journey, my friend,' said the gallerist, signing off. 'This bloody business could be your perfect ghat.'

Tara laughed, hearing the story.

'My father has a vision,' said Nupur.

She remembered one of their meetings in a café. Their coffee session had hardly begun and Salil Gupta was pacing up and down the small eatery, high on hot chocolate.

'India thinks differently,' Salil had said. 'It will behave differently if we allow it to.'

He was no expert on art but he was a keen observer of trends and he understood affluent people.

'Look at galleries and auction houses. They have gone online. Now we have online marketplaces that are hoping to form a bridge between buyers and artists.'

'What do we do?'

He drummed his fingers on the table. 'We will go back to physical auctions. We will up the game.'

'How?' asked Nupur, wiping the milk foam off her lips.

'Right now, auctions take place behind closed doors. Only the elite attend, by invitation. If you ask me, this is the colonial mindset.'

'You want us to bring in the new money?' asked Nupur.

'I want to bring in energy. We must expand the audience. These bidders must feel what gladiators feel when they enter the arena. The rush of a blood sport. It will happen if they know they are being watched by millions.'

Nupur was taken aback. Spectators at an art auction?

'We need television coverage of the auctions,' said Salil. 'Live coverage.'

'You mean each auction will be a television episode?'

'Yes,' said Salil, so excited he had to sit down. 'We will provide personality sketches of the bidders in the room. We will have stories on the major lots, written by screenwriters, not by critics. A professional DOP will handle the footage, capturing the drama.'

'And bidders will be our performers? Won't that turn off traditional collectors?'

Salil shrugged. 'Old collectors are part of the problem. They are anonymous, they squirrel away the best work, and they don't sell. Nobody benefits other than termites in warehouses. We need new collectors from new India. They may be less polished but, trust me, they will make better television.'

Nupur was doubtful.

'You want newbies and their foolish money?' she said, sounding worried.

'People will make mistakes. But this is a baniya country,' said Salil. 'There is native intelligence. They will learn quickly.'

'Maybe,' said Nupur. Her eyebrows had knitted. 'Most people are still clueless about art and afraid of it.'

Salil smiled. 'Indians are travelling, my dear. While others look up at the Sistine Chapel, my WPO gang tours Frank Gehry buildings. They eat plated desserts in Michelin-starred restaurants. One of them gave me an illustrated lecture on brutalist architecture. The buildings looked like bomb shelters.'

'Can good taste be legislated?' asked Nupur. 'We are good at legislation.'

Salil laughed. 'Let us not be cynical. I have realized one thing about India. People learn quickly so long as it costs them.'

'The media and social media will call us a tamasha,' said Nupur. 'We will be villains.'

'Possible,' said Salil. 'It might happen. Think about it. We will be unveiling this quiet, anonymous world to the general public. For a while, we will be interesting.'

'This will cost us some serious money,' said Nupur. 'If it fails, we will have nothing to show for it.'

Her father wasn't listening. He was a successful entrepreneur, confident in his ability to spot a market. Fair to say he was blinded by the clarity of his vision.

Anjana entered the glass building accompanied by her professor friend. She waited while her bag was searched. She walked through a scanner and it beeped. A lady in a security uniform attempted a body search but was rudely asked to step aside. The professor was stoic as gloved hands travelled his anatomy. They walked to a bank of lifts with visitor ID cards around their necks.

'What a nuisance,' said Anjana.

'Corporate world,' said her friend.

He was an academic from the US, one who wrote papers, spoke at symposiums. He was in town and Anjana had roped him in to meet this collector who wished to launch a project in the art world. Nupur had asked Anjana to have a frank discussion with her father on the risks involved in sinking a ton of money into the art market.

'The art world is Salil Gupta's latest jigsaw.'

They entered Salil's office, a tasteful expanse, and were ushered into the conference room. It was large and had mikes, projection screens, television screens, and coffee. Salil entered wearing a suit, shook hands, and ordered coffee for all of them.

'I am here at your daughter's behest,' said Anjana. 'I took the liberty of bringing my friend along. He is a renowned economist and behavioural scientist. Professor Robert Holmes.'

'I teach economic history,' said Holmes.

'In an Ivy League school,' said Anjana.

'What an honour,' said Salil. 'Please, have your coffee. What do you wish to discuss?'

'Money,' said Professor Holmes. 'It has a nose for people. It outs them. I always say: beware of what money can make you do.'

Salil was taken aback but did not show it. 'Go on,' he said.

'Every once in a while, money has a blackout. Call it a brain fade.'

'I see. For example?'

'There is the art world.'

'I see.' Salil was foxed. 'The market for art is billions of dollars. You call all that a brain fade, Professor?'

'All I am saying is reason and understanding are overrated in art. As are numbers, price graphs, and indices.'

Salil looked towards Anjana. She stayed silent.

'Well,' said Salil. 'The market exists. And it is growing.'

'It is a complex phenomenon,' said Professor Holmes. 'I wouldn't call it a market. Nobody has understood it fully. Nobody can. Even someone like me.'

'Perhaps a baniya like me can?' said Salil, looking towards Anjana.

'Sir,' said the professor, 'you have a good record in risk capital. I respect that. Are you an experienced collector?'

'He is a recent buyer,' said Anjana. She wouldn't grant him the title of collector.

Salil held up his hands. 'I am still learning.'

'I have studied the art market in great detail,' said Professor Holmes. 'And I have studied the corporate collector. It is a grisly record.'

'Ah,' said Salil, 'I get it. You are here to warn me.'

'A number of Big Bang companies that went bust were ones with art collections,' said Professor Holmes.

Salil tapped the table with his pen. 'Coincidence?'

'I don't think so. Let us forget the past. Tell me, sir, what drives you into the art world, if you don't mind my asking?'

Salil thought for a minute. 'This market plays by its own rules; it is the antithesis of economic theory. It is an opaque market with imperfect information flow. There are artificial barriers to entry, price discovery is unpredictable and can be manipulated. What else? Yes, there are other risks. For example, liquidity is poor. It is a classic imperfect market. I happen to love imperfect markets and honestly there aren't many left.'

'Is this enterprise an act of rebellion because you have been, so to speak, spurned by the art world?' asked Anjana. 'Rebellions come at a cost.'

Salil had heard enough.

'Don't take up a challenge just because—'

Salil held up his hands.

'A last word, if I may?' said Professor Holmes. 'Art and money are in some sense partners, and in some sense adversaries.'

'And in my world, one wins and the other loses,' said Anjana.

Salil named the venture Gavel. There was another player, also a local upstart, called Hammer. Both auction houses were 'desi', short form for postcolonial India. They were helmed by native entrepreneurs who believed India's time had come. They would deal in what was smuggled previously with impunity: temple sculpture, miniature paintings, Pichwais, Tanjores, Kashmir carpets, and antique jewellery. And they would also deal in modern and contemporary art. Their online sites were colourful bazaars. Their physical auctions were informal and friendly.

Girish was assigned by his newspaper to cover this phenomenon. His reporting was a mix of photographs and crisp captions.

At the unveiling party yesterday aam panna was dropped into champagne flutes. At the vernissage there was vodka in the pani-puris. And I was told there was a cocktail called Paati's Rasam whose glass was rimmed with its powder.

Gavel flew in money from tier-two cities like Jaipur, Indore, Vizag, Coimbatore, and Surat, and conducted tours in Mumbai, Kolkata, and Delhi, covering artist studios, museums, and private galleries.

Gavel's auctioneers are different. They do not wear suits or speak with clipped accents. Overseas auctioneers, as we all know, are thin-lipped and tight-assed. They look like Wooster and behave like Jeeves.

Auctions were televised for the first time.

The new bidders are not shy. They make it a point to show up in person wearing designer outfits. Among them are actors, industrialists, sportspersons, and others who buy lots as if they are paying entrance money – just so they can be seen. Erstwhile collectors have stayed away.

There was a red carpet when people arrived. Interviews took place as they do at film award functions. Inside the theatre there were bidding wars.

Winners of star lots are cheered lustily and interviewed after the auction. In no time, bidders have become television personalities. In a corner are government officials; there are whispers that they are tax officials.

Indian audiences loved these televised auctions. They were invited to vote on their favourite lots and even guess the outcome. There were prizes.

The new bidders are competitive and a little rash. Their aesthetic has not yet evolved. Yesterday, they spent good money on the pretty and the nubile.

The more experienced collectors and market players were aghast at their lack of discernment. Junk art was selling when it should not have been put up in the first place, they thought.

Dealers and art advisors arrived and spoke to the new collectors. Buy the established artists as well, they said. Soon good works by the moderns were bid into the stratosphere. There was so much new money in young hands, impatient money that began buying the gilt-edged.

The Gavel auction room has become a theatre where the addicted gather, their lives revolving around the next acquisition. They fight to stay calm. When their lots come up, they duel. A collective will drives them. New records are being set at every auction.

Gavel did well in the first three years of its existence. Its televised model was a winner. A couple of the other auction houses were quick to adapt to this new medium.

A new type of client has emerged from a new segment. Young, super-rich, and wannabe aesthete. An impossible category.

Anjana was aghast as she read Girish's reports. She held out the latest catalogue, one which offended her. 'I hate what is happening,' she said.

Girish's idiosyncratic coverage continued.

Last night in a plush hotel the well-heeled gathered for an art auction. There were eighty lots on offer. According to critics, it was a poor selection. All of them, serenaded by a suited auctioneer, sold, each sale marked by the sound of the gavel striking the podium. Make no mistake, in an auction house the sound of the gavel is the drumbeat of capitalism. The question that bothers the art world is the lack of discernment. They see it as a betrayal.

Speak to the entrepreneur behind all this, said Girish's boss. Get his point of view. Salil Gupta spoke with refreshing candour.

When Girish asked him for a quote, he said, 'This business will plateau soon.'

He told the same thing to his daughter when she was planning to take a breather. She had worked hard helping her father with the auctions. He gave her a handsome bonus. Now there was money in her bank account and she felt she deserved a posh sabbatical.

'What you have in your account is not money to burn. I call it risk capital,' said her father. 'Time to put it to work.'

'Any other pithy terms from your business world?'

'Yes,' said Daddy. 'Time for you to have skin in the game.'

'Let me decide for once,' said Nupur. 'For once let us do something more meaningful than making money.'

Salil Gupta looked at his daughter and realized how much of her mother was in her.

'I will use my precious little nest egg,' said Nupur. 'I am not asking you for money.'

'If I like your idea I will match your contribution,' said her father.

The Prize

The format was simple. Artists and their lives would be captured on television as a reality show. A shortlist would be made every year and the four or five chosen artists would come under the lens for a year. The public would be privy to the work they produced and the life they lived. The show would be called *The Prize.*

In the past the art world had produced catalogues on artists and their shows, and some books as well. The books were glossy, congratulatory odes written by respected critics. The catalogues were well-written but dense. Nobody read any of these. A frank examination of artists' lives, done the right way on television, would surely be more riveting.

Salil thought they should meet Anjana and get her opinion.

'She will shred the idea,' said Nupur. 'Anjana is a cynic. What she will tell you is that the consumers of popular culture are the ones with small brains. They have busy lives and every weekend they switch off. They want to be entertained, and they are easily pleased. I can hear Anjana say that these people need content like treatment plants need sewage. But this audience doesn't want to be told that they are consuming shit. This is your audience. Do you really want to give them a programme on high art that will have them over their arses and hector them about their inadequacies?'

'Yes, she is right. What is your defence?'

'The audience is smart. That is my answer.'

Girish was roped in to help script the episodes and provide background material. Tara would manage the production.

Initially, Tara was sceptical as well.

'High art and bohemian living in the drawing rooms of the middle class? You think it will work? It will be like the clash of civilizations.'

To helm the episodes, they chose a veteran called Shukla, who had directed many Hindi serials and then gone on to fulfil his life's destiny. He made a couple of art-house films, pouring his life's savings into them. He invited distributors to a preview theatre and screened the films. Their response broke his heart.

'Very hatke,' said one.

'We will get back,' said another.

Shukla lost most of his savings. In some sense, he did not mind because he did not respect the money he had made from the shitty serials he had directed. He put his feet up in his small flat in Bandra that had a balcony overlooking the sea, drank beer, and waited. He was convinced that someday someone would see his films and come and knock on his door.

The Gavel project excited him tremendously. It was an interesting premise and Nupur, who was piloting it, was open to taking risks. Daddy had deep pockets as well.

Nupur observed him closely as he entered the room where the team was meeting for the first time. Shukla had a peculiar habit. He viewed every space he inhabited as a set, and he was restless until he occupied that perfect spot where the director should be sitting. He chose a chair near the projection screen.

'I have a question,' he said.

'I go first,' said Nupur. She rummaged in her bag. 'I have a bunch of "No" cards somewhere.' She pulled out some cue cards. 'Are you listening?'

Shukla nodded.

'No clever stuff,' said Nupur, reading the first card.

'Meaning?'

'Let me read these out. No tints, no opera music, no super slow-mo, no super zoom, no art-house stuff.'

'I see.'

'What I want is a hardcore gaze.'

'You mean up close and personal?'

'Yes. Catch them when they are not looking. Go in, dig into their living quarters. Shoot what they consume. These are voracious people. Shoot their morning debris. Shoot under their eyes, inside their heads. Peel off the mask they wear. Describe them through the spaces they inhabit.'

'They might object.'

'Shoot them when they object.'

Nupur liked the fact that Shukla listened. 'You had a question, sir.'

'My first question is: what lens are we going to use?'

'I am not a technical type,' said Tara, 'so don't ask me.'

'I think he means something else,' said Nupur.

'I meant, are we going to shoot this with a neutral gaze?' said Shukla.

'Meaning?'

'Are we merely onlookers? Are we like spectators at a theatre?'

'Or?' asked Nupur.

'Or we have a script in hand. We coach the participants and they play out roles that we have already sketched. We control the outcomes.'

'No, no,' said Tara and Nupur in unison. 'We need accidents on set, we need surprises.'

'I guessed as much,' said Shukla. 'I think I know what you have in mind. I don't know how to say it.'

Tara took up the bait. 'We will be complicit observers. It is an art world term. Not abject bystanders, not enthusiastic participants, but something in between.'

'Catalysts perhaps?'

Nupur nodded. 'Yes, that sounds right. What happens in this programme should be important. We should be able to say, this is history in the making. That is our brief.'

'I like the phrase "history in the making"', said Tara.

'So full colour then,' said Shukla. 'Live sound and multiple cameras?'

'Yes. Recording the weird and the beautiful, the silly and the grotesque,' said Nupur.

'Strange lives, twisted thinking, the art itself,' said Tara.

'Greed on display perhaps,' said Nupur, 'and naked insecurity.'

'A reality that is self-aware,' said Tara. 'Everybody knows it is being recorded and nobody fucking cares.'

'I know something will happen,' said Shukla, excited by the minute.

'Something will,' said Nupur. 'There is a sense of mystery about the prize. We are not telling the artists everything.'

'Is there a lot to tell?'

'There is the prize money. It is a lot. It is more than they can think of making right now. It is large enough to push themselves for.'

'Meaning?'

'Well, do the best they can, you know. Not just the art.'

'And we will observe them, record them, evaluate them?'

'Yes,' said Nupur. 'You know what I want all the viewers to realize at the end of the season?'

'I don't think we want to get into that,' said Shukla, 'as long as they watch.'

He knew from personal experience that viewers were fickle and resisted manipulation.

'But it matters to me,' said Nupur. 'I want the viewers who are not into art. I want them to realize that they are suffering from a condition. If you are not into art, you are just... coping.'

'Hmm,' said Shukla, director of two flop art-house films. 'Good luck with that.'

The main room was called Adda. It was a cave with deep seating. You needed a strong core to get up from its low sofas. Adda bustled with people through the day. Nobody had a fixed spot. Nupur could be found in Adda from 10 a.m.

The room next door, a smaller one, had open windows and no air conditioning. It was the smoking den. Tara would hover near the window, take a drag, and stare. She looked like she was waiting for something. Her phone would light up often and she would ignore it. Every half an hour she would pick it up and return calls.

'Be patient,' said Shukla. 'It is taking shape.'

'Will you reshoot?'

'Bits and pieces,' he said. 'Gaps are building up. It happens.'

He slurped his tea. He looked happy.

'Do we need focus groups?' shouted Tara from next door. 'Someone is offering.'

'Do we?'

'Not now,' said Shukla. 'It will be too confusing.'

They had managed to rope in Anjana to chair the jury: a coup. She had refused when they first approached her, relenting when Ardeshir met her and explained the prize as a means to an end, the end being a wider interest in the arts in a country that had lost its aesthetic moorings, that did not understand or respect the creative process, was unaware of how artists live and how art got made, and was concerned purely with the market and record prices. In the UK the Turner Prize had kindled interest in contemporary art. This Indian prize would do the same; it was admittedly very different, but necessarily so.

Nupur was nervous. The first episode was important. They were to air it on the weekend. Airtime had been sold at low rates. If the episode did well, they could negotiate better.

In the end, the first season was passable. While the lives of artists were a fascinating contrast to the lives that the viewers led, the segments that showed the making of art were painstaking, at times ordinary. But some of it seemed to work in unpredictable ways.

A Mumbai artist made a slick presentation, unveiling his posh studio in Bandra for the first time. The next day his studio helpers, and there were many, unveiled themselves on TV. They were wearing overalls and carrying brushes.

'I am the one who paints his background,' said a young man holding a thick brush.

A woman wearing specs brandished a thin brush. 'I paint the faces,' she said.

They were carrying placards.

'WE are the real artists,' said one placard.

'He makes millions, he pays us daily wages,' said another.

It caused a public spat. Spurred by public attention and online support, the assistants filed for copyright and a share of the selling price. The matter went to the courts.

A Delhi collective, a group of three, did a complex staging at the National Gallery of Modern Art in Delhi. Few people could connect their dots. The three posed like New Age gurus, armed with obscure words and clever juxtapositions. A group of schoolchildren who were brought to the show in a bus made a spectacle of themselves by exiting from the show and collapsing in a heap. The next day a humorous takedown of the show appeared in a subversive TV programme called *All India Bakbak*. It was titled 'What the chhod is this?'

An artist from interior Karnataka poked fun at rituals and customs, and occasionally at art itself. When questioned on his simple drawings and his direct sense of humour that bordered on the naïve, he showed them two granite gravestones that he had ceremoniously planted next to each other in a cemetery under a mango tree.

'My latest work,' he said.

Carved on the first gravestone was 'Artist'. The second one said 'Art'.

A Chennai artist, a painter with an assumed name, quoted poetry when spoken to. His work dwelled on death. Amidst his sombre greys and maudlin browns, people found figures that harked back to the romantic image of the artist living on the edge, flirting with personal demons and financial ruin.

In the first year of *The Prize*, the rest of the art world was caught napping. When it woke up, the first thing it did was protest. Here was a commercial venture that was preying on artists' lives. To increase ratings, a torch was being shone on their peccadilloes. Worse, art was being dumbed down, brought to the level of *Big Boss* television.

'Be happy someone is interested in us,' retorted a senior artist. He had spent years down a rabbit hole with the dark for company.

The art community launched a resistance targeting Gavel. A boycott was on the cards. The fate of the auction business hung in the balance.

'They are giving the Nobel to behavioural economists,' said Salil. His investors had ring-fenced him at a bar. 'The world has changed. Today, stories explain the markets, not theories. Economics 101 now teaches us the importance of stories. That is what we will work with, that is what we will build: a narrative.'

'Can we have some hard numbers, in the meanwhile?' said his lead investor.

'Don't do the maths right now; be patient. All unicorns begin with a suspension of spreadsheets.'

'It sounds like a manifesto from the loony bin,' said the lead investor.

'That sounds like the art world, perhaps?' said Salil. Nobody laughed.

Gavel's financial backers were not impressed with the ratings *The Prize* received in its first season. The Guptas had a choice to make: give up the show and continue with auctions, or risk it all. Nupur fought with them.

'The art world has turned on you,' they told her.

She asked them not to climb down. 'Look them in the eye because that is what they respect. Right now, we are a nuisance, but trust me, this will become bigger than the auction business.'

'Tell us how you will improve the ratings?'

'I have learned,' said Nupur. 'We have all learned how this medium works. We are confident that art and artists will make good television in the format we have. We will execute better. And yes, we will increase the prize money.'

When she mentioned the figure, they were stunned.

'A million dollars? Isn't that too much?'

'Exactly,' she said. 'People will question it just like they question three million dollars for a work by Tyeb Mehta or Gaitonde.'

'What will a million dollars do?'

'Mark my words,' said Nupur. 'It will make artists do things, will make for riveting television.'

The investors allowed her another year. The announcement of the prize of a million dollars was splashed across front pages.

'Do we know what we are doing?!' asked Tara. She was in a state of delirium.

V

Overheard Snippets

I am unable to write like Anjana can, dwelling on the elegance of the quotidian and the sumptuousness of the banal.

Girish

I could very easily write like Girish says, if I chose to. I do so sometimes just to keep him in his place and get under his skin.

Anjana

We are different from artists whom you recognize and accept so easily. Painters are obsessed with light. Sculptors with negative space. We are obsessed with imbalance, with societies and their movements.

Brown Sahib

Critics are harmless, curators are not. Critics maintain distance, curators nudge and poke. Critics tell you where art comes from, curators tell us where it should be going.

Anonymous

If it is a good work, why have just one of its kind – that only one person can enjoy?

Suleiman

What were the bidders smoking?

Ardeshir

There were habits in the auction room that people mistook for tics.

Nupur

There is no good reason for making art, but committing a crime is rarely senseless.

Inspector Pandey

Auctions and their prices are very real. As narratives they are between farce and satire. Strangely, the numbers, their sheer magnitude, make the art not valuable but weightless.

Anjana

The art world is paying the price for subjectivity, Anjana. You are to blame.

Girish

In childhood, Marwaris watched a trail of ants and learned that by using their fingers to wipe that trail, they could confuse the army that followed. Marwaris know that scrutiny of the prosperous is inevitable. Which is why they dislike phrases like 'footprints on the sand of time'.

Salil

In my time painting was considered a feminine pursuit. Like needlework. I was like you. Music played in my head. But I was easily dissuaded. I was bombarded by the view that life was harsh and the odds were against taking chances. Artists were a bedraggled lot those days. And writers? They had no means.

Salil's chacha

I went to a place that made me cry. The serenity, an age preserved. It did not take me long to realize I had come to a special place. It was so quiet you could hear a slight breeze, distant bells, birds as they flew overhead. I wondered if the people who stayed there were aware of what they had. And how could anyone get used to something like that?

Tara

Live like a prodigal. Puff of dust, and the fairy tale begins. I learned to ignore a few things. There is beauty around us here amidst the rubbish. You know, deep down we are all creative. The worst thing in this quest is daily life.

Maya

My friends went to resorts and game reserves while I was hauled off to galleries. I began hating these large colonial buildings set in large estates, dotted with misshapen objects and bloated egos. Really, most of these artists had pompous material written about themselves and their precious work. Precious puff, if you ask me.

Nupur

VI

Nupur

There is a business in Mumbai called Flood Mart. It opens its shutters in June when the clouds come in, and over three months it thrives, counting the days when the city shuts down. I asked a hawker once what he did when it poured: did he curse, did he flee? Where did he place his belongings; in which crack, in which crevice, did he hide them? He laughed, as I have seen people do in Mumbai. I cannot describe that laugh or explain what it means: it is not fatalistic or defeatist; it is a knowing laugh. It includes me in a kind of fellowship, the kind that stays in the city despite everything.

More than any other city Mumbai questions the idea of permanence.

I was sitting in the middle of my small living room because the ceiling was wet in two corners. It was raining; I could hear it beating down. The monsoon was an invasion. The annual waterproofing ritual had failed; the black tar we poured on the roof tiles had probably cracked. Plop, said the water. Plop, said the rain. Plop, said my effing brain.

I called Tara. 'Life is bloody useless,' I said. 'Will people remember all this?' I asked her. 'Is it worth it?'

Tara said something rude about how she had been dealing with the same question far longer than me, staying with a fragile artist who looked at life as a rite of passage.

'My roof isn't leaking,' said Tara, 'but, ha ha, this ship is.'

I called the contractor, the damberwala, the annual failure. He was busy; the whole city was out looking for him and he was on a terrace.

'We cannot fix any leak now; we have to wait for a dry spell,' he said when I tracked him down.

'What should I do till then?' I shouted.

He was silent for a while, as if to say life must go on; then the phone cut off.

I pulled the drapes and the mechanical curtain rose. It was dark outside.

I had been to a palmist, against my best instincts. It was a new low to climb stairs in a Dadar colony into a modest abode where an elderly gentleman in a white veshti – no shirt – sat on a low chair. He wore thick glasses and was bald. He played bridge in his spare time at an establishment called Brahmin's Club at two rupees a point.

'There are lines that lead out of every palm,' he said. 'This tracery points to decisive moments. You need to be aware.'

There was of course a decisive moment in every palm, that was supposed to be fatal.

'If I pay heed to such things I won't go very far,' I said.

'Why have you come then?' he asked.

'I have ceased to care,' I said.

He looked puzzled. 'It is not my place to give you advice,' he said.

'Something is holding me back,' I said.

'What holds us all back?' said the old man.

I was asking people, but nobody cared. Anjana the sage was so wise; she had the right words. It is not knowledge, she said, that impedes progress, but allegiance. She was so good with words; she could shit on me and I would be fine.

'You will go far,' said my palmist.

'I will, really? Pray, what will egg me on?'

'The spirit of the survivor,' he said. 'Which is why you must stay in Mumbai.'

His eyes twinkled. I could have hugged him. I counted out the amount I was to pay. He took it gratefully.

I went out into the rain. I walked, water running down my clothes. There was a faint smell of flowers; there was water collecting on the roads, cars were splashing their way through. It was twenty-something, the year that was, a strange year, an untutored year that was full of idiot boasts. Something was amiss in its makeup. In fact, the whole decade was nonsense. Scientists were struggling; economists were agape. The new theories in physics were making no sense; they were beginning to sound mystical. And no economic theory could explain what was happening in their world. The repeated implosions in the financial markets had spooked participants, governments, and the PhD think tanks. Was this all a blip or two, or was this worse? Was the failure of capitalism nigh? Was this the time for me to be taking serious risks?

Mumbai was too busy; it had no time for such questions. It was smug, as if its very existence were proof of something. I mean, what did the city really have?

Soot, for one, that soiled collars and cuffs. The moisture in Mumbai's air married carbon particles and smoke flakes. The effect on skin was like the erosion that the salty sea air caused to buildings. Concrete rusted in Mumbai; the surface gave way. Every few years scaffolding climbed the crumbling facades and green gauze flapped around the structures like a Christo wrap. The road-facing boards proudly proclaimed that 'Guniting' had started. Guniting was a repair job where concrete was injected to protect the steel rods by filling up the cracks and crevices. In high society this process was called Botox.

This was my mood, call it blue, when my Delhi boyfriend called. That tone of voice! A mild, complaining tone that spoke of what he was entitled to and wasn't getting enough of. He had come to Mumbai, ostensibly on work, and was calling from the airport. We met at a Chinese restaurant over coloured dimsums. He was still very good-looking, so much so it hurt to look at him. He complimented me, said I looked busy and purposeful. And what has happened to your hair?

We walked that evening on the Marina, held hands. The breeze briefly swept away the months between us but we realized the gap that had formed was unbridgeable. His trip was successful. We knew we would not meet again.

I broke a little the next day. I called my mother. 'Come,' I told her. Sarla Gupta needed no second invitation.

'I won't go away in a hurry,' she said.

There were a few lines on her face, despite care and attention and her creams. Her underarms hung loose. Her posture was as it was. She looked alert; her eyes had her mischief.

'Who said anything about going away?' I said.

'Nobody. It is best to address the unsaid.'

Her visit to Bombay, her Mumbai, was a renewal of a lifelong love affair. She came and then disappeared for a week. She met people and renewed her acquaintance with roads, shops, and some trees. She was glowing, her skin ablaze, and the moist, warm weather showed up as a red tint.

'I fought with Salil before I left,' she said.

'About what?'

She had tried to spring-clean the house and remove accumulated deadwood. There were so many things that would never be used that were choking her existence.

'Salil is a keeper. His family throws away nothing. They have a huge room that is full of the most useless things. Old batteries, car tyres, toasters, mixies, radios. The room stinks and it looks like the next edition of *Mad Max*.'

'What about you? Are you a keeper?'

'Well, Salil is still around, ha ha.'

She was a good distraction. I needed someone to fill my days till we got going with our project. Tara was travelling in the hills, getting stung by bees and chased by dogs.

Tara was upbeat when she returned. She sensed my unease. 'Why don't you say what's on your mind?'

'I don't know,' I said. 'You have seen firsthand so much that has happened. Right? Hidden in all that is the real me, forgotten because the cameras are out there. Nobody is looking at me.'

'We could remedy that,' said Tara.

'Seriously,' I said. 'I feel nothing is happening in my life.'

She dismissed it. 'No worries,' she said. 'Season 2 will begin and we will all be fine.'

'I am not so sure,' I said. 'I feel I am going to make a mistake.'

'How do you know?'

'I am due,' I said. 'I have no illusions. The road is parting and I will take a wrong turn.'

She was quiet for a while. 'Do you feel the art world turning on you?' she asked.

'They are waiting for me to make a mistake.'

I could sense it. In my reality show, the lives of artists would be under the spotlight more than their art. One year is a long period in a reality show that has regular episodes.

'What do you fear, behen?'

'Very soon art and performance will meet; posturing will begin. God knows what will happen. Engineered events? Threatened careers? Perhaps lives in danger?'

These questions were bothering me. Would artists' behaviour change if their lives were being closely observed, and would they do something bold or rash if there was a prize to be won, a prize that projected their lives on the small screen, that had to hold the attention of a fickle audience? I asked my father.

'Depends on who you pick,' said Salil.

'Who should I pick?'

'Pick a wild card, one who is unpredictable, who has been repressed by the elitist gatekeepers, who is good, mind you, but in their eyes will never be good enough.'

'Is there shame in scandal?' I asked.

'Hain?'

'We pick a wild card called Praveena.'

'I have heard rumours about her. Who else?'

'We pick Tara's mother.'

'Why her?'

'Because she is a brilliant artist going through a bad phase. And she needs the money. I am worried, though. She lives on the edge, and the edge is where strange things happen.'

'Who else?'

'We pick a performance artist like Krishna Kumar,' I said, 'one who will make things happen. And last of all?'

'Someone who makes art that I do not understand. I mean really do not. What you call cutting edge. I don't see the point of it; neither will the majority. I would love to see the public respond.'

I thought of who that would be. 'Someone like the duo Brown Sahib?'

'What are they into?'

'Revolution,' I said.

Brown Sahib

Brown and Sahib were an artist duo. Jamie Brown was based in London. He had a shared studio that was on the verge of a railway track. When trains passed his table shivered, his teacup rattled, and his bones lost density. The studio had a large glass window that for the most part let in what he called a grey light. This grey light infused his work like coffee colours infused the works of Rembrandt.

Brown exercised by walking to his studio from his small studio apartment, which was sublet to him by a Pakistani who ran an electronics store that made money on SIM cards. Occasionally he missed the rent; the arrangement was that he paid 5 per cent extra for every month of delay. Three months' arrears and he could let himself out.

Brown bought a SIM card that he used to call Sahiba. She wasn't talkative but at a pinch she would send some money; she had the stash because their work sold in India. Their art was showcased strategically in the UK. They managed some local coverage which they then highlighted on social media. This helped sales in India.

Most of the saleable stuff was posters. The duo adopted the Shepherd Fairey approach of making large editions of posters that had a lot of red and a Mao-era sensibility popularized by Wang Guangyi. Fairey had a great following for his resistance-styled offerings which carried words like OBEY. Another one said HOPE, referring to the Occupy Wall Street movement.

The duo also liked the anonymous surfacing of the graffiti king, Banksy. They knew that this approach could work in India despite the high noise levels on its streets. A subtle mural in a Mumbai street would be pissed upon without anyone objecting. But a serial intervention near railway stations' ticket counters would find attention.

Their first anonymous street sign said CAST(E). In smaller lettering below was 'your vote'. Their second was a poster that said HARTAL, with the subtext 'should be complete'.

What exactly do you think you are doing?

This was the question posed by Mumbai police. Art, they said.

Their considered view was that art had to be political; the undertone had to be subversive. In the twenty-first century the world was connected and sneezed as one. News headlines were ubiquitous. On social media people were signing on to causes with which they had no physical connection. Crowds were forming online and their activity was now virtual: crowd-funding, crowd-voting, crowd-willing.

'Geopolitics is impacting lives on a daily basis. How can art stay away from it?'

In one of their interventions, they set sail on the Thames with a large quantity of opium, in a boat called Columbus that had a galley with white men in chains. In another work they occupied a pedestal in Trafalgar Square, setting up a small booth that supposedly issued residency permits to immigrants.

Tara studied the duo. She thought they were interesting, and they would also polarize opinion in India around the question: is this art, or some more New Age shit? Nupur wondered about the impact they might have on television. Conceptual stuff could be boring, she thought.

It was time to meet them and settle the issue.

Nupur and Tara smoked some weed in the duo's studio. There was a Pye radio on a teak table, a Grundig spool player, a grandfather clock, and an Art Deco side table. Brown was standing erect, a cigar between his teeth.

'Art is my fourth career attempt,' he said, in a clipped accent. 'My most successful.' He looked at his cigar. 'By the way I cannot draw or paint.'

'That is so sweet,' said Nupur.

'Such refreshing candour, sahib,' said Tara, biting her lip.

'I make the money in the partnership,' said Sahiba.

'How, please?'

'I have a million followers on Instagram,' she said. 'There is mayhem when I am online. And there is advertising.'

'Wow,' said Nupur. 'Have you ever heard anything like this, Tara?'

'Not in little India.'

'You won't believe how much money you can make out of an online presence,' said Sahiba.

Nupur stared; Tara blinked.

'Every day we brave a new world,' said Nupur.

'Ha ha,' said Brown and Sahiba.

'Do I sound jealous?' said Nupur. 'I really am.'

'I want to kill myself,' said Tara.

Their hosts brought out whisky, ice, and cut glasses. 'On the rocks?' Nupur nodded, Tara poured slugs, they both sniffed, and sipped. Nupur coughed; Tara's cheeks reddened.

'58 proof,' said Brown.

'Cask strength,' said Sahiba.

'You are just going to stand and watch?' asked Nupur.

'We don't do alcohol,' they said, smiling.

They sipped aloe vera from tall stems. Some goji berries floated into their puckered mouths. They kept smiling.

Nupur loved the whisky, and Tara began to acquire a taste for it as well. 'So woody, such a nice colour.' Soon they were ready to speak their minds.

'Things have failed in India,' said Nupur.

'We began with a welfare state,' said Tara.

'Nehru,' said Nupur. 'Noble man among wildebeests.'

'More whisky?' asked their hosts.

'Theory deceived us,' said Nupur. 'We tried everything; Marxism, capitalism, socialism.'

'Primitivism,' said Tara.

'Look at what we have become: a nation of shopkeepers, a baniya state. All our high hopes were dashed by Lakshmi.'

They slumped in their chairs, the liquor swirling in their heads. Their hosts stood like cool cucumbers and said nothing.

'Artists here are suffering,' said Tara, 'from feelings of neglect.'

They were served some dry Italian pasta and some leafy salad. Tara couldn't bear to look at her plate. The dry white wine made her cough.

'Seriously, how do you afford all this?' said Nupur, looking at the wine label.

'We got a grant last year,' said Sahiba. 'A genius grant.'

'Genius grant? Did you take a Mensa test?' asked Nupur.

The duo laughed as one. They were holding hands.

Tara kicked Nupur under the table. She knew her friend was on the verge of saying something indelicate.

Praveena

Money is hard to come by in Mumbai; this was a common sentiment. It was true – more so in art. 'Be patient,' Praveena was told time and again, till the phrase gave her a rash. She wanted to pay for the studio and her living expenses herself. She hated asking her father for an allowance.

Suleiman understood her plight. He spoke to his neighbour in Pasta Lane, who knew someone in the studio that made copies of well-known artworks of the Impressionists. There was a big market for these copies. People did not care for originals; they were quite happy to have a grand-looking painting that looked authentic. Praveena was aghast when her father broached the idea.

'Copy?' she exclaimed, shrill and caustic. 'You have any idea what you are asking me to do?'

Her father let her stew for a while. 'I am not asking you to,' he said.

The proprietor of Galleria told him that copying was different from faking. It was craft at work, avowedly, and not art. What was wrong with that? It was a comedown but one that could be rationalized.

'Think of it as practice,' said Suleiman. 'It is like a musician doing riyaz.'

Praveena needed the money. 'How much per day?' she said.

It was a handsome amount, enough to tempt her. If she put her mind to it, she would produce good copies. 'Fine,' she said, 'but nobody should know.'

Her goal was perfection and she achieved it by forensically examining the technique, sourcing the right materials, working, reworking, and repainting till she got it exactly right. Her father could not believe how good a painter his daughter had become.

Her copies found ready buyers and very soon she was paid a percentage of the sale price. She found time to read, attend shows, and continue making her own art. But things moved slowly on the exhibition front. CDs of her work kept coming back from galleries.

The marriage question popped up now and then. There were liberal families in the community that would gladly welcome her. But boys were apprehensive of her reputation as a 'free spirit'.

Despite her best efforts she could not manage a solo show. She participated in some group shows and did get a special mention or two. That was it. It hurt her when her mates, especially men, got solo shows and began to make a mark. Their work was nice, just not great, so why them? There was no answer. There were fits of rage, naked suffering on her thirtieth birthday, jealous raves on opening nights, and sullen drinking. One hot flush, then another. She had no shoulder she could lean on, and no companion in misery.

One fateful day she saw some copies of Indian moderns. In the corner of her small space in Galleria, she sat up. She was appalled. Such bad copies they were. And then she saw some that were not copies. They were true fakes: amateur attempts at making something new. And they were signed Francis Newton Souza, Syed Haider Raza, and Maqbool Fida Hussain. Each attempt was worse than the other.

'What do you think?' she was asked by the proprietor.

'Fakes,' she said.

'Are they good ones?'

She laughed. She hadn't laughed in a while so she made up for it. She laughed till tears rolled down her cheeks.

'Please kill me,' she said. 'Take that palette knife and do it before I drink up this can of thinner.'

Something spoke to her, something wicked. There was so much inside her that had accumulated, stuff that she needed to purge.

She studied the work of three of the moderns, choosing the prolific ones who had a ready market and established prices. She read about their lives, saw films of their time, met people who knew them, and studied hundreds of works, making detailed notes. By the time she put brush to paper she knew where to begin.

She destroyed many attempts till she got it right. At the end of a year, she had made a set of works that passed muster. Some Souzas, some Razas, and some Husains. Each was documented meticulously, and she kept images and records – for 'provenance'. She showed them to the proprietor of Galleria. He was a charlatan but even he could sense he was looking at something special.

The only correction required later was in the signatures. Praveena's handwriting skills fell short. Or maybe signing the forgeries proved too much for her. Maybe she was ashamed to be doing this work when she knew, in her heart of hearts, that she could do so much more with her life.

She fell sick, was unwell for a couple of days. Listless during the day, confused and depressed when evening arrived. She was conflicted, her feelings alternating between anger and low self-esteem. When she recovered somewhat, Zubeida asked her, 'How are you feeling now?'

'Read my tweets, Mausi.'

It was wise of her to have taken to Twitter rather than Facebook. Among her friends on FB her posts were guarded and infrequent. On Twitter she was anonymous and in her element, posting measured sentences. Two of her tweets made waves.

The first was mistaken by some as an artist's credo they could adopt. It said: Art that fills my pocket hurts my pride.

The second was more pointed and poignant. It said: If the death of Modernism has a gravestone you will find fakes there instead of flowers.

When her tear ducts stopped flowing, she handed the fake documentation of the paintings to her father. 'Keep this with you. And don't show it to anybody.'

The old man put the material with his property documents. He felt sad.

'Why did you do this, beta? There was no need.'

What could she say? That she wanted to show up the system? Establish her credentials in some screwball way?

The works entered the market; in good times it was a vast sieve through which all and sundry slipped. The works changed hands and provenance was established. Nobody suspected a thing and a couple among them came up for auction at Hammer. It was a significant test. They achieved good prices. They carried authenticity certificates signed by the reigning diva among curators: Anjana.

Suleiman cut out the auction results and filed them. The dossier was now complete. Once the works sold at auctions, and that too at prices higher than comparable works, a great calm descended. His daughter now seemed at peace, no longer angry. She focused on her own work, closing a chapter that she hoped would remain undiscovered.

One fine evening when Ardeshir was at a loose end, he remembered Praveena. He had a nagging thought that he may have been too dismissive about the pieces of embroidery the girl had shown him. He had half a mind to ask Suleiman for a studio visit, assuming Praveena had a studio somewhere.

Suleiman had said nothing since the rejection. It had hurt him beyond measure but he knew he could not force the issue. He pretended nothing had happened between them.

After the forgery episode which he knew had affected Praveena at a subliminal level, Suleiman thought of exiting the slush fund arrangement he had with Ardeshir. He needed to do something. He asked to meet, and when he landed up, there was a surprise waiting for him. It was a wild card entry. For *The Prize*. Ardeshir had organized it. 'I may have been a little rushed when I said no to your daughter,' he said. The old man's face lit up. He could have done anything for Ardeshir at that moment. The rush of emotions broke through. He hugged Ardeshir. 'Bhai,' said the latter, 'I wish you would join me for a drink. Just once.'

VII

Season Two

The team decided there would be four episodes for each participant. The first was to be an introduction, in the form of an interview or discussion at a location that would be mutually agreed upon. The second episode would cover the art that each was making. The third and fourth would evolve as the show went on. They discussed the concept with the chosen artists.

Initially, Maya would have none of it. She was old school. She thought the art and the artist needed distance from each other. Nupur had to work with Tara to get her mother to agree. She also spoke to Maya's friends, people like Girish. Girish and Tara were convinced by Nupur's reasoning. Maya would finally see the life she was leading once it was shown on television. It was an ugly life, and the rude shock could help Maya mend her ways.

'We will be playing with fire,' said Tara. 'My mother isn't what she used to be.'

In the end what convinced Maya was the prize amount. That shook her. 'What the hell!' she said. 'The money would be so welcome.' She had a debt mountain to deal with.

'I don't trust myself,' said Maya, when she was told the first episode would be live. That too in a bar where she could pretty much do what she was prone to. They were at her studio where Nupur kept staring at Maya. Having heard so much about Maya's debauched lifestyle and habits she was taken aback when she met her. Maya looked quite normal and was smiling.

'You look happy, despite everything,' she blurted.

'Shouldn't I be? I don't understand why I shouldn't be.'

'There is so much happening in your life,' said Nupur.

'So? Should I be perpetually sad? Should I be weighed down by every small thing?'

'That's not what I meant,' said Nupur.

'There is no posthumous life, young lady.'

'Nice,' said Nupur.

'There will never be a lateness to my greatness.'

'Oho,' said Tara.

Brown Sahib were more studied. 'We usually work with a script,' they said. 'Can we write one?'

The short answer was no.

Praveena did not respond to their requests. Her father Suleiman said he would convince her. Her practice was interesting. Her proposed solo show had portraits of Suleiman. It was titled 'Parental Advisory'. She continued with embroidery as a medium. She liked its imperfection. Instead of perfect knots and patterns her work had cut threads hanging loose. They are like broken links, she said when some clients complained.

Krishna Kumar invited them to Kerala. 'The setting is important,' he said. 'You must shoot my segment in the backwaters and on a boat if possible.'

'Well, what do you think of our foursome?' said Nupur.

Tara shrugged. 'Maya is all bravado, our Malayali Krishna Kumar exudes chutzpah, Brown and Sahib have the smarts, and Praveena? God knows what she is all about. The fact is that she's lying low. I can tell you one thing. Each of them is a nervous particle.'

'Can you hear the music?' said Nupur.

'What music?'

'The music that is playing. I can hear it.'

'Is it an incantation or is it a dirge?'

There were supposed to be some interviews with others in the art world. They weren't easy to shoot. The art world had ganged up and erected barricades.

Nupur needed a good gallerist on the show and she set her sights on Ardeshir. He was the most dynamic and interesting among the new breed of gallerists. He would set the show alight.

Nupur spoke to Girish. 'Help me, and I will compensate.'

Girish, no admirer of the ways of the art world, was happy to help if he could in some way show this world to outsiders.

The stage was set for the second year. Maya's episode was televised first. She had a reputation as an enfant terrible, an artist whose colourful life made the papers for the wrong reasons. 'The interview will be a blast and the show's ratings will go through the roof,' said Nupur. Cameras followed her as the team took on Maya.

The Maya Episode: The Fugitive Years

'You are so young. Are you still in college?' asked Maya as she ordered a classic martini. It was a lowly bar in the suburbs that had a gritty atmosphere and a passable bartender.

Bharti, the journalist chosen to conduct the interview, looked flustered. Her age belied her ability to get under the skin of her subjects.

'Have you titled this episode?'

'I was thinking of "Inside the Mind of an Artist".'

The drink arrived. Maya sniffed it and frowned. Something wasn't right.

'Is there any difference, Maya? I mean, inside your head?'

Maya narrowed her eyes as she sipped her martini. 'We like to fuck with it,' she said.

'Sorry?'

'What a shitty drink. Has the interview started?'

Bharti looked towards the cameras. 'Yes, we are rolling.'

Maya searched inside her drink with a toothpick and speared the olive.

'Look at her eyebrows,' said Nupur, standing behind the camera. Maya's eyebrows met, like Frida Kahlo's. 'Look at her skin.' She was noticing how tight the skin was across her cheekbones.

'Inside she must be smiling,' said Tara

Bharti soldiered on. 'Artists see differently, in ways that others don't. Do you agree?'

'What we see is visible,' said Maya.

'I see,' said Bharti, looking towards the camera, towards Nupur and Tara. 'Were you brought up differently? Would you say that?'

Maya looked surprised.

'Do you seriously think we are what we are because of upbringing?'

'Yes,' said Bharti.

'We are what we are despite our upbringing,' said Maya. 'I am not being clever. Nobody nurtured me.'

She paused and looked down at her hands. 'My house was an immigrant's house, a basti in a mohalla. Our so-called yard had a rubbish dump where dogs fought with cats for what flesh remained on bones.'

'Wow,' said Nupur.

Maya tilted her head back, looking into the lights.

'My father was always away in the Gulf, my mother sat at home, morose, and life went on.'

Bharti licked her lips. 'Could you tell us more about your growing-up years?'

Maya smiled. She tapped some invisible ash into the small ashtray that was shaped like a frog. The weed had taken hold and she began speaking.

'Imagine being a nail in a horseshoe, imagine being strung up like empty cans in a soup kitchen. That is what we were. We lived in a poor mohalla. It was cramped, so cramped people couldn't spit. At the entrance was an iron pillar of unknown origin. Somebody had strung a loose rag on it as a flag. It was rumoured to have been green in colour. The rain took care of that.

'In the oval of our enclave was sand, grainy sand that you could feel on bare feet. Our measure of Earth was thirsty and rainwater seeped through the sand never to be seen again. Strung around this oval like a bunch of cans, we rattled in the wind, each of us. The wind howled in the hot summers of Amritsar.'

Maya lit another cheroot. She inhaled and her eyes were distant.

'Half the mohalla was empty at all times. The males had gone to the Gulf of Oil, to the receptacle of His Lord's munificence, the one who gave wells of black gold to the tribesmen of the desert and left us soot. The men went for months together and returned once every year. Women and children stayed behind, uninvited or denied visas. The old folk stayed put, counting what came every month.

'My mother had a word that described her state. "Ardhangini," she said. Entitled to adha, half. Ardhangini was a curse.

'She bought half loaves of bread for as long as I can remember. Half of her bed stayed neat and vacant. She lived half a life.

'There is a theory of optimism that I have come to understand. It was founded by the legion of adversity. These legions had good, honest people who worked hard during the day and then went to bed. Illness and inflation were periodic visitors, like the seasons, and they tested them – and us. Mother had a nose for illness; she could smell it coming. She would start bumping into doors and muttering about partitions and about men who went away to fight wars. My mother could smell inflation too. We would start living on smaller portions and we would spend more and more time outdoors, as if trouble could be shared. There was a maidan nearby where we children played among fowl, and dogs fetched our sticks and stones. The weather would sense the times and be kind.'

'You mentioned a theory of optimism,' said Bharti.

'Ah, yes,' said Maya. 'The theory of optimism says that illness and inflation will pass like the seasons. It makes no mention if good times will come.'

'What about neighbours?' asked Bharti.

'Salim uncle was our neighbour on the right. He gave us credit at his provisions store. He would peer at his ledger when Ma went to the shop and make yet another entry. He wrote a string of two-digit numbers, one below the other, in the manner of a Chinese scroll. Five columns fitted on a page and there was a total carried forward.

'On our left was a butcher. He was a burly bundle of fun. Nothing in this world could faze him: not the job of knife against neck, not the peeling of skin, or the stringing up of muscle flanks by thread. Every evening he would call out for me and tell me stories that had good beginnings and never ended.

'We were vegetarians, just us. On Bakrid day we shut our windows and drew the curtains. My mother would sit hunched in a chair in the mornings and grip the sides. I wanted to peek and did so once. I am not telling what I saw. I never peeked since but every year we sat and I could imagine the quiet goings-on.

'After an hour in the chair my mother would be on her feet and she would be stumbling into doors and muttering about the Partition thing and about men who went to war and I would wonder about the connection. My father certainly wasn't fighting and it was only goats that were dying. I realized later that in her mind there was a muddled metaphor. She kept returning to a pre-Partition Punjab, a place I would never see.

'We would emerge in the afternoon when the cooking smells arrived. We would hug the mohalla and take it to heart. We received coloured sweets and wishes for the upcoming festival. This was a civil society we lived in. This for my mother had been life before Partition happened. As before, we were the flies in the horseshoe. We were happy campers and native survivors.

'After spending years setting up a farm and reaping its slow dividend, my father went to seek work in the Gulf. He was reluctant to begin with. He returned once a year bearing gifts, but when we stopped keeping count, the frequency fell. He began to like it there. He earned a good sum and we paid the tax. He had a goal, a financial target. As a child I never knew. My mother must have asked him the question in her own way. How much money did we really need?

'My mother found Shiva. She became a bhakt. Framed pictures were strung up in the rooms and small sculptures that looked like a pestle and mortar were placed before them. She was a stringy lady, not the usual Punjaban who caught the spread in her thirties. She missed out on a few things in life and she found expression in her bhakti.

'She plied me with books of all kinds and they were mostly in English. There was a young boy in a small bookstore that lent books. It was called Parshuram Lending. I waded through abridged classics, and as I entered my teens, I found romantic fiction pressed between well-worn covers.

'On one of his visits my father brought me a camera. I held it in my hands. I turned it around. It had a black casing and a snout and it had numerous dials and knobs that needed to be turned or pressed. I put my eye to the viewfinder and the face of my mother came into view. She looked happy.

'My father noted my interest in photography. Every succeeding trip I got a new lens and they were bigger and bigger, and each snout when fitted threatened to topple the camera with its weight. One day at the bookshop I was shooting the small boy and the lens grew and almost reached his face.

'After Mother and Father came Susan Sontag, the third important person in my life. As a young girl I was impressionable and I was looking to be influenced every day. And a life like Sontag's and her book *On Photography* made a big impression.

'I took her instructions to heart: "Do stuff, be clenched, curious. Not waiting for inspiration's shove or society's kiss on your forehead. Pay attention. It's all about paying attention. Attention is vitality. It connects you with others. It makes you eager. Stay eager."

'I never consciously paid attention to anything. But I was eager, curious, wanting to do something noticeable and break out of our anonymity. In a few years I could see my parents die and disappear from the face of the Earth. All that would be left of them would be my memories. That was scary.

'If I were to walk at an anthropological dig and all I saw were terracotta bits, stone shards, and metal implements I would sit down and cry. I would want a name, just one name. Tell me about one person who lived at that time and let me know her story, her small victories, what made her laugh, and did she cry as she aged? I do not want to learn about faceless civilizations.

'I wanted to write a diary, a diary I could call "My Growing-Up Years". That is what everyone calls them. Some call them "The Best Years of My Life". I didn't mean to be different but the truth is these were my fugitive years. Fugitive is a nice word if you know the range of its meaning.

'What else?

'I must tell you about my time in Mumbai.

'My father had given me advice. He wasn't aware he was giving any. One long day in the hot summer he was lying on his charpai in the courtyard while dinner was cooking on a hearth. He said daily living can take up your life. In his words it sounded better.

'Beta, guzare ke khoj mein zindagi guzar gayi.

'It was simply said and I took it to heart. Amidst industry I needed to find meaning. In my life there would be romance, there would be pain, and there would be very little time to reflect. I needed a city like Mumbai to discover what life had in store for someone like me. Mumbai was a fugitive city that had been written about with passion. Where I came from was very different. Amritsar. A place I called Ambarsar, home till then.

'I was a Bachelor of Arts from the Ambarsar Arts College. We were provincial in some ways and contemporary in none. My arts teacher Mrs Bhatia had her own methods. She sent me to the streets and asked me to observe. After a day in the field, I was back.

'She asked, what did you see? Show me your drawings.

'I had none. I wasn't very good at drawing.

'So, what did you do the whole day?

'Ma'am, I went to a tailor, a restaurant, and the hostel. I took notes, I told her. I pulled out a quarter notepad, ignored her frown, and read.

'When you thread a needle, you curl your lip. When you see someone eat you smack your lips.

'What was it with lips?

'And when you tie your pyjama string your tongue hangs out because your kurta is under your chin.

'I shut the notepad and feared the worst.

'Lovely, said Mrs Bhatia.

'Lovely? Lovely was the name of my friend, her pet student. Mrs Bhatia said, Lovely, please show her your drawing book.

'Lovely shrugged and opened her neat sketchbook.

'I want you to copy what she has done, Mrs Bhatia told me.

'Copy? Ma'am, you want me to copy?

'My shrill indignation was wasted. I wasted two days of my life copying some Lovely drawings. Just as well, I thought to myself. On its own, my line didn't move; it carried the enormous weight of my confusion and did nothing to the page. I decided to chuck drawing and painting for a while and pursue art history.'

Bharti smiled, glad to be back on camera. 'Before Mumbai you went to Baroda and did an MA in art history.'

'Yes.'

'But you are an artist.'

'Yes.'

'What is your art about, if you will excuse the naivety of the question?'

'Just this once, I will answer it,' said Maya. 'The art is always about me.'

'Do you ever consider the viewer?'

'The viewer is second fiddle. You understand?'

Bharti flipped to the next sheet, hunting for a safe question. An image of a painting by Maya spilled out.

'I love this work even though it is quite grotesque,' said Bharti.

Nupur and Tara looked at each other, raising their eyebrows.

'I don't get the work, you know?'

'What don't you get?'

'What were you thinking?'

'Ouch,' said Tara.

Maya made an impatient sound. 'You think this is what I do in my studio? Think?'

'You don't?'

'I don't know,' said Maya. 'I am sorry. I don't know what to say.'

She wasn't happy with the question.

'Thinking is natural, isn't it?'

'Yes of course. Thinking makes us human. I forgot.'

'Look at this work. It poses all kinds of questions.'

'She is good,' mumbled Tara. 'I think she is pretending.'

'You want an answer from me?' asked Maya.

'You don't know?'

Maya shook her head.

'Then how do you expect the viewers to know?'

'I don't care,' said Maya.

'Did somebody buy it?'

Maya shifted in her seat. She was here against her will and she was in no mood to cooperate.

'Are we on camera all the time?'

'It is supposed to be a live interview,' said Bharti.

'Have a drink, Bharti,' said Maya. 'It's on me.'

A waiter arrived and Maya ran her finger down the cocktail list. 'This is awful,' she said. 'What kind of names are these? Sex on the Beach. Penicillin. Between the Sheets. Do you have gin and tonic?' They waited for the drinks to arrive.

'What have you read about me?' asked Maya. 'Have you done your homework?'

'As I said, you started as an art historian. You weren't very good at it because you lacked the scholarly approach. You decided to revisit drawing and painting and found your niche. You have done well.'

'That's it?'

Bharti was just warming up. 'You got married, had a daughter, and then you broke up for no reason. Since then, you have dated a series of men and never had a serious relationship. You act like you are tough but it is an act. There are rumours you have been in and out of rehab for drug dependencies.'

Maya closed her eyes for a while and said nothing.

'You are a rebel, Maya,' said Bharti. 'There is a group you belong to that looks at rebellion as a reason to exist. You have done a work after Marquis de Sade and this is as close to your heart as any work will get. For in bondage and play, blood and games lie your release and fulfilment.'

Maya downed her drink. 'Who wrote your fucking notes?'

'Me.'

'Try this other gin,' said Maya. 'Bombay Sapphire. That is a proper drink.' She gestured to the waiter.

They drank; the next ones arrived. They went down as well.

'Wait for the bill,' said Nupur.

'You will shortly get your money's worth,' said Tara.

'The morning after,' said Maya, lisping slightly. 'I never regret the morning after. It is true I am interested in Marquis de Sade: in whips, masks, corsets, the lair, in animal spirit, and the shriek. The shriek as a form of human expression fascinates me. The pulsating fear, the rush of blood, and your hair on end. We die at that moment of fear.'

She paused. 'Am I making sense?'

'A little,' said Bharti.

They looked at each other and smiled.

'I was supposed to find the real you,' said Bharti. 'That was my assignment. Why do you hide?'

Maya smiled. 'I don't hide,' she said. 'Ask the cops.'

She was truly high. She sent the barman off for a missing ingredient and in a moment that would remain etched in television history she drew a line of coke on the counter, bent over it, and snorted. Her face came up and her eyes shone. She dusted the counter hurriedly.

'Can we edit this?' whispered Nupur, dismayed by what she had seen.

'Yes, we can,' said Tara.

Maya puffed out her cheeks and held up her right hand to the light. She frowned at the sight of tremors. She was bright, glowing, as if a bulb had lit inside her.

They ploughed their way through another round. The liquid felt dense to Maya; every sip was laboured and she was slurring, speaking with her tongue on the roof of her mouth.

'Have you read Walt Whitman?'

Bharti nodded vigorously. 'Listen, can I have a toke?'

'Ha ha, of course, my dear. Here, easy, easy.'

'The blood in my veins,' said Bharti, leaning back, blowing a plume of smoke. Her head was bursting.

'One hour to madness and joy,' said Maya softly, taking a puff.

'O furious! O confine me not!' shouted Bharti, holding her temples.

'What is this that frees me so in storms?' said Maya, the last puff taking her into the clouds.

'What do my shouts amid raging winds mean?' asked Bharti.

Maya laughed. There was a momentary pause. 'Now you can ask me about art,' she said.

'Art is so banal sometimes,' said Bharti.

'Now you are talking!' said Maya.

'Who shall we blame?' said Bharti. She was holding on to the bar counter for dear life. Maya's jaw rested on her glass.

'Say something I can understand,' said Bharti.

Maya smiled. 'What can I say that is new, that is different? Art, poor thing. Lost in a porn-filled world.'

'Thanks,' said Bharti, barely sitting up, too dizzy by now to even shake her head. 'I can't watch porn any more. Who wants to see over-sized equipment and such good faking?'

Around this time the police arrived. Somebody it seems had tipped them off about bar-girl activity. The posse rounded up everybody, asking for identification, and asked the barman to produce the licence. Maya and Bharti were trying hard to stay on their feet. The television crew stood around with their footage, hoping it wouldn't be confiscated.

Nupur spoke to them. 'This is a television set. We were shooting an episode.'

The man in charge looked at the women around him. He was apologetic. 'Sorry,' he said. 'We were told this was an illegal dance bar.'

The KK Episode

Nupur and Tara met Krishna Kumar after the tree incident. They sat on round chairs in an Irani café, had beer, bun maska, and keema with egg, and went through his portfolio, a visual record of his performances.

'You are like a boy who never grew up,' said Nupur.

'On the contrary,' said KK.

'You were born grown-up?'

'Yes, with a moustache and well-combed hair.'

'And your nice accent as well?' said Tara. 'Is it authentic?'

'Yes. I am mimicking myself,' said KK.

'We would like to film you talking about your childhood,' said Nupur, 'and where you grew up.'

'Why? Actually, why not?'

'It is for *The Prize*,' said Nupur. 'When can we do it?'

A week later they filmed him.

It was a stilted episode. Krishna Kumar the performance artist was for some reason self-conscious.

'Face the sea.'

'In Kerala, sea means backwater.' It looked like the sea.

The camera panned the countryside, then moved along on the back of an SUV into the streets.

The SUV paused in a village setting. It was evening; the light was fading. They shot a set at the back of a traditional dwelling where an old lady was seated; her hair was loose and her earlobes hung an inch.

'My mother,' said KK. She turned towards them. 'Look at her. What do you see?'

'Kamala Das,' said Tara.

'She is no poet. She is an eternal optimist.'

'Why do you say that?'

'She never tires of telling me that there is a day in her life waiting to happen.' KK shrugged, his shoulders sloped. 'What day and what life? As far as I can see, every day of her life is the same.'

KK's mother waved a fan to stir the air. The family dog was curled by the door and he emitted a low growl that announced the patriarch's arrival. The old man was unsteady after his evening shot of country liquor.

'Every day in my father's life too looks the same. Yet my mother has this sunny view that the best is lurking somewhere nearby and needs just a gust of wind to come her way.'

'Tell us more about her.'

'She is simple, she is complicated. From close up she looks old, older than her age, which she actually doesn't know. But she knows so many people who are now dead. She is fond of cooking and cursing. She curses while she cooks; she smiles when I am eating. I eat well, she says, but not enough. We sit on the floor; our utensils are the ones we cook in. Bugs flit about, some fall into the thoran. My mother notices and says nothing, does nothing. I am lazy too. I continue to eat as if nothing happened.'

'And your father?'

'My father has presence, not in a nice way: he comes into a room and the air curdles. It seems darker when he is there, and quieter. He hardly speaks. He eats quietly without looking up, doesn't say a thing, good or bad, and burps at the end of his meal. He sits with legs folded below him and picks his teeth. Look at him, his stringy grey hair, the bony shoulders, and his recessed eyes. He has led a common life. You can't blame him for that. But my mother, she begs a question.'

'Which is?'

'Should I admire a woman who has spent as much time with him as my mother?'

'You can't choose your parents. Is that a cliché?'

'I am caught between my father and my mother, between other useless things, like tradition, customs, religion, ritual, and all our dance and drama. There are so many stories in my head and they all speak; sometimes they peck at my brain.'

He knocked his head with his knuckles. The others flinched at the sound.

'Stories,' he repeated. 'They are meant to fritter away by day's end and die. They don't. I pick up the pieces and enact things. As a child, as a teenager, and as a young man I have had an enduring passion. I wish to perform; I want to transform the space I see, the time I spend, and the people I meet.' He looked for some reaction. 'That is my life, quite useless you know, sometimes.'

They shot some scenes inside his college. They shot Girish speaking about his friend.

'KK has wrestled with a few things all his life. Right since his childhood he was at loggerheads with rules and authority. He hated these figureheads who could toss him out of class. He couldn't belong to anything for very long. Some people aren't meant to be in college yet that is the place they find themselves. College becomes a post-adolescent holding area where your career chooses you. Art chose KK; it promised him an anarchic existence.

'Once he got branded as an artist, so much became acceptable. A permanent stubble, shoulder-length hair, well-worn jeans, T-shirts that said clever things, poor eating habits, cheap cigarettes, and endless black tea were signs that he had donned the mantle. He learned how to challenge authority, fray their nerve ends, instil in them the feeling that he wasn't always in control of himself, and that made them wary.

'He did his BFA in Trivandrum at a time when the state of Kerala was in ferment. The country was wrestling with the political misdeeds of the emerging political class. It doesn't take much for a Malayali to take up cudgels and KK was in the company of creative rebels. They could take down anything. No system and no dispensation could satisfy them.

'He arrived in Baroda for an MFA with a history sheet of creative misdemeanour. It was a badge that made him proud and gave him meaning. He arrived after trawling the West Coast. He took his time, touching upon places like Mangalore, Ganpatipule, and Goa, places of pilgrimage for the young. He lived on coastal curry and fine spirit, locally brewed. He ate red meat that was tenderized by vinegar and Diet Coke. And he smoked some weed and some tobacco, and felt forever young.

'He returned after his MFA and spent two years in Kerala without a job, without income. There was acid from the family that ate into him, questions from those who paid his bills. People thought he was idle; he did not agree. All this while he was sleeping and dreaming up incidents. Even the nights were places for narrations; episodes awakened him and illuminated nothing. Things needed to happen for KK. He needed to prod and push the idle and subvert the still. He needed to disturb those caught engaging in reality. For him a landscape was a jigsaw that needed to be disassembled for it to yield its essential truth.'

'And in the end?'

'Finally, he did what Malayalis do. His compass took him to Mumbai. It is halfway to the Gulf.'

They visited his studio apartment in Mumbai, carrying their cameras.

'Come in, come in, please.'

They entered with some difficulty.

'This place looks like it has seen only bachelors,' he said. 'Doesn't it?'

Clothes were strewn on the sofa. The sofa was at an odd angle in relation to the wall. A painting hung on a visible nail and needed to be straightened.

'But before me, there was a young couple that stayed here and they fought bitterly and ended up separating. When they left, they wrote ugly things on the wall about each other. The woman used a knife and carved words into the plaster. When I came to inspect the place, all of it was still there. It was like an art installation, really. My landlord was quite upset and he hired a mason to clean up the writing. I wish he had let it remain.'

'Shall we sit?'

'Of course. Sorry.'

KK picked up the clothes, bundled them up, and took them into his bedroom. He returned quickly and patted down the sofa.

'Would you like something to drink? Juice? Let me check what I have.'

He opened the fridge and a couple of packets fell out.

'Rice batter,' he said, and laughed.

Nupur and Tara sat on the sofa a little gingerly and drank orange juice. KK showed them some photographs.

'Stills are not an elegant way to capture performance art,' he said. 'But my gallery insists on producing them. They even try to sell them.'

'Do you travel a lot? I guess you must be.'

'I live out of a suitcase,' he said in a matter-of-fact tone. He looked at a corner where three suitcases were stacked on top of each other. 'I wear white shirts and dhotis so laundry is a problem. They get dirty so easily.'

'Your last performance was interesting,' said Nupur. 'Let me try and describe it. You went back to your old school and attended class for a month. It was geography class, I believe. And the tenth standard.'

'Yes,' said KK, running a hand through his luxuriant hair. 'It was awkward in the beginning but everybody got used to it. I made new friends and the teacher liked me in the end. In a sense, at the end of one month, I was no longer visible.'

'I believe you asked a lot of questions?'

'Yes, I did. I was not trying to act smart. I honestly did not know so much.'

'So, what was the point of this so-called performance?'

He scratched his head. 'I am not supposed to explain,' he said. 'The performance was for the children in the class.'

'I am so sorry, I shouldn't have asked,' said Tara.

'It's alright. It is a natural question for performance art. For all art, actually.'

They laughed.

'I spent one month in an enclosure in a zoo,' said KK. 'Did you hear about that?'

Tara had read about it. She wondered how the authorities had allowed it. People stood and stared at him, looked around the grassy enclosure, and at the tree in the middle, hoping to see some animals. Many of them started talking to him; some called him names, and others took photographs. He did nothing in particular and at no point did he look at them or respond to their urgings. He grew a beard, did not bathe, ate only raw fruits and vegetables, and his clothes shredded from his attempts at climbing the tree. After a few days, he looked a sight, a genuine curiosity worthy of an enclosure in the zoo. He began to draw large crowds.

'Your work steers clear of so many things. There are so many distractions for artists: politics, religion, sex, death, lust, geometry—'

'I remember you now,' interjected KK. 'You unfriended me on social media. Right?'

Tara nodded. 'I was about to say what I do not like about you.'

'You mean that like the others you are also turned off by my—'

'Aggressive behaviour online.'

'And yet you are here.'

'It is a job. You remind me of somebody.'

Krishna Kumar looked puzzled. 'Do I know him?'

'Where were you that day, that evening, Mr Krishna Kumar, when my mother overdosed on pills?'

'I was nearby. I was in a restaurant. You know Mr Pandey, the policeman?'

Tara nodded again.

'Mr Pandey asked me that question in that same tone. I told him I had no alibi.'

'That's not what I meant,' said Tara.

He smiled, looking rueful. 'Of course,' he said.

'My mother says you are a true performance artist.'

'Bless her,' he said. He was seated on the floor and Tara was on a cushion. He raised himself slightly and remained expressionless. 'Artists like your mother and me are performers. There isn't much that separates our life and art.'

'I see,' said Tara.

'We are not into drugs for recreation,' he said.

'Hmmm,' said Tara.

'But it has become a trap for Maya. She keeps increasing her dosage. I shouldn't be telling you but she is quite deliberate. I have a record.'

'You have a record?'

'Yes, a daily record,' he said. 'I could give it to you but don't share it.'

'What will I do with it?' said Tara.

There was one last recording in his apartment.

'Tell us about yourself, in no particular order. We will edit later.'

'There are many clichés when it comes to Kerala and Malayalis. The artist from Kerala is another cliché. We are omnipresent in the art world, just like Che Guevara is in God's own country. Che did not know how big he is here. Men here like to be macho and imagine revolution.'

'Your personal life. I sifted through public domains and there is very little on your personal life.'

'I am a small-town person. The whole of Kerala is a small town, between a village and city. I am not a city person by upbringing. I am not rural either. If you know Kerala well enough you will understand there is no urban–rural divide there.'

'Middle class?'

'I hate the middle. It is defeating. We are relentlessly distinct in every little thing. Mallus can be cussed. By just being themselves. We don't care too much what you think of us because we are very sure that when you visit Kerala, it will win you over.'

'Your mother. Tell us more about her.'

'My mother came from Tamil Nadu, from a place called Palghat. Every damn Friday her daily life was an offering at the ritual altar. She went in for an elaborate head bath after marinating her whole body with turmeric. This was native hair removal and it left a yellow stain. I watched her preparing herself for her husband. In turn, the least he could have done was shave, freshen up, and wear a decent dhoti.'

'Was she weak?'

'No, I never thought of her as weak. Maybe when she was young, in the first flush of youth as they say. Later, as time passed the equation changed. My father became less of a force, a little defeated by what he foresaw, I think. You know, the realization that dawns one day that not much is going to happen in this life. And all he could see in the eyes of his near and dear were our expectations.'

'And in old age?'

'In old age, she is his pension. She has rescued him from an early demise. She is strong that way. There is no love left but she is loyal to him like she is to everything in the house she has spent her life in. I dread the ending. When his end comes the house will be hers and with my father gone, she will be left with the furniture.'

'Does she enjoy her last years?'

'Yes. Like the telecom companies promise, she has her postpaid nirvana, all alone, a doorstep, a backyard, some hens, cows, and dogs. She meets me when I come. No welcome, just a simple acceptance. We sit and I talk and she occasionally listens.'

'And this is your family life?'

'Yes. And I carry this with me wherever I go. A small island that I realize I have become.'

'It sounds empty and lonely, Krishna Kumar.'

'Strangely, it is not. I feel protected by this life, this intimate cocoon that is mine and mine alone, and I can't share it. The associations are so beautiful and they spring up at me. It is my particular place, with its sounds, its flavours.' He looked into the camera. 'I love Kerala not because it is God's country,' he said. 'I am not a tourist. I love my state for its dogged habits, its unjustifiable customs.'

The Praveena Episode: The MFA Girl Gang

Praveena held up her latest creation. It fluttered. 'Step aside, Abba,' it said. It had been embroidered on a white square cloth.

'That's it?' asked Nupur.

'Yes,' she said. 'It sounds like a slogan, doesn't it?'

Would the earlier generation step aside? Would that be the essence of this wild-card artist? Nupur was looking for conflict. She could sniff something building up. They worked hard, and after week-long parleys in an Irani café on Cadell Road, they had some pointers.

'Are you sure you want to do this?' said Nupur.

It was daring, the whole idea. What would happen to this young lady? She was slim, graceful, and so reckless. Where did that streak come from?

'My father will kill me,' said Praveena. 'It is only a matter of time.'

Nupur shook her head. She had to give this more thought.

'Are you still a virgin?' she asked. 'Sorry, please excuse me, I shouldn't have asked.'

'Does it matter?' said Praveena.

'It doesn't,' said Nupur. Fuck, she thought, I sounded so medieval. 'So shall we go ahead?'

Praveena nodded and started speaking into the camera.

The Society had three members, just three. We were MFA students in our final year, each seeking a way out of this question that popped out of every parking lot, every back seat, every garden bush, and every cinema corner seat.

Our meetings discussed progress. Usually, we laughed a lot. Besides me there was Sukanya and Kalki. We saw ourselves as not traditionally good-looking. The rest of the MFA girl gang were better looking. We had thin lips and short hair; one of us even wore glasses. Lipstick was beneath us. We could not wear a saree nor a salwar kameez even though our families packed them in our bags. As kids we had all worn braces.

Of the three of us, Sukanya was the sexy one. She was dusky and had dark eyes that she highlighted. She would wear kurtis all the time. It had a careless front that flapped and there was a promising curve. But she had a deep voice and a loud laugh. And she ate heartily. Boys watched her eat more than them, laugh louder than them, and when she spoke they sounded like pipsqueaks. The closest anyone came to hitting on her was when the shy Aakash kept staring at her for a whole week. Aakash made no move and so that was that. Sukanya wanted a big, bad boy who would brook no opposition. The first guy who came on strong would get her cherry. Sometimes I wished I was that guy.

Kalki was frail and given to sneezing. She had an aroma about her, the aroma of Vicks VapoRub, of eucalyptus oil, and other medical colognes. She was the one with glasses and in her right hand there invariably would be a handkerchief that drooped as the day progressed. Kalki was flat-chested; there were no props in her armoury. She was ignored till it hurt her enough to try something new. She returned after a vacation with a makeover from Mumbai. Sukanya and I stood in the station and blinked. She had green eyeshadow, red-rimmed glasses, and a blue scarf wrapped around her neck. She looked stunning. And then in the rickshaw she sneezed and sneezed till she had to remove her spectacles, hide her face in her scarf, and watch her eyeliner run.

We were tragedy queens with stories to tell. I was the bold one who made the moves on the boys. I had trouble finishing. Round the bend I sprinted but down the straight I was a lame duck. By then I had seen too much, heard too much, and spoken too much as well. Whenever I said something, it was misunderstood. What was wrong in telling your boyfriend as you saw it?

'Your nose hair is showing. I could trim it. It is easy. Just a minute, where are you going?'

Or:

'What do you think you are doing? No, no, I don't mind but you should see what others think of your eating habits. What? Nothing wrong? Maybe I heard somebody else chomping.'

Or:

'Why do you have to pull out what is stuck in your teeth with your fingers? No, no, I am not ultra-sensitive. Forget I said it. Are those actually gaps in your teeth?'

And:

'Yes, I can smell honest sweat. How was your game? You won? Terrific. Sure, we will go to the after-party. Like this? You are not having a bath? No, just asking.'

Once a month the Society discussed the Close Encounters. They were few and far, and in between were hot musings that we felt would reflect in our art. We came from the Narrative School after all and this was dinned into our pretty heads. We were from a section of MS University, Baroda, where you painted stories, or else. And stories come from experience so we felt our escapades would give us the meat. Ha ha, how I wish.

Sukanya was the breathless one and a great one for description. Whatever she narrated went to our heads. She had this thing for dreams where a billowing ghost, a Bhoothnath, hounded her, asking for her licence and her virginity. In real life she pursued this gangling boy called 'Attar' Ahmad. Ahmad's family was in the perfume business and he applied his family franchise on himself. Most times he smelled of earth after the first rain. Petrichor. After a month-long dalliance, she was frustrated by his lack of finesse.

'Why do men spend half their life thinking about sex when they spend 0.1 per cent of their life doing it?'

The Age of Kalki, or the beginning of the end of our Society: a dark moment whose history I will now narrate. The Society refused to believe that sex was preordained, that we should just wait. Nothing is preordained about sex, said Kalki, other than imagination and chaos. Our Kalki resided in between these two states. She was forever dreaming and frittering her life away. She said sex needed grandeur, some theatre, when all it called for was some grammar.

She was an elf of a girl, restless one moment and fast asleep the next, folded up in the midst of a book. She evaded all questions on where she came from, who her parents were, and who had brought her up. According to Sukanya she was hiding a mother in Delhi. Kalki was my best friend – only because she came up to me before Sukanya did.

Semesters changed with the seasons, mood swings followed. The first semester was hot and dusty, and the second semester brought a dry chill. No matter; Kalki was always an affected person. She was an all-weather sneeze. We advised her to marry a quack who would cook up some homemade remedies and apply them on her forehead, like they did in Hindi films. In normal circumstances she would have ended up in a small town that had only three train services every day. But the girl had ambition, and she was tenacious. If nothing else, she would leave the world in shreds.

One day in Baroda her life began.

She met a yoga teacher who gave her a genie bottle that had a long snout. It was filled with water and as she bent forward it went through one nostril. The water travelled, irrigating the canals; it was meant to flow out from the other nostril. In her case there were blockages; there were dams and mucous trenches. She coughed, she spat, and she sneezed, and the water came out in dribs and drabs. She persisted and the snout went into the other nostril. After the bottle was empty, she looked up and lo and bloody behold, there was clarity. She did not sneeze for a week. That was amazing.

Gone was her shyness, her listlessness, and her dreamy gaze. This was a new Kalki, alive, clear-headed, confident, and with a new vocabulary. Her outfits changed and her style quotient leapt. The boys looked at her anew and liked what they saw. All she needed now was grammar.

The Baroda of those days had a municipality that was doing a poor job. The roads and lanes were in a bad way. There was no order or planning, and excessive construction had brought with it some peculiar problems. After a hot summer in Baroda heavy rains followed. On the third day of such rains the Vishwamitri river began to rise. The water found no place to flow and so it collected on the roads, in the maidans, and inside people's homes. People gathered on terraces and watched their cars float. After a few more days of rain the army was called in to help. They came in helicopters and dropped food packets. They came in boats and caught crocodiles. And one of the army men broke Kalki's heart.

Kalki met an army captain who was part of the search-and-rescue effort. The young man strapped her to a winch and held her as they were lifted into a chopper. Earlier Kalki had waved her blue scarf to attract attention. He took it with him as a token. Two days later he swung by in a jeep and she took a good look at this man who had held her close. He was a strange fellow.

Captain Rastogi was selfless in rescue. But he was unpredictable. Even his colleagues kept their distance. For reasons best known to them women found him irresistible. But he had eyes only for Kalki and he seemed overly attentive. He stayed back after the ops were over. In the space of a week Kalki was a wreck.

There are three types of danger that you confront: when you know what awaits you (a snake under the bed), when you know something awaits you (a rustling sound), and the third is when you don't know why your hair is standing on end. Captain Rastogi was the third, an unknown, dangerous something. The way he held her, the way he pressed himself against her, the way he held her hands behind her back, and the way he looked into her eyes. Things had reached a stage where she wanted a way in, despite herself. The handsome young man looked good on her arm, had a way with her that spoke of experience. The way he gathered her up, the deceptive lightness of touch, and the expert arousal of her nerve ends that she never knew existed – she wished she could travel the distance. Arousal competed with a nameless fear.

Kalki disappeared for a week with this captain. Nobody knew where they went or what transpired. She returned after a week and knocked on my door. She looked different. I must confess she did confide in me.

The Society met one last time. We shared a bottle of rum, and we shed a few tears. We promised to meet again after ten years.

The camera zoomed in on Praveena's face. She looked into the lens long enough and she sneezed.

The lens moved to Nupur. 'Turn it off,' she said. 'Shukla ji, could you give us a moment?' She waited till he left, then sat next to Praveena.

'You haven't answered my question, Praveena.'

'You haven't asked,' said Praveena, sneezing again for some reason.

'Does Kalki exist?'

Praveena looked vulnerable. 'Yes, she does.'

Nobody said anything for a while.

'What do you want from me?' said Praveena. 'You want a sound bite?'

'A simple acknowledgement, just for me.'

Praveena disappeared for a month after the episode was aired. She did not answer calls. Nupur read newspaper reports that spoke of a protest in Praveena's community. They came at her and the show. It was labelled 'media exploitation'.

Finally, when she could not bear the silence any longer, Nupur visited Mahim and knocked on Praveena's door. A stone-faced Suleiman greeted her. She was ushered into an anteroom. Praveena rushed in, looking none the worse. They hugged each other.

They spoke for a while and ate some keema samosas and drank some sweet milky tea. As she was about to leave Nupur asked, 'Are you working on something?'

Praveena's face clouded over. 'Yes,' she said.

'Can I see it?' said Nupur. 'Please?'

She waited and Praveena brought something. 'I have been doing this for the last month,' she said. 'I have made twenty of them.'

Embroidered on white cloth were four words in uneven handwriting: 'Abba set me right.'

Nupur felt as if someone had kicked her in her stomach.

The Brown Sahib Episode: Artist Proof

Nupur and Tara went to the Jaipur Literary Festival. It was January. Oprah came that year but they didn't manage to see her.

They didn't see Salman Rushdie either. He threatened to show up in Jaipur like his Gibreel Farishta and Saladin Chamcha, falling from the sky 'like titbits of tobacco from a broken old cigar'. But then lots of other people threatened to show up as well and protest. After the ban on his book *The Satanic Verses*, India had donned the mantle of 'protest nation', and amongst the powers that be in the government, Rushdie was persona non grata.

Inside the festival the hullabaloo over 'will he, or won't he' had little impact. Some authors did read aloud from the banned book and were shepherded away, never to be seen again.

From Jaipur the pair went to the India Art Fair in Delhi. Till the previous year the art show was held in Pragati Maidan, essentially a site for trade fairs that wasn't suited for art because pigeons came in through the skylights, flew about in the cavernous space, and, on spotting standing sculptures, did what came naturally: they shat on them. The sculptures were misshapen and nude, and the proportions were wrong. The pigeons were agnostic; they still shat on them.

That year the India Art Fair was held in a sports field in Okhla. The large tract of land was levelled, flooring was simulated using plywood, and air-conditioned tents were stretched atop. As you walked in, your step was springy, the air was cool, and the flooring just about held.

Outside the main arena was another enclosure where the real gladiators sparred. This was the panel discussion arena where words were used by critics and curators to bludgeon stray visitors who had paid for entrance and wanted to experience everything. The flooring in this space was made of lighter ply, had more give, and every step made a sound that resembled a human emission.

It was a short journey from the Jaipur lit fest to the Delhi art fair. The similarities were many. There were pitched tents in both locations and the public arrived in numbers at these annual events: hungry seekers, selfie hunters, excursion parties from schools and colleges, gawkers, and the amateur practitioners who came to see and hear, deride the famous, and, in the case of the art fair, ridicule the high prices. Unlike Jaipur, where you could spend the whole day seated comfortably in the various enclosures at Diggi Palace, in the art fair you had to keep moving from artwork to artwork, booth to booth, and hall to hall till you emerged into the cold outside after an hour or so. The art was displayed in three tents, and while collectors were shepherded by gallery assistants and dealers, the public had to fend for themselves.

There were no chairs. The only proper seating available was in the smaller tent where panel discussions were held. The chairs here were taken up by a loyal coterie of scholars, global curators, and museum directors who came in early and sat respectfully. Stragglers who came in for some much-needed rest from all the roaming were stung into leaving by the terminology used in the discussions and the stares of those who could understand it.

Nupur and Tara were in the small tent, seated. Nupur's team was filming. Brown and Sahib were on the podium along with two important local curators and the owner of a private museum who had funded the duo for a project.

'Let's sit near the entrance,' Tara had said.

'You mean exit?'

Tara scoured the programme sheet; the topics were daunting. The current topic was 'Political Art'.

'That is short form for victims and villains,' said someone in front.

'Who is the victim this year?' said Nupur.

'Art itself.'

'Who are they blaming?'

'The private galleries and the auction houses. They are the villains.'

'And the saviours are these critics and curators?'

They looked around. 'Who are the two curators on the podium?'

One was a smooth-cheeked, boyish, earnest lad, and the other was a bearded, middle-aged grizzly with jowls. Both wore specs, shawls, and a slight frown to denote the required pre-seminar intensity.

The discussion began with a poser.

'Imagine an art that is temporary and disjointed,' said Sahiba.

The mike promptly acted up and screeched.

'Imagine art not as a car but as a head-on collision.'

'What?' mumbled Nupur. She looked towards Tara for help. 'Is that a good line?'

'India has strong potential for breakaway art because of its vibrant politics,' said Brown. 'It has a complicated caste system, an active left that has ruled two states, and a right-wing Hindutva movement that is pitting itself against intellectuals and secular thinkers who have written the country's history.'

'Thus far most of India has been excluded from art,' said Sahib.

'Is that a good line?' whispered Nupur. She needed a tagline like a dog needed a bone.

'I am trying to rectify that,' said the museum owner.

'Left to the market economy, art has become a commodity; it has lost its edge, and become repetitive,' said one of the curators.

'Art has been poorly served,' said the other curator.

'That's a good line,' Nupur muttered. She wrote it down.

'We need a collective resistance,' said the bearded curator, leaning back. He looked quite capable of orchestrating one, preferably a sit-in.

'Censorship is a form of political art,' said Brown. 'Censorship rewrites our cultural output. It is invasive.'

'If artists do not engage in political art, the government writ on culture will prevail,' said Sahiba. 'And we will all be poorer.'

'CAMP, the Indian artist collective, made art from the political sting called the Radia tapes,' said the museum owner. 'We need more such initiatives.'

There was a collective pause at this stage, and the duo shifted gears. The tone was now personal.

'Our art is not optical. It's political,' Sahiba proclaimed.

So, one excluded the other?

'But we don't do street art. We don't do posters, or graffiti, or videos. We don't write blogs and we feel Facebook and Twitter lack teeth.'

Brown was nodding vigorously at the crescendo of don'ts. 'We have broken away from video and moved onto live feeds,' he said.

'From blogs into online petitions,' said Sahiba.

'From likes and shares into crowdsourced content,' said Brown, completing the chorus.

By now Tara was gripping the sides of her chair, trying to hold onto this cutesy vision she had of a painting on a wall and a sculpture on the floor. Her idea of art was slipping away into the dark reaches of pre-modern history.

'We are the new curators of art,' said Sahiba. 'Not these critics.'

'We create audiences, not art objects,' said Brown.

By then he had acquired a halo in Tara's eyes. He had bad teeth, she noticed. When he grinned, he looked like a villain in a Bond movie who was about to bombard the world with a secret weapon.

Brown Sahib drew them into a web of connected devices that were blown up on four large screens. Things were happening as they were speaking. A dynamic listing of black money accounts across the world, changes in surface temperature in the Arctic, oil price movements, the movements of Edward Snowden, extracts from the writings of Arundhati Roy, and the completed biography of Subhas Chandra Bose flashed across the screens. As did citizen reports on things unreported by media; this included videos, photographs, and other material.

Was this the real underground?

'Our user base is connected with handheld devices, and content is being streamed 24/7.'

Brown Sahib did something and the audience in the tent could see themselves reacting.

'What the fuck just happened?' said someone.

'Artist proof,' said Brown. 'Something just happened that would have gone unreported, for all time to come. This is the future of art: a sustained campaign, an intervention, and sometimes just an incendiary phrase.'

Tara could feel the weight of collective breath. Her thighs trembled.

'The insidious power of new media,' whispered Nupur. 'What potential!'

Later, Nupur placed a mike before the young curator and asked a question. The young man brushed his wavy hair from his face.

'For a while artists had ceded the stage to us,' he said. 'Now they are trying to oust us by learning our ways and gaining mindshare. Art is a power game where we have to compete for public participation.'

'Isn't he cute?' said Nupur.

The handheld camera kept rolling as they entered the high-speed lift. The Mitsubishi cubicle rose smoothly and rapidly. Nupur's ears contracted as they reached the twentieth floor.

'We wanted to buy an apartment where the floor rise charges were 20 per cent of the total cost. We had to be on the twentieth floor or above.'

They had to use a swipe card at the glass door that was half an inch thick. They entered to the sound of a hiss and a couple of beeps. Nupur could feel security cameras train themselves on the nape of her neck.

'Only glass, no bricks,' said Brown.

'We wanted Minimal,' said Sahiba. 'We love Extreme.'

'We had to get a Distanced Feel. The sense of being Cut Off.'

'Free from the Earth. A living space where Ideas could take Wing.'

The view was breathtaking, and as was usual in Mumbai, the sea showed up.

'From here we look down. We call this the Perch.'

From the Perch, people looked like ants, cars were little toys. Everything seemed more civilized.

'You should come here at night. In the dark the lights flash; you can see flights stacked, descending slowly into Santa Cruz.'

Tara panned the sleek apartment, dwelling on the imported shelves and fixtures, the profusion of electronic devices that were blinking. Nupur looked at the bank of buzzing equipment and raised an eyebrow.

'Revolution never sleeps,' said Brown.

'You know what,' said Nupur, 'I attended your session, I read your documents, and trust me, that was heavy going. I waded through your biodata, all twenty pages of it, and let me tell you, it sounds pretentious and smug. I also sat through your early art that was video, your later performance pieces, long and dense as they were. And I have to ask you – and we are on camera, mind you.'

'Yes?' said Sahib.

'What are you made of? How do you practise a flagrant mockery of the market and yet live like this?'

'You suspect something?' asked Brown, sounding tart. 'If you are—'

'I don't know,' said Nupur. 'Maybe I do. That's the honest truth.'

Brown and Sahiba looked at each other. 'At least you are honest,' said one of them.

'And hard-working, don't forget. Listen, you don't have to answer my questions.'

'No, no, we will. We have to. Who will do this? Sahiba, how do we make a living?'

'How have we lived?' echoed Sahiba.

'Universal grants. Project grants. And the Genius grant that is a large amount, in dollars. It was embarrassing but we were one among fifty others; each was called genius.'

Tara butted in. 'I spoke about you to Anjana. You must know her, everybody does. She said that among other things you are good at writing CVs and making applications. If you need a place to stay for a month you apply for a residency. If you need to fund your work you go to a bank with a big art collection put together by someone you know. Or you go to a museum with a proposal.'

'Everybody works in this manner,' said Brown. 'This is Modus Operandi 101.'

'What else did Anjana say?' asked Sahiba.

Tara should have kept her mouth shut but she was happy enough revealing Anjana's private opinions.

'She said you dress well and you travel well. You look like global citizens. You are sociable when it matters, and relentlessly friendly with those who matter.'

'I think you should also know that she gave us a single-sentence summary of your work, and it is not dismissive,' said Nupur. She read it out from her phone.

'The use of technology in innovative ways in a connected world to trigger social upheaval ostensibly for society's well-being.'

'Nice,' said Brown. 'Ideas move us ahead. Every project encapsulates an idea. Our first paper was "An Oral History of Angst". It was an oral history with music notations. We had two performers who played the cello for an hour in a manner that really moved people. We publish a paper on every project. We invent terms. Every term we invent is a stepping stone that moves us into a smaller circle. You arrive in this business when you are among the very few on what we call the same plane. We understand each other through a cryptic code of annotated references. After ten years of relentless pursuit, we have arrived amongst the rarest of the rare, part of an aesthetic cult formed by exclusionary forces. You know all other art forms are the has-beens. What you are seeing in the auction rooms and galleries are capitalist leftovers. Painting, sculpture, and all such objects now have a shelf life. The power belongs now to the idea itself.'

'Is there a point to all this? That is, is it connected to the real world? To this country, for God's sake?'

'Yes, there is. Of course, there is. We can share it with you when the time comes.'

'And till then? Are we all supposed to believe you? Why?'

'We can't tell you too much. Only this much. All the political art you have seen so far is kindergarten stuff. I mean, what does it achieve? Merely highlighting the plight of people? Some academic excitement and self-serving accreditation? Our political art is what shakes society, attacks its very roots, warning us of what is possible

– purely because it is possible. Call us nutjobs because that is what we are trying to be and yet so close to reality that it frightens even us. It is a bad time to be blissful.

'There is a loose thread that runs through every society. The fabric forms when warp and weft tighten themselves into cloth but there is always that one thread that is broken. And we hold this thread. It is a virtual thread that runs deep, that is interconnected, that can be triggered, and it can cause social upheavals.'

'Are you trying to scare us?'

'Fear is so outdated. We believe in hate, the only truly resilient social binder. And paranoia. Paranoia is so useful and it is so easy to arouse tribes using this and then plant fear for each other.'

'What is your goal? Why would you?'

'It is a fair warning. A world so connected is a dangerous one; it is ripe now for collapse, for the next extinction. There is no such thing now as highly unlikely. You need to spend time on research like we do. We studied social disasters like fascism and we tried to project its next manifestation. Then we realized we could not say how and when but it was clear it was imminent. We hold our future hostage; it is in our hands. We have the power and yet we are powerless. Governments cannot change it. Nation states will not. So, who will? It is better then to trigger something ourselves, something big that frightens us all once again.'

'You sound pretty juiced up. You could be arrested.'

'That would only accentuate matters. Our physical presence is not very important.'

'What would you call this? Art?'

'Art that is invisible. Invisible art is the completion of the circle. Its after-effects are strong, powerful, and visible. Its truth is in the experience. The rest is stupid capitalism.'

'Could you tell us the end game? Is there one?'

'What we have in mind is a test project. It is political. You have heard of the Arab Spring? Of course, everybody has. Well, we are going to do something similar with the tools at our disposal. We plan to engineer a Dalit Spring.'

Episode: Krishna Kumar

It was a dark stage, with a single spotlight trained on a puppeteer. He was seated; his shoulders were hunched, and on his left knee was his foreshortened accomplice. The puppeteer wore a black-stained shirt, black-frayed trousers, a dark overcoat, and a hat jammed low, covering his forehead. A shadow formed a hood around his face. His accomplice was dressed in rags and wore a permanent leer. His head looked like produce from a cabbage patch.

There were no other props on the stage. Black cloth had been stretched on the sides, giving the place a spare and funerary appearance. The vibe was that of a memorial service. Strange music was playing, a barely discernible tune. It sounded like a cello piece. It was a death march from the film *The Constant Gardener*.

It was a half-full house; there were people scattered on the seats. Those who came were friends and their friends. There were no well-wishers. According to the puppeteer, well-wishers should go to a well with coins and follow their wishes.

As the murmur subsided and the audience settled in, the music stopped and the puppeteer spoke. He had a gravelly voice.

'I live a lie,' he said.

'He is an artist,' said the puppet, pointing without looking. 'It comes with the territory.'

The puppeteer shrugged.

'How I wish this was a dream. Last night I was sitting in my studio with my head in my hand. I was looking, like Rodin's Thinker, at yet another unsuccessful work of mine. I was wondering why despite my best efforts it remained a lump of clay.'

The puppet spoke. 'He looked awkward. Have you seen a lion caught eating goat cheese in the jungle?'

One person in the audience laughed out loud.

'It was a student work of mine, a pimple from my college days.'

'A time when he was a twit,' said the puppet. 'A bad time to have a visitor who came by in a tourist taxi.'

'It had white number plates,' said the hooded puppeteer. 'It was parked outside my door, the door open and shut, and in she walked, with her polished shoes that squeaked on my cement floor. She was wearing red-rimmed spectacles but her eyes were elsewhere. I realized she had already seen me by then and had scanned my work as well. Both had fallen into categories before she spoke.'

'Both had fallen,' parroted the puppet, gesturing downwards with a hand.

The puppeteer looked crestfallen and stayed that way long enough for the audience to get restless. Someone coughed and someone else laughed nervously. The spotlight dimmed. Out of the dark the puppet spoke up.

'My name is Lalit Kala,' he said.

A few eyebrows were raised. This was the government institute that supported the arts; some would say it was on life support.

'I am not an Akademi,' said the puppet. 'You think I am a puppet?'

'Yes, you are,' said the puppeteer.

'You don't know what a puppet is,' said Lalit Kala. 'The Akademi is a puppet.'

The audience laughed.

'Don't listen to him,' said the puppeteer. 'He has got me into enough trouble.'

'This artist is dead,' said Lalit Kala, pointing to the puppeteer. The audience looked at him. He stayed motionless, his eyes still invisible.

'This man was an artist,' said the puppet. 'Till this woman came to his studio. In five short minutes she wrote him off.'

'And how!' said the puppeteer.

'She said he would not feature in any history book.'

'I grovelled,' said the puppeteer.

'He did, the snivelling beast.'

'I pleaded for a mention.'

'He said even an addendum footnote would save his life.'

'But no, the one with the legs walked away.'

'She left her perfume behind.'

They sat in silence for almost a minute.

'She looked like a Goldsmiths graduate,' said Lalit Kala.

'She was the kind that writes for *Frieze* and attends the Venice Biennale.'

The puppeteer slumped further down in his chair.

'What was her name?' shouted someone in the audience.

As if on cue a woman walked onto the stage. She was wearing a skirt and her shoes made a squeaking sound. The spotlight moved to her.

The puppeteer turned and looked at her, and the puppet swivelled in her direction. She stood there unaffected, impervious to their gaze.

'Her name is Sahitya,' said Lalit Kala. 'Another Akademi.'

'Sahitya writes history,' said the puppeteer. 'She told me every twenty years there is a Movement.'

'Roughly speaking,' said Sahitya. 'There were the Progressives in 1947, the Group 1890 in 1962, and the Radical Collective in 1987.'

She had a tone of finality, one that was accustomed to making pronouncements.

'Each Movement had five to ten names,' she said. 'The Progressives had five. The Group 1890 had ten. The Kerala boys had somewhere between the two.'

'And me, I don't belong,' shouted the puppeteer.

'Not even to the Mumbai boys,' said Sahitya.

She moved to the side and lit a candle. She cast the light on a nearby wall. A draft from the side of the stage made the flame flicker.

'I wish art was just a celebration,' said the puppeteer.

'I wish it was destroyed every now and then,' said Sahitya.

'I wish the money merchants cast their eyes elsewhere,' said Lalit Kala.

'When currency roams, the produce surrenders,' said Sahitya. She held the candle flame between thumb and forefinger till it died. The stage darkened.

VIII

WPO

It was a seven-star hotel near Bandra Kurla. The common areas were like football fields; they housed sculptures, a fountain, and some rocks. Every surface was different; the material used could be described as single-origin. When asked about his particular style, the architect smiled and said, 'Planned accidents.'

At the entrance, there was a revolving door where children played merry-go-round and adults waited politely for each other, enacting a pantomime called pehle aap. A young woman in a lovely sari welcomed her and shepherded her to a bank of silent lifts. There was one with a liftman in uniform and polished shoes. He made her nervous, so she tipped him. She hurried away, worried the tip was small. Her heels clicked on the granite floor.

The function was in the ballroom. The WPO was a large organization. It described itself pithily as a 'global leadership community of extraordinary chief executives'. They had gathered in strength, wearing smart casuals.

'Will you pay?' she had asked the organizer, half in jest.

A small honorarium.

'Why me?'

'Maya ji, we wanted a speaker from the arts. Someone with a worldview different from ours.'

She wore a black dress, a pearl choker; her hair was tied, her nostrils bore traces of what she had chased. Maya's eyes were bright, her manner composed; one hand held a piece of paper, the other an unlit cigarette in a holder. Smoking wasn't allowed inside.

'Don't do this, don't do that.'

'House rules, madam.'

'And yet your mother bit an apple.'

The hotel manager led her into the room. Men, a few scattered women, rose and clapped till she sat down on the podium. She held a hand over her eyes and looked down at them. She did not recognize anyone.

'Some of these people have your work, madam.'

'I am sure; I mean they can easily afford it.'

They tested the mike.

'Can I have a drink before we get started? Fine, later then. If I stay, that is.'

The sponsor for the evening was Sarla, wife of Salil Gupta, a senior WPO. The compere, a grey-haired gentleman, read out a thank-you note.

'Sarla Gupta is a connoisseur. Her interest in music is deep; her understanding of its grammar is remarkable. How does one travel so far as a listener? I have seen musicians look up to her. They seek her approbation. In my experience, very few people listen with the required mindfulness. In Sarla Gupta's world, it is a form of surrender. Her good ear comes from an interesting life: from a variety of experiences, from an ability to nurture one's senses, and, dare I say, from a degree of recklessness. Listening to an hour-long alap in a distracted world is a form of daredevilry. I have always treasured our moments listening to the masters together, completely absorbed, oblivious to the rest of the world.'

Amidst loud cheering, Sarla stood, bowed towards Maya. 'This is your evening. I just love your work. I would also like you to hear a few words from Salil on his journey in the art world. He is here and he is not prepared; perhaps it is best that way. Salil, will you, please?'

Salil rose slowly, walking even more slowly to the podium, collecting his thoughts.

'This could be headlined "Baniya in the Art World"', he said.

A few of his friends laughed.

'I will try to be brief. It has not been a smooth journey for me. I had no expectations. Most of you know what baniyas are like. We are careful with money; we don't like waste. What we mean by waste is peculiar and at times strange. In my parents' home fruit that was overripe had its takers. Clothes that were too tight were altered and it did not matter if the look was outdated or a style was out of fashion. Nothing was thrown away. The large valve radio that had stopped working was still there; retreaded tyres piled atop each other, expired batteries, even school study material. There was pride in this kind of living. No certificate was needed. The smaller the amount saved, the better was the payoff. My father argued endlessly with coolies at the station. His tips at restaurants were occasionally returned.'

There was more laughter.

'But times are changing; there are some baniya labels now in the fashion industry.' He took a deep breath and puffed his cheeks. 'And there are baniyas like me. In the baniya world I am a kind of horror story: a successful man, well educated, sensible. And what am I doing? Throwing money away by buying for millions what took a few rupees to make and perhaps a couple of hours. My community says Salil is a joker, pagal, sanki, victim of mixed marriage, perhaps of a daughter who studied the wrong things abroad and thought spendthrift ideas from rich countries could be imported.'

Nobody laughed. One of his friends spoke up from the audience. 'So Salil, after this long journey, please tell us, what is art?'

'Ouch,' said Nupur, worried for her father, facing this difficult question.

'Let me see,' said Salil, quite at ease. 'There were three stages in my journey with this question.' He held up three fingers and folded them one by one. 'What is it? Is this what it is? And the last and most important was, it is what it is.'

'Nice,' said Maya, a little surprised.

'Let me say something more,' said Salil. 'I have to describe what my daughter and I have been up to in the art world. My daughter and I have tried something different; we have persevered, and we have learned. Ah yes, one more thing. Legitimacy. For the longest time I sought legitimacy. Legitimacy seeking is a medical condition and I had it. I wanted to be accepted in the art world. I hungered for acknowledgement. It was quite pathetic.'

Nupur spoke up. 'Dad, I think you have had your say.'

Salil held up his hands, smiling. 'You all know my daughter. She runs this business. I think we should hear from her. She is a winner in all that she does.'

'I am not,' said Nupur, 'and honestly today it is not about us, but I must confess to you all, it is not me but art that is winning.'

There was a short break after which Maya was invited on stage. They seated her on the podium and tested the mike. There was a brief introduction, some details of her shows; the last, panned by a leading critic called Anjana, wasn't dwelled upon. In the quiet that followed, a spotlight lit a halo around Maya. She remained seated, her head bowed; she paused till she had their attention.

'Consider a land that is a garden of weeds. Somebody carved out a nation and the weeds were fine with it. Weeds survive without tending or nourishment. They have learned to spread, mingle, ride roughshod, and care little for presentation. This land of weeds is my country.

'The partition of this place was ugly and will remain a festering wound. When will they learn? You cannot tend weeds that have no respect for maps. They will capture territory till you submit to their reality. You cannot manicure this land in the name of civilization.

'If you want to look for character, look amongst these mongrel plants, these non-thoroughbreds which have not been granted pedigree. What a bloody mess they make. Who cares? They know the garden plant will die. The imports will stand in rows, flower and fruit, fuck the soil, and finally wilt.

'Weeds have names but do you know them? It doesn't matter really if you don't. If you really like pansies and dahlias, don't bother finding out.

'I am a garden weed. That is what I meant to tell you. Maya. My name is Illusion. You may not have noticed me. I was there standing amongst these flowering plants and manicured puffs looking a little rough and a little randy.

'Somebody once told me, I am trying to place you. I could see his confusion. I have tried to put my finger on it too. That really is my life and my art.'

She looked around the room and looked a little lost. 'Sorry,' she said, and coughed. 'Let's see, what else can I really tell you today? Let us continue with nature. What does it tell us? These daily sunrises, the rainstorms, perfectly formed petals, astonishing creatures big and small. What do they tell us?' Nobody responded. 'This is a grandstanding universe we live in. People try to capture it but all they can do is make cruel approximations. In their phones, in cameras, and in art.'

She looked up at them.

'Nature is perfect in every way; it is beautiful even in its anarchy. The likes of me are filled with foolish courage. We set out to make art. Art is fallible; artists like me even more so. There is no shame in saying it. I have lived a fallible life. In all these years of drawing and painting, I have been drinking, shooting drugs, and smoking weed.'

There was an audible intake of breath in the room. People shifted in their seats.

'I have built myself a private hell. I feel secure in it. In my unkempt, disorderly world, my body wastes faster than time.'

There was a whole lot more she had written down on the piece of paper, avowedly confessional, precious in her estimation.

'Sorry, you have to give me time. Allow me these pauses. I like to frame my thoughts like I frame my pictures.'

A long pause later, she said, 'Look.'

She held out a hand. It was shaking; the light and shadow exaggerated the movement. 'I am shivering. This happens when you are addicted. I am afraid of the fact that I am addicted, that I will never kick these habits. It is what it is, a kind of prison.'

She paused again. 'A question bothers me. If I kick these habits, will my art suffer? Will it?'

There was a hush in the hall.

'I lack the courage; I cannot answer these questions. If you asked me what I set out to do many years ago when I was young, when there was a bright light in my eyes, I would have probably said, I want to make a difference. Now, many years later I can tell you: in the best of times that is all we can hope to achieve.'

She turned towards Sarla Gupta. Sarla is a seasoned listener. 'I listen to music as well, music that comes from the wellsprings of ustads and pandits, from decades-old riyaz, from light, from shadow, from summer and rain. Music does things to me; at times I feel like breaking free, dancing; at times I am mute. At the core of art appreciation is the very same fallibility that afflicts its creators. This is our secret pact.'

'Lovely,' said someone in the audience.

She looked again at her piece of paper. 'And why is this relevant at all to you? Because it is possible that you, despite your affluence and visible goodness, may be building prisons of your own, that there are chains that bind you, that you become aware of, and are helpless. Is it possible?'

Nobody answered.

'I don't have a solution, mind you,' said Maya, smiling, 'but at least I know the problem. What else can I say? Perhaps just this. In my worldview there is principally me. This is the narcissism that gives me hope. This is human DNA. Each of us has to count. I believe in a state of mind that denies the ordinary as a way of life. Art can never be ordinary. If you cannot make art, at least learn to appreciate it. Give it time. Give your heart and soul some time. Give yourself a chance because we live in mean times. Be generous.'

She finished on that note. Nupur and Tara stood and led the clapping.

Maya left soon, complaining of a headache. She looked drained.

Tara heaved a sigh, looked towards Nupur, and nodded. They had been nervous, Maya wasn't predictable but this had gone so well.

'The most lucid I have seen her in a while,' said Nupur. 'How does that happen?'

Tara shuddered; she knew more, so much more. 'She was like this before her drug overdose,' she said. 'A burst of clarity before the implosion.'

The Incident

'Talk to me about it, Tara,' said Nupur.

'It began with the dog,' said Tara. 'The neighbour's dog went berserk. He ran up and down the stairs, his nails clicking loudly as he scampered. He scratched at people's doors, and he barked his head off. The sound bounced from wall to wall and brought out all who were in their homes enjoying a Sunday evening.'

'How did the dog sense it?'

'The smell.'

'What smell?'

'The smell of blood?'

'Which the neighbours couldn't smell.'

'But the dog could. This wasn't just some nosebleed. It was so strong the dog couldn't handle it. They followed him and barged in.'

'The front door was open?'

'Always. Everything was so frantic because of the dog. Try and imagine the scene. The dog was everywhere, running from person to person, pawing at the wooden bathroom door. The marks are still there.'

Tara remembered what people said. 'She had a strange expression on her face. Some called it a smile. Others thought they saw tears. I don't blame anyone for these versions. They had walked into a small room with a big tub. There were flowers in the water, scented candles in the corners, there was music playing. And blood. Never had they seen so much blood, red that was turning pink; it had spilled out and spread onto the floor. The taps were on and the water kept flowing. She was near her end when they barged in, petering out, ebbing away. She breathed her last while they watched. It was a horrible helplessness.'

'Did she say anything?'

'She was barely alive. She couldn't speak by then but she knew that people had milled around her. She sensed the commotion and probably resented the intrusion.'

'And you weren't there?'

'No. I wasn't there because she made sure I was away. She chose a quiet period.'

Tara's fingers were digging into her palms. Nupur watched her, afraid she would draw blood.

'Can you believe it? Music was playing. Wagner and the bloody cellos. You know what, I try to imagine that evening: my mother pulling off her pretty shoes that she had left outside the bathroom, removing that floral gown that was her second skin, lowering herself into the water, smoking that last weedy cheroot, drinking from the small bottle of vodka, taking that half razor that barbers use and slicing her light green, delicate veins, two cuts in each hand, letting them drop to her sides. And then the ooze, the slow, interminable bleed.

'That's how she went. The cuts were clinical, so quiet and so peaceful, but the commotion brought the closure to its truthful form: a butchery. I am glad people barged in; she must have realized what she had inflicted on herself was butchery. She would have seen it in the eyes of those that came in, the horror of the death scene played out through the eyes of unwelcome visitors. People screamed, some fainted, a few were led away. They froze for a few minutes, numbed by what they saw. Nobody touched her; the fragility was such.

'They did call a doctor finally. He came from the depths of the colony, huffing and puffing, holding his chest and breathing gulps of precious air. Good God, he said when he arrived. Even he was overcome. He would never have seen such a death, such a spectacle.'

'Try not to imagine it,' said Nupur, holding her friend's hands, unclenching them.

'I can't help it. There is an image in my head, like a painting.'

'Lucian Freud?'

'Just the man for such occasions.'

'People are such ghouls. I believe some took pictures.'

Nupur had seen them. She had received the images from her team. There were hesitant suggestions about using them for the show. Some part of her wondered if this was what Maya had in mind: a parting performance worthy of a prize. Was this Maya at her Lucian best? Was this her stairway to Lucian? Surely not!

'What could have prevented this? Isn't that a question people ask?'

'Yes,' said Tara. 'I ask it all the time.'

Nupur held her friend. Tara was lost in the moment, her thoughts colliding.

'I am so sorry,' mumbled Nupur, now knowing if she should own up in some way.

'The whole thing is so sick,' said Tara.

'You mean?'

'Everything,' said Tara. 'This prize, my mother's life, all these people around her.'

'Right now you must be hating me,' said Nupur, fearing the worst.

Tara went into hiding. Nupur had to unearth her now and then. 'Spend time with me,' she told her friend. 'Has this really happened?' Tara kept asking, 'Tell me this is just a dream.'

She came over one day looking haggard; she looked at Nupur barely and said many unsavoury things. They drank some and lay around.

'Are you taking some medicine?' asked Nupur.

'Too many,' said Tara.

Nupur grabbed her friend's bag and pulled out a pillbox. There were sleeping pills of different dosages, there were pills to calm her down, there were muscle relaxants, and there were some anti-depressants.

'I hope you aren't mixing the pills.'

'I do, sometimes.'

There was a cocktail for her every mood. One for an ordinary day, higher dosages for when she was worked up, and a potent third for when she was manic. They were evening dosages. Every day that passed affected her and the long night ahead scared her.

'I don't like this,' said Nupur. For a while they stared at the box.

'A drug overdose is an accident waiting to happen,' said Nupur.

'Look at me,' said Tara. 'Do I look the type?'

Nupur wasn't convinced.

'Don't worry,' said Tara. 'I don't see myself checking into a hotel, locking myself into the bathroom, and cutting my wrists.'

'I couldn't have imagined your mother doing it either,' said Nupur. She could not understand what had happened. Wasn't suicide for jilted lovers, the indebted, paupers perhaps, or victims of abuse? Wasn't it for the terminally ill and the seriously disturbed? How could Maya have done it? She was smarter than that; she wasn't the type who would revel in a posthumous high.

When Tara left the room, Nupur rummaged through her bag looking for answers. She found some handwritten letters and a single photograph. A black-and-white gelatin silver print that captured the profile of a man. Written across the frayed print were the words 'Why so sad?' It was a photograph of Maya's father. The letters were from him; he had a good hand.

Even as she opened one of them, she heard the door opening. Tara stood in the doorway. Startled, Nupur stood up as a reflex, feeling mortified. There was no point in saying anything when caught this way.

'Still looking for reasons?' said Tara.

'Yes,' said Nupur. 'It sounds awful but I wish there was a silver bullet that explained everything.'

'There isn't,' said Tara. 'There never will be.'

The doorbell rang. It was Girish. He hugged Tara and sat quietly. He looked awkward. He was so unsettled that he lit a cigarette. Then he remembered and offered her one, lighting it for her; they smoked in silence.

'Your mother was a lovely person,' he said.

He lit another cigarette.

'I never knew you smoked,' said Tara.

He shrugged. 'It is temporary,' he said. He looked at his cigarette and then abruptly stubbed it out. 'I can live without them,' he said. 'Is it that easy for you?'

'Tara,' he said, 'I should tell you that your mother had many sides to her.'

He was weighing his words and struggling to say whatever it was he wanted to.

'We thought we knew her. We all thought so. But in the last few months she wasn't the person we had spent so many years with. It was almost as if she had crossed a line.'

'You mean she had lost it?'

'I don't know. I don't think so but others certainly felt that way.'

'How was she the day before?'

'Manic,' he said. 'Bad. Awful. It was so hard to see her those days. She was going down rapidly and it was so bad we all decided to call Varadarajan, our landlord from Baroda, hoping an older person could talk to her and convince her.'

'Did it help?'

'No. On the other hand, Varadarajan was deeply affected. He spent more than a month with her while she tried to kick her habit. You have no idea, you were away. She was down to shooting herself between her toes before that. I had seen her do that and it was painful and degenerate.'

Degenerate.

'Varada and she fought, and they both suffered through her rehab attempt. She was wild. She would beg him, she would steal, and once she offered herself to Varada. And he hit her. The old man actually hit her. He knocked her off her feet.'

'KK told me you stopped meeting her?'

He nodded and looked defensive.

'So it's true? I refused to believe it when he told me.'

'What was I to do? Your mother was hard to handle in the best of times. She started targeting me, she—'

Tara shouted at him. 'I can't believe what I am hearing! You stopped meeting her? Why?'

He got up and retreated. 'I wish I could tell you.'

'You bloody coward.'

'What?'

'You selfish bastard.'

'Hey.'

'You left her when she needed you the most?'

'Listen,' he said.

'Listen? You listen.' She got up as well because she couldn't sit around.

'Tara,' he said, 'I can understand you are upset but—'

'Is this what you do when your friend is in trouble? How could you? You look so calm, so well rested, so bloody composed.'

'You are… hey. Hey.'

She had had it with him. She threw what was around, an ashtray, a bowl, and she could have beaten him up if he hadn't left in a hurry. He turned and ran.

'What a fuck he is,' said Tara.

'Easy,' said Nupur.

Tara was told Girish had a number of works that her mother had done in the years before. He claimed they were gifts. She wasn't so sure. Her mother wasn't the gifting type, no sir, she wasn't. They had had issues with ends not meeting. Fair enough, no one was weeping; it was an artist's life but there was a daughter to take care of, remember? She asked that the works be returned and Girish refused.

What was she to do now? This mission was harder than she imagined it would be. She wanted to speak to Pandey because she thought she had a lot to report that was new. She felt she had made progress.

'Mr Pandey, so far I have heard two rambling accounts but in between I have struck gold. Krishna Kumar confessed he could have been an accessory.'

'That's what he is telling the whole world. I don't believe him. It is like he is taking credit. You can guess why.'

'Because of *The Prize*?' she asked aloud. Was that possible, ghoulish as it sounded? She didn't know what to believe any more. 'Sir, do you know that Girish has many of her works? I have proof. He is a lowly thief. He has some of my mother's best works. Could you get them back? How? I don't care how.' She was disheartened. 'Is this worth it, Mr Pandey? What are we trying to dig up?'

'You know what we are trying to do,' he said.

She wanted those works back. They were worth something, and if they were really as good as she had been told, then they were worth a lot. Girish was at the top of her hate list. The arsehole had called the wrong ambulance agency that evening when someone called him and they took more than half an hour to arrive. He was the one who had helped her mother source drugs the week before the incident.

She confronted him about that.

'How could I refuse her? You should have seen the state she was in after three weeks off,' he said.

'Dumb fuck,' she said. 'I don't believe a word you are saying.'

Girish couldn't take it any more. He had a piece of paper with him, precious and private. He carried it around with him; it was frayed, handwritten, and some ink had smudged. He pulled it out and handed it to Tara.

'Careful with it,' he said.

Tara recognized the writing. Her hand shook; she couldn't bear to look at it. She spread the sheet on a table and smoothed it out. Most of what Maya had written had been blackened, and by design there were a few clear sentences. She read them slowly, pausing after each.

> There is a beast in charge of my life. A cunning creature.

> Can someone burn these photographs. This isn't me. I don't look like this.

> Sleep deserts me. It has been a month since I have slept more than an hour.

How useless it all seems.

Where I am is very far. I can't get back. I have ceased to care.

My daughter eggs me on. Poor girl. Will I survive this?

All Tara could do was sit and stare. Really, Maya? Could it be true? Was this the truth you were seeking?

Nupur

Inspector Pandey dropped in at my office. He wasn't in uniform. He looked closely at the artworks on the walls. He asked a few questions; he seemed genuinely curious.

'The inspector general's wife paints,' he said. 'She held an exhibition and the IG made sure we all turned up. She had painted scenes from Shimla and Manali: mostly watercolours.'

'And that is the only exhibition you have seen in your life?'

He nodded. 'Yes,' he said.

I handed over three catalogues from recent shows to him. He held the catalogues and looked at the covers one at a time. 'I saw your TV show last year. My wife watched it and she forced me to.'

I offered him tea or coffee. 'Tea,' he said.

I poured the tea and he sat back, crossed one leg over the other, and let his eyes roam around my place. 'You live alone?' he asked.

I smiled. 'Mostly,' I said.

We sipped some tea.

'Miss Nupur, Maya's suicide was like a performance,' he said.

Inspector Pandey had been reading magazine articles about art and a feature on performance art had caught his eye. About the artist sitting in the Museum of Modern Art in New York for more than a month so visitors could sit opposite her and stare. Some of them cried while staring, some were photographed, and most of them tweeted, Facebooked, pinned, and Tumblred their few minutes of public exposure. Hundreds stood around and watched this performance that was titled 'The Artist Is Present'. A simple world it was, if you ask me, with simple-minded people.

And what did the inspector think about it? 'Time pass,' he said. 'What people in Mumbai do when they are unemployed.' He was surprised that artists could actually cause a public commotion abroad by merely sitting in one place and staring.

'Suicide as performance? You sound very dramatic, Inspector,' I said. 'Some more tea?'

He nodded. 'I have seen many crime scenes,' he said, 'but this was hatke.'

'I have seen many art installations,' I said. 'This was very filmy.'

'Yes, the correct word,' he said. 'It was very disturbing. She was smiling, lying in the tub, bleeding to death, and smiling.'

'She was drunk, wasn't she, and she had taken some drugs?' I said.

He frowned at my easy explanation.

'Have you registered it as a suicide?' I asked.

'No,' he said. 'She couldn't have done it by herself.'

'Oh, so you have booked it as a murder case?' I said.

He looked unhappy that I was asking the questions; perhaps the very questions that were troubling him.

'Someone had helped her,' he said. He held my right hand, turned it so I could see my palm, and traced a line across the wrist. 'Deep cuts in each hand. Trust me, it is very hard to cut yourself that deep. But there were no signs of struggle.'

'So it wasn't a suicide and it wasn't murder?' I said.

He threw up his hands in frustration. 'The last time she attempted suicide I asked Ms Maya, I questioned her, and she said she couldn't remember anything of what happened. She said something silly, like – I am too old for that.'

We sat in silence for a while.

'Art and crime have so much in common,' I said.

He raised an eyebrow.

'The idea of authorship and the question: how did it happen.'

The inspector was very clear in his head about art. 'There is no good reason for making art but committing a crime is rarely senseless. And yet look at this case, Miss Nupur. It is a mockery.'

I showed him some video footage I had uncovered. A neighbour had shot the scene. It was gory and riveting.

'Footage for your contest?' he asked.

'Is that a serious question?' I said. 'Tara, her daughter, is my colleague and best friend.'

He shrugged his shoulders. 'I think she did this for your show,' he said.

It sounded like an accusation.

'You call your show reality TV, right?' he said.

I nodded.

'You are dangerous people,' he said. 'Your show is promoting this behaviour. Will you accept responsibility?'

I said nothing.

'My boss asked me to watch the series *Fear Factor*,' he said. 'I saw some episodes. The contestants were forced to take risks they would not have in daily life. They signed a contract that said even if they died in the course of the show, the network was not responsible.'

'Nobody forced them,' I said.

He wanted a copy of our contract. I said I would send it to his office.

'Does it have such a clause?' he asked.

I hesitated. 'It does,' I said. 'But Inspector, we do not force our contestants to do anything. In fact we ask them to lead normal lives.'

'I am sure,' he said. 'My boss also asked me to see the TV series called *Survivor*. You must have seen it. It is astonishing how people behave when placed in a competition.'

'You haven't heard a word of what I said. We expressly tell contestants not to—'

'It doesn't matter what you tell them,' he interjected. 'What matters is what happens, not what your contract is or what your intentions are. That you can discuss in a court of law.'

I shivered. Where was this going? 'Are you going to arrest me?' I said. I was joking.

'Not now,' he said. And he smiled when he saw my expression.

'It isn't funny, Inspector,' I said. He shrugged his shoulders.

'If your contest promotes such behaviour and something happens, then you will be an accessory,' he said.

Before he left he asked me about Krishna Kumar. He knew he was a performance artist. 'These artists are strange people,' he said. 'In my experience in Crime Branch I have not come across people like them. Can you explain them?'

'No,' I said. 'They live in your Mumbai; you explain them.'

I was unnerved after that meeting. I was happy that my ex called later that day. 'I am in town,' he said. 'Your town.'

He came an hour later, looking like he always did, achingly good looks that he barely seemed conscious of. We hugged. I actually held him for a while. He sensed something and looked down, an eyebrow raised.

'This is not the beginning of anything,' I said.

He smiled. 'I am too old for you,' he said.

'And yet?'

'And yet we get along.'

We went for a walk along the bay; the breeze was refreshing.

'You know it's been months?' he said. 'People are asking questions.'

'You are still single? Is that what they are asking?'

'Yes.'

'Since when did that bother you?'

'It never did,' he said. 'But somehow, I don't know, the last few days I have been bothered. I just feel uncomfortable.'

I understood what he was getting at. Every now and then he raised the question. He was ready for a commitment. I wasn't; I did not want to give up what we shared: time mostly, a good few moments, time I wished would never end, in which somehow everything and everyone would stay the same.

'Nupur, I think I know you.'

'No, you don't,' I said, removing my hand from his.

'You want us to be like your parents.'

'Maybe,' I said. I had no time to get into all that; there was too much happening and I told him some of what was bothering me. He heard me out, quiet and attentive; at some point my head fell on his shoulder.

'You can't be in control all the time,' he said in the end. 'Things happen.'

That was fine, that much was fine; it would do. I had this battle and it was mine.

My father called the next morning, on cue. I think he knew who I had met yesterday. I told him about my meeting with the inspector.

He sounded worried. 'This could spiral,' he said. 'Should I come down?'

I said he should.

'Are you okay?' he asked.

'I don't know,' I said. 'I am just feeling a little low. It looks like I have bitten off more than I can chew.'

'Are people supporting you?' he asked. 'Surely some in the art world are rallying around you?'

I laughed. 'I am fighting a battle on many fronts,' I said. 'Most of all against this invisible creature that seems to throw things in my way and waits for me to stumble.'

'Creature? You mean…' he trailed off.

'Yes,' I said. 'There is something intangible that seems to work its will on all of us. I can feel its presence, the force of its intention.'

'Nupur…' said my father, now seriously worried.

'I have not lost it,' I said. Maybe I had. 'Don't worry,' I said.

'Is your friend holding up? Are you in touch?'

I acted instinctively; I called Girish and asked him a favour. He was reluctant. I assured him I wouldn't let anyone know. He took me to his uncle's place, a large apartment in Dadar. In a room stacked against a wall were works of Maya; early works, and a few she had worked on before she passed. We turned them around, cleaned them as best as we could, and arranged them against the four walls. It took us an hour. Girish left the room at my behest. I pulled up a chair, shut my eyes, and waited for my pulse to settle. It wasn't the best display but it was a unique exposition. How she began, how it ended, and a yawning gap of years in between that I could fill in with what I remembered. The works spoke to me as I savoured them. I have no idea how long I was in there. It was precious to be with Maya again; she was there as alive as she had ever been. 'Kya?' I could hear her say. 'What do you want?'

My journey with art was complete. More than anything else, this experience was life-affirming. Art is a living, breathing thing, someone had said. This display was proof.

Curtains

'I wish I could say she picked the wrong profession. She chose to become an artist and that came with its baggage. With its uncertainty. With its illusions.'

'But she was successful.'

'True, and yet she took her life.'

'Exactly.'

'I think she chose the wrong company.'

'From what you have described, the other three…'

'… are fine people? You don't understand. I don't blame you. It's hard for me to explain. Each of them is a good person. Yet this happened. That's what I meant. You are looking for a cause after the event. Have you realized it could be you, that you are also in some way responsible?'

'I see.'

'Sorry, I did not mean to be so direct. She had attempted to kill herself before, right?'

'Yes. And nothing changed. You may be right. What the hell, I am not some life coach or therapist. She was the story being written. Each day a loose leaf. Nothing that I could do would change the narrative. At best I was a sort of paperweight. You know it was beginning to affect me? I had developed a nervous tic. It was weird, some muscle in my body, a small one, decided to fire up on its own. A psychological response – a physical manifestation.'

'It's gone now?'

'Yes. It left with her. She was the source. She never did normal things. We were not a normal family. It was a peculiar life. So much abuse, and I had to put up with it. Her habits, the disarray, the bloody mess. And she, walking around saying, I am an artist,

I have to do what I do. Even if it means walking up to the edge every now and then.'

'What did she teach you?'

'Strangely, she taught me patience. I learned to live through small moments, handle inconsequential days. Counselling helped me. You need to be anchored, my counsellor said. Find a core, be strong. It is hard, believe me. I feel like I am fighting.'

'Fighting what?'

'I don't know; it's so hard to describe. It feels like I am being dragged down by a death-defying gravity.'

'Was it all worth it?'

'Ask Nupur. She has her hands full, there are court cases. There is one against Brown Sahib for communal disharmony. There is a case against Krishna Kumar, Salil, and Nupur herself for aiding and abetting. And she is being threatened about *The Prize*. Praveena's father is threatening to expose Anjana's certification mistakes. She is on the jury and that will jeopardize the prize. KK is threatening to come clean on God knows what.'

'What does Salil say? Does he have a solution?'

'He told Nupur to let the dam burst.'

'What?'

'Yes. He also said, let's get the prep going for Season 3.'

'Because the ratings of the programme are through the roof?'

'Yes. Father and daughter are in trouble but they are also raking in money. It is amazing how, when it comes to making money, Salil Gupta has the Midas touch.'

'So, who do you think will win? And don't tell me art will, in the end.'

IX

Some Artist Briefs

Anita Dube
She likes words: the sound, what they look like when carved, and their power in dissent. Words bristle when she clothes them with wire; they can be ominous when cosseted in black velvet. Her résumé includes art history and a manifesto that finds a place in it.

Atul Dodiya
Stalky figures in awkward predicaments. Assemblages of quotes and references in curiosity cabinets. Metal shutters with street cred roll up to reveal sly metaphors. Atul plays with your mind.

Badrinarayan
A born storyteller who illustrated situations, dwellings, and creatures. The rendering is simple, the subjects seem naive, and everything is out to lull one and all with their idyllic ways.

Bharti Kher
Kher's two-dimensional works are energetic mosaic patterns that use bindis and sperm notations. They raise notions of fealty and motility, and refer to the gravitational pull on planets, the plentiful universe, its creation, and its energy.

Bikash Bhattacharjee
Bikash came from the Bengal School, which has a romantic history. He had a sensual view that was tempered by Calcutta's edgy tonality

and coarse palette. His forays into surrealism were an extension of what the city represents.

K.P. Krishnakumar

He is present in spirit in this narrative, though the character by the same name in the book isn't him. He, too, is an evangelist for lost causes.

Krishna Howlaji Ara

His still lifes and nudes, with their charcoal outlines, emerged from the streets of a city that valorized the dark. Mumbai is at its arresting best when Ara's vignettes reveal the impersonal yet intimate view of bystanders.

Lucian Freud

Paintings that are old school, by appearance a bloodless coup. They challenge you to look away even as they will you to not do so. He managed to look at his friends and relatives in ways they were ashamed of. Naked is a form that his palette knife wields while his subjects sleep.

Manu Parekh

Painter of Varanasi, of street temples and imagined deities. Sparks from shorting wires crisscross the canvas, revealing layers of unsubtle colours that the city has taken to heart.

Mark Rothko

Rothko in another life stayed in Chidambaram where he visited the temple and its sanctum and gave meaning to the Chidambara Rahasyam. His work is in museums, salons, and chapels where it resonates with the present-but-invisible, with all that is considered spiritual, with Maya.

Nalini Malani

A meld of myth and lesser-known tales of heroic impulses and feminist credos, the body as a site, as a ship, as a battlefield.

Not much that is going right is conveyed through a European palette and contemporary mediums.

Nasreen Mohammedi
She constructed patterns, simple at first glance, that deconstructed wind, space, and sometimes the sea, which she took to heart. For viewers, her pared-down geometry could be just that, or it could be a liminal form of poetry.

Ramkumar
For him, a landscape was as much about subsoil and topology as it was about terrain and manmade structures. Trees were featured as an essence of green, water as blue, and history was writ in the impasto layers rendered by knife.

Subodh Gupta
Gupta uses everyday objects in his work, principally kitchen utensils, travel accessories, cycles, and bikes. One work mystified many. It had blank canvases on the floor, made of fibreglass. They raised three questions: Were these paintings? Was it a piece of sculpture? Was this art?

Vasudeo Gaitonde
If you can reduce a language to a private alphabet you can reduce the world to a colour field, and people to helpless abstraction. Gaitonde's work is the viewer and the artist in an endless quest.

Zarina Hashmi
Hashmi's is a pared-down world of notations, script, marks, and absence. Personal history mingles with maps and localities. The lens is up close, at times in your face, at times an eagle in the sky. Acutely sensitive to materials, she recreates them using paper pulp, rope, and gold leaf.

Acknowledgements

One hour to madness and joy! O furious! O confine me not!
(What is this that frees me so in storms?
What do my shouts amid lightnings and raging winds mean?)

'One Hour to Madness and Joy'
by Walt Whitman

The term 'complicit observer' in the context of art was coined by the poet, curator, and writer Ranjit Hoskote.

A few lines from K.G. Subramanyan have been quoted and acknowledged within the novel. They are from 'Excerpts from a Notebook', *Art Heritage*, No. 11, 1991–92.

About the Author

The art world has been Sanjay Kumar's muse since 1988. As a director of Sakshi Gallery, he has been privy to the growth of the Indian art scene and global developments in the last few decades. His experience in setting up finance and software businesses came in handy in his bid to understand the art market. This then has been a long journey from philistine to novice to participant and now to gadfly. *Artist, Undone*, his first novel, was an outsider's journey. This second foray is an insider's view into this opaque, mysterious, bristly, yet beguiling world of art.